I0778215

Published by Deeds Publishing in Athens, GA
www.deedspublishing.com

Printed in The United States of America

Cover and interior design by Deeds Publishing

ISBN 978-1-966641-43-8

Books are available in quantity for promotional or premium use.
For information, email info@deedspublishing.com.

First Edition, 2025

10 9 8 7 6 5 4 3 2 1

For Riaz.
With you, I found my world.
J.C.

Without a trace of sympathy, the woman sneered. "Horses can't tell time."

"Wha—? There's people…"

The woman's lips pursed tight, and she tilted her head. "Even better. He's got company."

"N–o–o. It's worse. I can't be late!" *Think you're funny? You're not!*

The woman put her hand on her hip. "It's been fifteen minutes! I called the 1-800 number. I'm late too! Now I'll be stuck in rush-hour traffic and I…"

June's fingers clenched tight. *Lady, please. I can't take another word.*

The door burst open from behind the desk. A frazzled middle-aged woman stepped forward. "Next."

Looking straight at the clerk, June spoke up. "I'm locked out of my room! I just need a key card." *I hope these people don't jump me for that.*

The woman in the line glared and raised her voice. "We were here first, and we all have issues."

June waited while the clerk helped the people in front of her. And waited some more. The lobby reeked of burnt coffee, but burnt coffee was better than no coffee at all. She looked hopefully at the carafe—empty, *Darn.* And she'd left her full travel mug next to her keys too.

Finally, minutes later, her new key card in hand, June raced back to the room. She pressed the card to the door sensor, no luck. She waved the card, no luck. She turned it over and boom! The light went green. "Good grief. I better calm down." Looking around, she muttered, "And I better quit talking to myself."

They're here! Grabbing the keys, she hurried to her car. *Gas! I didn't stop for gas last night. I'm going to miss Sarah's ride and Mary's going to change her mind about me. I'm about to lose again. No. Please no…*

Leaving the parking lot, she looked at the gauge. *On fumes…* She pulled into the first station she came to and waited. Reaching the pump, she put a few gallons in. *My heart is pumping faster than the gas going in! Just enough to make it to the barn. I'll fill up after my ride.* She sped off.

Bumper to bumper for a mile ahead and behind at seven in the morning? Now at a dead standstill? Come on! She squeezed the steering wheel. *Is there a wreck up ahead? This is awful. That lady was right.* Trying to not be reckless, she changed lanes and pushed the pedal as hard as she dared. *Yes! Moving! Make up some time, get to the exit. There it is.* She looked in her rear-view mirror. "Uh oh." A red flashing light and a short whoop of a siren got the message across, and she slowed to pull over. *A ticket? Oh geez.*

Approaching her side of the car, the officer looked down at her with a stern expression and his right hand near his holster. "Do you know why I stopped you?"

June gulped. "Yes, sir. I uh…I'm so late. I think I was going a little fast."

"It's better to be late, than dead. License and registration please."

Handing them over, June gripped the steering wheel. *Thanks a lot for the advice. You sound like my parents. 'Finish college, June. Give up riding those horses, June.' Hurry up, guy. Get it over with.*

He stared at her license. "Southern California, huh?" Opening his ticket book, he peered inside her car then started writing. "Must be used to driving like this."

"No sir. I'm just late." He finished writing and she left. *I can't training you. Let's show her we're good together. We can do this here and we can do this at home in the show ring too.* She gave him a little pat on the neck. "You're amazing."

2

"Kismet."

"Excuse me, sir?"

"It's kismet, Preston. Your availability to hop on a jet and be here just in the nick of time to get the Bentley ready for its show. Now that's impressive." He ran his fingers through his thick, graying hair.

"It's my job. I'm happy I was able to help."

"You sound identical to my son. Philip was always ready to step up to the plate. God, I miss him. Your father must be so proud of you."

Preston tensed. *My father, proud of me? A car mechanic? I don't think so.* "I'm sorry for your loss, Axel. Philip was great. No doubt about it."

"Thank you. It's wonderful just hearing his name." He dabbed his eye and stopped a teardrop. "Anyway, just get this other bad boy out on the road and 'make my day,' as they say." He grinned.

"My pleasure, sir."

Preston closed the hood of the car with a gentle touch. *Ah. Good car. Good day. Nothing like getting this little beauty ready for the road.* He patted the car. *Makes enduring the family expectations a little bit easier.*

At twenty-nine, he wasn't a kid anymore and didn't have many of his wild ways left or allowed any interference with his business plans. Moving from town to town accomplished more than keeping his business operations in the black, it kept him from being obligated or controlled by anyone, in any way. Freedom was his biggest necessity. Never had it as a child and didn't intend on letting any of it slip away now or anytime in the future for that matter.

Getting the keys, he looked at his clean coveralls. Glancing at his hands, he grinned. *Nice and clean too.* He got in and started the car. Listening to the purr, he turned off the radio. *That beats any song. Silence on the road makes my ride even sweeter. Nothing can top my job.*

3

Before June knew it, warmup morphed into movements and soon her ride was underway. She headed onto the centerline, mirroring Sarah's straight-line finish on the long-axis line running down the middle of the arena. Facing the judge, the centerline is a rider's calling card of first impression and ability—and one that starts and ends all tests. June's spectators' eyes were glued on the pair. Riding through the upper-level sequence, she commanded her Hanoverian stallion's three gaits of walk, trot, and canter into mastery of all that could only be topped with the award of a blue-ribbon win.

Praying D would continue the perfection; she sat as quiet as a feather in the wind, enabling her seat to follow the powerful thrust propelling his legs forward while hindquarters pushed under his center of gravity. His back was relaxed, and he carried out each trained movement of collection, extension, passage, and piaffe. The sight was easy on the eyes. His moves were rhythmic, balanced and as expected for a ride that was one notch away from the Olympic level of dressage competition.

Reaching for calm persuasion, she coaxed D's Diamondaire to power through and give it his all as though the world was her stage, yet only two spectators were here to watch her test in the isolated arena, and they chatted quietly nonstop on the sidelines.

Moving into the halfway point, the horse's canter was collected and exuded the push as required. Lifted strides brought him into a canter pirouette to the right with the rhythmic balance of a metronome sitting atop a soloist's grand piano at Carnegie Hall, ticking in perfect cadence with each note. Turning, D completed the pirouette and the twosome moved into the three-quarter mark of the FEI Intermediate II dressage test. Deep in show mode, white foam lathering on his hindquarters and streaming from his double-bridle bits spattered an enviable amount of white foam into the air, some landing on June's black breeches.

Sneaking in a touch of a pet of encouragement on D's withers, she eased him to accept her cues as he moved onto the diagonal line of the dressage court, following her aids to begin the first of seven flying changes every second stride. Her optimism was over the top and her heart—pumping with exhilaration, was balanced by steady contact of hands and legs to execute move after move. The horse was nailing every movement and June focused to control her breaths. The canter lead and the slight flexion of the neck would support the moments of airtime coming with each flying change and transition to the new lead.

Officially, only five test movements and a couple of minutes including and ending with a halt and salute at *X* on the centerline were left to go for a letter-perfect ride. June's heart was beating so hard her chest pounded while her eyes focused on every letter in the arena guiding her geometry and steps of the ride. *We're almost there, boy…*

4

At the same time, Preston's yellow Lamborghini sped down the country road as if the world was on fire. It wasn't—only the rear tire was smoking. Looking back into the rear-view mirror, he saw the smoke. *Not good.* He looked to his right and saw a horse and rider majestically gliding through the air. The rider's blonde ponytail's flicks caught the sunlight and shimmered for an instant. *Wow. A horse can skip at the gallop? Almost looks like ballet on stage.*

In the next second and before he could slow down, the tire blew, and a large, shredded piece flew up and into the dressage arena as the car jerked to a stop and a loud backfire boomed as though a cannonball had been fired. The bay horse, in response, flicked his solid black thick tail, reared up, and raced wildly through the sand, bucking and zigzagging sideways until he catapulted the rider off.

Preston slammed on the brakes. Opening his car door, the sudden upward lift of an unfamiliar, large yellow object caused the horse to look, snort, and gallop the perimeter of the arena bucking in panic-stricken speed with kicks flying. Preston stared at two women sprinting across the sand toward the horse and rider's motionless body stretched out on the sand, oblivious to the hooves that were coming close to her head as they thundered past. For a split second, his dad's voice dominated his mind—*Run. That's what you always do. Just call for help instead.* He gritted his teeth and fisted his fingers. *Not this time. I'm stepping up to the plate!* He bolted from the car. He ran to the arena railing yelling, "I'm so sorry!" The horse ran even faster.

The two women kept running—one to the rider and one to catch the horse. The horse spied the gate halfway open and raced through it, heading off to the roadway with the reins, saddle, and stirrup irons flapping while the woman remained in hot pursuit. Soon the two were out of sight.

Preston looked at the silent body and yelled. "Is she breathing? Should I call 911?"

"She's breathing. Yes, call! I don't want to move her."

Preston jumped the rail and dialed. "We need an ambulance. Rider thrown by horse. Unable to move. She's unconscious."

The authoritative voice issued commands. "Stay on the line. I'm calling for an ambulance. Don't disconnect."

"Okay." He turned to the woman kneeling at June's side, "I'm staying on the line. The operator's calling it in."

The voice came back on the line. "The ambulance will be a helicopter due to your location."

Preston gulped. "Okay." He stayed on the line and told the woman. "They're sending a helicopter."

The woman choked out, "Thank you." She started sobbing. "June, help is on the way. Please, June. Don't move if you can hear me. Stay still."

Within minutes, the sound of the chopper's blades came closer and the rhythmic thuds louder.

Preston's voice trembled. "Can you go with her?"

"I can't. My children are home alone, and I only came to watch her practice test. I don't know her."

"Can the other woman go?"

"Mary? She can't. She's from out of town—the horse's owner. She came with me. I own two horses boarded here. I hope she caught the horse. That one can run forever. I hope he doesn't cause an accident or get hit by a car. He might get hurt and need a vet. He could've pulled a tendon. She won't know until she finds him."

The helicopter landed a safe distance away and two EMTs ran to the arena. One carried a backboard, the other a medical bag.

Preston turned to the EMT. "May I go with her? I feel responsible. My tire blew. It's my fault. Please let me."

"That's not protocol. Hey, she's got an allergy bracelet on. Get her I.D., purse—whatever you can find. We need to know what she's allergic to. Hurry!"

Heading to the arena gate, Preston turned and shouted. "Where's her purse?"

The woman pointed. "Her car's over there. See? Next to the big oak tree. Should be unlocked. No one's ever around here."

Preston ran, then yelled. "Hey! I got her purse." He ran back.

The woman called out, "We'll check with the hospital. Thank you! God bless."

Waving him into the helicopter, the EMT closed the door behind him. "Buckle up. We don't usually allow this, but you have no other way to get to the hospital and it would take you too long by ground. Search for her driver's license and allergy information. Check her wallet for an emergency contact or next of kin. Her allergy bracelet's too faded to read. Here, take it. I need to start an I.V."

Preston reached for the bracelet. Shoving it in his pocket, he searched her purse. "Got her wallet, but no contact or allergy information. Her cell phone's locked. Found her license."

"That'll do. Tell me what you know."

"Her name's June Tarlin. She's twenty-seven. California address…San Diego."

"Okay, far from home. Organ donor?"

"Yes. Oh my God. I'm so worried about her." He wiped beads of sweat from his forehead.

"Hang in there. The hospital has a great trauma team."

The helicopter landed on the trauma center's rooftop and a gurney and trauma team awaited. Transferring June to the gurney, they whisked her off to the Trauma Room with Preston trailing behind and heading to the waiting area.

* * *

A nurse came to his chair. "Hello, sir. Preston, right? June's going to Room 362. Third floor. Give your name to the unit secretary and they'll let you in."

"Is she awake?"

"Not yet. She has pain medicine on board. Talk easy to her if she wakes. We don't know if she'll remember anything. That goes for her name too." She walked off muttering. "Horses…."

"Okay, thanks." His voice trailed and his steps quickened. He entered her room and sat in a chair next to the bed. The bracelet bulged and he fished it out of his pocket. *It's not an allergy bracelet.* He turned it over. Squinting, he read the tiny inscription, '*Reach for the Stars.' Poor woman. What if she's paralyzed or, God forbid, has some other permanent injury?* His head dropped into his hands.

5

June moaned and stirred. *I can't lift my right arm high enough to put your bridle on, D. Come on boy, open your mouth for the bits. We need to go warm up. You're pushing your neck against me. My right leg is stuck. I can't move. My God. What's wrong? Nothing's working. Keep trying…*

She groaned and brushed her hand across her face and felt lumpy hard plastic brush against her cheek. *What's going on?* Her eyelids fluttered open. *Oh, just a bad dream.* She looked up. *I'm inside a room?* She looked at her right arm and saw I.V. tubing taped to the back of her right hand. Her right leg was on something and tied down. She looked left and saw a man sitting in a chair sleeping.

"Where am I? Who are you?" Her eyes opened wide, and her chest heaved with deep breaths looking at the handsome, muscle-bound stranger in the room. She pulled the cover up to her chin with her left hand and covered her eyes.

"Please don't be scared. You're in a hospital. You had an accident. Do you remember anything?"

He's still here. She uncovered her eyes. "Who are you?"

"I rode in the helicopter with you to help them find out who you were. You were unconscious."

"So why you? I don't know you. I don't even really know what happened…" her words slowed. "I think I fell off D."

"Is D a horse?"

"Yes."

"I'm sorry. My car tire blew, and the piece of tire flew into the air and…"

She finished his sentence. "Oh my god. My leg. Do you know about it?"

"No, June. I don't."

"How do you know my name?"

His face got hot. "I had to search your purse for your license."

"And you are?"

"Preston. I'm uhm…Preston—uhm…. James." His face burned.

"You hurt me, Preston." She gasped. "I hope my leg isn't broken. If it is, I might as well be dead."

"I'll keep my fingers crossed."

"For what? Me to be dead so I'll be quiet?" *I'm being mean. Who cares? I'm in pain.*

"No, God no. So that your leg isn't broken."

"Nightmare…I don't know whether to say thank you or get out!" She stared at the ceiling and grimaced. "Hand me my call button or just push it for the nurse. I need to know more." Her eyes filled with tears.

"Of course. I'll push it for you."

* * *

Preston spoon-fed June a few ice chips. She waved Preston away. "That's enough. I feel sick to my stomach." She sighed. "No one's ever babied me before." Her eyes glared. "My leg is killing me."

"I can see that."

The door opened. A man in a white coat entered her room. "Ah, hello. You're awake. I'm Dr. Ralph Carson. Your orthopedic surgeon. Nice to meet you. How's the pain?"

"Surgeon?" She bit her lip. "Ow. My leg hurts and my head feels like someone swung a bat at me, but other than that, I'm alive."

"Good to hear. Do you remember how you got here, June?"

"No, doctor but I think I fell off my horse. At least that's what he," she pointed, "said."

"That's correct from the history 'he' provided, and 'he' is?"

"I don't know him. He caused this." Her arms flopped on the bed, and she closed her eyes. "Ouch…"

Preston stood and extended his hand. "Preston James, sir. My car's tire blew and caused her accident. I am her uhm…uhm…no relation, but a helping bystander."

"Yes. It's all his fault. His car did it." June bit her lip.

"It did doctor, and I'm so sorry. I'm here to help her since she told me her family lives in Florida. I can be here, no problem. I'm uhm…self-employed. Yes, I can be here. If I'm needed."

"Okay, Preston. Good to hear since Discharge Planning will need to know how she's going to get around after her surgery."

"Surgery?" June wailed. "No way. I have to ride."

"And you will. But not for a while. After reviewing your x-rays, I have a diagnosis and a plan. Is it okay to continue our discussion with Preston in the room?"

"Might as well. He already knows so much about me, what difference does it make?" She groaned.

"June, you have fractures on your tibia and fibula, the two leg bones that are in the calf portion of your leg. Quite a hefty break, but day after tomorrow—surgery, and we'll get your bones fixed up. But the good news is, you'll mend with a cast and most likely won't need any permanent hardware. However, you'll need recovery time and most likely physical therapy to get back to your uhm … active lifestyle, I must say. You'll have a full-length leg cast for the first four weeks and a cast change to below the knee for the second six."

June brushed a tear. "Ten weeks of this? My God. Please make me okay to ride again."

"I will use my years of experience and thousands of cases to guide me, June. Please rest and try not to worry. Time and good care will heal your bones. I'm glad you are young and healthy. It makes it so much easier."

He turned and left the room muttering under his breath … "Why on earth do women like to ride horses?" He continued as he walked down the hallway. "Men too for that matter. Then, there's bikes, motorcycles, snowboarding. That's my practice, summed up in a nutshell."

* * *

June covered her face with the inside of her left arm. "This stinks. I'm stuck. I was only up here for the weekend. What am I going to do?"

"I was only here for the weekend too. My client's car isn't wrecked but I need to finish it up for him."

"Are you a mechanic? I see you have coveralls on." *Doesn't even talk like a mechanic and his hands are clean? No wonder his tire blew. He never touched it to check it! He probably never does his job right, so he won't get dirty.*

"It was a test ride for the car. I am a mechanic of sorts."

"What does that mean?" *Tall and blonde. Piercing blue eyes. Chiseled jawline. Good looking, I'd say. That's irrelevant. He must not be a very good mechanic; he almost got me killed.*

"I'm a concierge mechanic. I go to my clients and take care of their cars."

"Excuse me? Don't cars have to go to a garage?" *The world would be a safer place without him loose on the streets.*

"These cars are not the usual cars on the street and my clients aren't necessarily ordinary either. They're busy and need custom care for their collections. I travel to lots of cities. I was just up in Portland, Oregon. This was my last stop before heading to San Diego."

"I live there."

"I know that." His cheeks got hot again. "Saw your license ... I'm from San Diego but I don't live there anymore."

"Oh. Oh no. Well, I do, and I need to check out of my motel here." *My God. And then what?*

"I can help you check out of it."

"Wait. I can't checkout. After surgery, I'll be on the street if I do."

He stood and came next to her bed. "Should I call your family? Parents, maybe?"

"No! My parents are in Florida, and they'll know I failed. I'll hear, 'We told you ....'"

"You didn't fail. You had an accident." He pulled his chair close and sat next to her.

"If I was a better rider, I wouldn't have fallen."

"What? The way that horse took off?"

"Hey. It wasn't his fault."

"Go ahead. Say it. Blame me. I'm strong. I can take it. It's better than thinking you failed."

"You look strong, but I'm living proof that I failed. I'll have to figure something out. This broken leg has really messed up my plans. I should just give up." Tears bubbled in her eyes.

"Can I help you?" His eyes riveted on hers.

"You can't help me. If I can't ride, no one can help me."

"I could take you back to San Diego when you can travel or …"

"Ten weeks from now? No. I've lost everything, including D." Tears rolled down her cheeks.

6

"Don't you have a girlfriend that's going to be looking for you? I mean, technically, you are with a girl."

He laughed. "Don't you have a guy that's going to get jealous that I'm hanging out here almost 24/7? You're the first and only one I've done that for, June."

"Why? Because I haven't made you?"

"That's one reason," his cheeks pinked, "and the other is, besides the fact you're quite beautiful with gorgeous blonde hair, you're a rebel just like me. Ran away from home and didn't want to fail. I admire your spirit and I gotta uh…step up to the plate this time."

"Thanks. No one's ever appreciated that side of me. In fact, no one's ever noticed that and given me any credit at all."

"Well, I see it and I like it. You're bringing out something new in me too, June."

* * *

June smoothed the blanket. "How come you're a mechanic and your hands are so clean and unmarred without a speck of grease? Most mechanics have hands with wear and tear lines. I'm a rider. I don't have painted long fingernails. They'd get ripped off with my riding gloves."

"Oh, those cars, and those owners, many of them are just collectors. They sparkle and the owners need me to take them out and run them. I have shops that I work with in various cities if something major needs to be done; people that work on specialty cars. It's a pretty nifty set up."

"How'd you come up with the concept?"

"Well, long story, I've always been around motors, but not cars. My father builds boats and has some manufacturing factories in different places. I liked the mechanics, but I wanted to be on dry land and move around, not sit in a corporate office, and watch the invoices come and go. Paperwork, yuk. Would you like traveling?"

"Never thought about it because it would mean I couldn't ride every day. I want to have my own training barn and my own horses. Maybe to breed them, but for right now, I just want to ride Grand Prix. That's all. I couldn't stand being out on the road unless I was driving my truck and trailer, which I don't own yet, to a show with a couple of horses. What about your father's business? Doesn't he want you involved?"

"Yes, but that's the last thing I want to do."

"Well, my family owns real estate. They don't get the horse thing, so any property they own is not for a horse — apartment complexes, duplexes, reno houses to flip and all that. We're miles apart, and it's not just the distance. It's just the way it is."

* * *

Two days later, June went to surgery and Preston went out on a mission. Wheeled back into her room, her nurse adjusted her bed settings and brought her ice chips. Minutes later, Preston returned.

"Hi, June. Looks like you have a nice white cast on."

She moaned. *He's still here. I'm surprised he hasn't run away. I've been a total meanie to him. Can't help it. My leg is encased in concrete.* "I hate whiners, but this is miserable. At least I like white. White and black. Great dressage colors, you know? Could you hand me the ice chips? I feel like I've eaten arena sand or something."

Preston stood and filled a spoon and offered it to her. "I have news."

Accepting the spoonful, she swallowed. "About?"

"Us."

"What do you mean 'us'?" *This is unexpected. Now what curve ball is life throwing my way?*

"I'm staying here to help you get on your feet. I booked two ground-level suites right next to each other in an extended stay motel. I can't leave you stranded."

"Because you feel guilty?" *Has to be why. I certainly haven't encouraged him to stay.*

"Because whatever. I know you want to make it on your own and so do I. We've had plenty of talks about that. There's a lot to be said for breaking away from your family ties and making it on your own. I get it. Same situation here. My businesses are my own and I don't have to follow my father's marching orders anymore. Besides, I can't stand living in one place."

He stood and paced. "By the way, I finished up my client's cars here in town, so I'm free as a bird for a while. I hope you like the plan. I did it just for you." He pulled a chair next to the bed and took her hand. "Glad that I.V. needle's gone." He patted it and let go.

"Oh gosh. Me too. Another step toward freedom. Thank you for sharing your guilt trip." Her hand flew to her forehead. "Mamma Mia. This cast is an anchor and a reality check. I accept your offer, however because I must and yes, I appreciate it. I can't even drive! I'm sorry I'm just still mad and can't get past it. Having said that, are you sure there's not going to be a jealous girlfriend? Wife? Lover? Anyone going to come and pound on my door for taking their man?"

He offered more ice chips. "You're funny. No, there's not. How about you?"

She swallowed another spoonful. "That's enough. Thanks. Nah. My boyfriend had big dreams and they didn't include me once the owner of a big fancy barn spotted him. And Tanner moved on to the rich and richer; horse buying trips to Germany with her. She let him pick the horses and they flew them back to the States. Top-level, six-figure competition horses. You get the idea? It was all money, money, money.

"I moved on too and just about had a great arrangement, but I'm sure Sarah Jones, not me, will get D to ride now. At least she's a decent person and a great rider. She always beats me though, and she did it again. Lucky girl. Oh well. I may have to give up on all this. But I'm going to fight like no other to get back to what I was if my leg cooperates.

"Just to be clear," she continued, "you're not into staying in one place after this, right? My life will consist of nothing but riding and making up for lost time."

"I won't be around."

"Good. I won't be in your way. I need stability and a training barn. Cars travel, but barns don't."

"I understand. Truth be told, being near horses is the last thing I would ever want. And as far as women go, no woman would ever put up with my travel lifestyle. That's a fact from experience and I don't object. My cars are my freedom."

"Fair enough. Just so you know, an inanimate object like a car can't hold a candle to the warm body of a horse. I can't live without horses. If I can't ride, I'll clean stalls or just give lessons. Trying to face reality, my friend. Few people make it to the top in dressage … and this is a classic example of derailment."

"A freak accident?"

"Whatever. We're just two people, in a situation, trying to get through it, right? Let's see, twenty-four hours in a day, seven days in a week, ten weeks of being stuck, uhm … Do the math, Preston. We're about to waste 1,680 hours of our lives getting nowhere, meeting no one, and doing nothing that we love, or used to love. To be honest. This layup is going to drain every red cent I have in the bank and I'm not going to beg one dime from my parents. No way. Good thing I've always been a saver.

"So, no need to lie about anything to me. Your life is your life and mine—whatever shred of it is left, is mine. Deal?"

"Putting it that way, 'trying to get through it,' is a perfect description. Deal. Now that we've cleared the air, we have a plan."

"We do. I'm going to have to tell my parents I have an injury, but I'll make sure they understand my care is not a problem and all I need is a little healing time. Well, a little is stretching it, but so what. It'll keep 'em happy."

"Your call."

* * *

June dialed her mother's number. Please go to voicemail! Opening her mouth to greet her mother at "Hello," she smiled in relief when it was only her voicemail. " … leave a message … "

"Hi, Mom. It's me. Just calling to let you know my leg got a little banged up when I was riding. Well, the ground banged it up, I guess." She grimaced and forced a little chuckle.

"Anyway, I'll be taking a little time off riding. I know you and Dad are glad I won't be on them, uh, horses and, uh … resting for a few days. Yes, I'll be resting. I'll call you soon so we can really talk. Love ya!" She hung up. *Liar, liar, pants on fire. I have no choice for now.*

* * *

Two postop days later, Preston walked into June's room. "Hey, you're smiling!" *She's seeing the hope and feeling better. Poor girl. If I was in her place, I'd be a miserable wretch to deal with.*

"Discharged and on my way out of here. I can't wait! They cut the leg off my one and only pair of sweatpants, and this white top has seen its better days. But I made them let me wear clothes instead of a gown. I could care less what I look like."

"Ah. You look fine the way you are." *Still a little hottie no matter what you're wearing.* He grinned. "Be back soon."

* * *

June grabbed her phone and called her sister. She blurted out the words as soon as her sister answered. "Hi, Brianna. I can't talk long."

"June? Hi! Okay, I'm listening."

"Don't freak out, but I fell off a horse and broke my leg."

"What? You? Oh my God! That's terrible! Is it bad?"

"Uh … ten weeks of recovery, but no metal in my bones, just a couple of casts to get me healed. I'm being discharged from the hospital right now as we speak."

"Hospital? Ten weeks! Dear God! When did this happen? Mom and Dad haven't called me—June? June!"

"Uh…A few days ago."

"Oh no. Days—This is serious! Have you told them? I can't believe Mom wouldn't…"

"Sort of. Okay? I sort of told them. I'm telling you the full story, but I'll let them in on it slowly. I don't want them flying out here and taking over or making me go to Florida."

"How on earth are you going to manage? How are you going to get home? You are home, right? In San Diego?"

"No, I'm not home. It's sounds crazy, I'm near Sacramento—close to where the accident happened. I've got my care planned. I'll explain more later, but there's this guy…." *Don't give my secret away, Bri.*

* * *

Pulling up at the hospital entrance. Preston jumped out of the SUV and called to June. "Hey, they wheeled you to the door so fast that you beat me." He knelt and took her hand. "Allow me, my lady, to help you into the car." *If the circumstances were different, this is one girl I would date.*

"You're funny. But yes, I could use your help getting out of this wheelchair. This cast is so heavy." Her eyes looked into his. "Still feel guilty for all this?"

"Yes, but we'll survive." *She's close enough to reach out and lift her into my arms. Oh, that would feel so good. Her body next to mine.* He bit his lip. "Anyway, let's get in the car. I have a wheelchair place to stop at to get one for you, and some crutches. Then, we'll get lunch and go to our place."

"This is such a good day! Mary called and I told her about my ten-week plan, and guess what?"

"What?"

"D isn't hurt!"

"Did she say you'll get him back?"

"No, but we're going to call each other when I'm better. I'm okay with that. Besides, she didn't mention Sarah."

"Sounds good."

"There's hope. I'm just glad to be getting out of the hospital."

* * *

"Ah, yes. Home sweet home for the next two and a half months?" She reached out and punched his arm in jest and leaned into him. Preston's pulse quickened. *She's happy.* Her blue eyes looked deep into his and overwhelmed his thoughts, starting a battle between committing to responsibility and losing control. His chest tightened. *Relax man. She's not pressuring—yet. But what if she does? I could kiss those luscious red lips.*

"It's okay. I do appreciate the fact that you even stopped your car to help. Of course," she huffed as she got into the car, "your car couldn't go without a tire."

"I know. But even if it could, I would've stayed until help arrived." *No, Dad. I didn't run. And I didn't let my money buy my freedom this time. And guess what else, Dad? People can change, you know? But you'll never know about all this. No way.*

"That's nice to hear."

* * *

Evening came and dusk brought a sense of peaceful calm to the suites. Preston knocked on the door. June called out. "Is that you, Preston?" Her heart skipped a beat.

"It is."

He's still here. I'm not alone. "Come in."

"Hi. Want to go for a stroll in your wheelchair? Fresh air before I go pick up dinner?"

"Sounds good. I miss being outside. I miss D. I wonder how he's going to do at his next show with Sarah; probably a 70 percent or higher. Darn. I missed out. Mary could've picked me to ride him. I wanted to show him and try to earn a high enough score that moving up a level would be a logical move. Most of the shows in the San Diego area are going to be over by the time this cast comes off. That's okay because I wouldn't have time to practice for them anyway. But you never know, maybe there'll be a late show I can ride in." *Not likely.* She sighed and thumped her cast. "Solid as a rock, God. Grand Prix horses don't come a dime a dozen and neither do riders."

"You'll get back in the saddle, June. Just a little bump in the road. Wasn't there an Olympic rider who fell and broke her leg? She came back. Didn't she? I mean, before you I never paid attention to the dressage and now..."

Her head lolled back. "No more horse talk. Come on, let's get out of this room before my pity party turns into a sobbing mess."

"Your chariot awaits. Here, let me get you in the wheelchair. No falling and breaking your other leg."

"Oh my gosh. That would kill me off."

"Good thing you're tiny enough that I can pick you up if I have to."

"I was wondering about those biceps of yours. All for show?"

She reached out and squeezed his arm. She hesitated to let it go. *Hot and strong, just like him.* She eyed him and couldn't stop herself from feeling her cheeks getting hotter.

"My hobby. You noticed, huh? I work out at gyms wherever I am. Let's go." He stretched and held her in support of the transfer. His hands held her body without hesitation, and he grasped her anywhere he needed to, and she relaxed into his hold. The space between their bodies was evaporating into thin air. She was all his for now. "I love your smile."

Oh boy, June. This is a stranger, and you are putty in his hands. Oooh, those hands.

* * *

They stopped at a grassy spot and looked at the fountain.

June wheeled herself a little closer. "I like the sound of water. It's so soothing. Like the sound of horses' hooves on sand. There really isn't much sound when you're riding. I get lost in the moment up there."

"I get it. I've always liked the power of cars. Good thing my job lets me be around them. That's enough talk about my work. How about we take a little break from reality and make our weeks an experience that even a girl with a broken leg could enjoy. What do you say?"

"Just hiding out from the world…and no pressure?" She toyed with the wheelchair armrest. "So different from my sunup to sundown routine." Her eyes lit up for a second.

He reached out and gently lifted her chin. "No pressure at all. I'm twenty-nine and I've never taken some real time off."

"And no set plans?"

"None."

"Would be a first for me too."

"Let's go for it. And let's go for real, and I mean now. You look tired."

"I'm exhausted."

"I'll push. Breathe in the fresh air. I'll take you to your room so you can rest."

June touched his hand. "Good thing you're so strong." *This cast is as heavy as my heart.*

* * *

The door closed behind Preston, June reached for her crutches. Grabbing them, she huffed and stood. She breathed hard with fear. *I'm not steady. Gosh, this is tough to do. I need my phone.* With turtle speed, she put them under her armpits and moved toward the table. *Purse, phone, got it!* Using her body, she pushed the chair out enough to sit down, with her full leg cast extended out and her other leg firmly planted on the floor for balance. *Dear God. I hope I don't pass out and fall off the chair. Not an ounce of softness on this hard carpet.* She brushed her sweat away, dialed, and gripped the phone when her call was answered. "Hi, Mom." Her voice, as cheery as she could muster, almost cracked. She bit her lip and fought tears.

"Hello, June, honey. How nice to hear your voice. I'm glad you called. I was just getting a cup of chamomile tea before going to bed. We went to the beach with friends and I'm exhausted. How are you? How's your leg? I wasn't sure what you meant by 'banged up.' Is it cut and bruised?"

"Oh no. Nothing like that. You know me, Mom. Keepin' busy

riding and it's been fun. I uh, traveled up north for a client to present her horse in a test ride so she could watch and compare my riding to another rider. I was hoping to work more with her horse and get her to choose me to keep riding it and even move it up a level."

"Oh, yes. That sounds just like you. Always working those horses. How did it go? Did she choose you?"

"Well, unfortunately, the horse heard a tire blow, and he got spooked and I fell off. So, my leg needs some healing time now, as I mentioned in my message."

"Honey, you rarely fall. That must have been some spook. Did you go to the doctor or a clinic?"

"Oh yes, Mom. I've been well taken care of. My leg's wrapped up and, like I said, it needs time. I'm in the Sacramento area. I'm going to stay up here because I do like the doctor I saw."

"Are you sure going home wouldn't be better? Isn't it going to be expensive staying there in a motel?"

"No problem. I got it covered. Um, Mom, I need to run to the bathroom, so, I just wanted to let you and Dad know. I'll keep you updated."

"Okay honey. I'll let you go. If things change, call us and we'll fly out or fly you to Florida. I know you need to be giving lessons and it sounds like you won't be able to for a little while. June, I wish you had a desk job or at least worked indoors in a safe job like your sister does."

I know you do. Why do you think I'm not telling you the truth? Ugh! "A little while's right. Thanks, Mom. Great offer, but I'm okay. Bye." She groaned and put the phone down. Standing, she managed to shove the crutches under her armpits and hobbled toward the bed. *I can't do this.* A tear rolled down her cheek and she couldn't wipe it. Her nose ran a little and a tissue was out of the question, and nowhere in sight. Her shirt sleeve worked. Just as she sat on the edge of the bed, one crutch fell to the floor. *I hope there isn't a fire. I'll die right here in this bed. Not a bad idea, actually. June!* She managed to support her cast leg with both hands and using core strength and her arms, lift it and lie down. *Thank God I'm a strong rider. This is bad.*

7

Preston used his key and opened the door an hour later. "Dinner's in the bag. June?" He walked over to the bed. *My little Sleeping Beauty.* "Fast asleep…June," he whispered. "The food's here. Want to eat?"

June opened her eyes. "Oh, okay."

"Let me help you up." He moved the crutches out of the way and struggled to get her up without letting her cast drop. "Chinese takeout and then I stopped at the grocery store and got some fruit and some ice cream for dessert."

"Sounds good."

"Look." He pulled two things out of the bag. "Battery candles for the table. If we can't go out yet, we can have some ambiance without setting off the fire alarm."

"How did you know I'm into candles?"

"I just guessed. I'm getting a little more sophisticated as the years pass."

June rolled her eyes and shook her head. "Oh yeah. Twenty-nine, almost thirty."

"Yes, mam. Don't forget, I know you're twenty-seven."

"You and my license. Geez. Good thing I didn't have tax papers in my purse or give you my cell phone code to check my contacts and photos. I would be completely exposed."

"Hey. I helped save your life, didn't I?"

34

"More like helped end it!" She snickered. "Keepin' the guilt goin', that's all."

"Are you ever going to let me off the hook?"

"How about when my cast comes off and I can be back to the way I was?"

"Funny!" He brought her crutches and helped her get steady with them. Guarding her as she walked, he got her closer to the table and helped her sit and propped up her leg. "I'm going to be an expert attendant. You think Grand prix horses are hard to find, what about good help?"

"Mister, you have a lot of proving to do to support your claim of 'good.' We'll see. Day one, done." She took a bite. "Sorry to talk with my mouth full, but yum!"

"I can do better than Chinese takeout." He laughed. *I've just never tried to impress. Never had to.*

"Prove it. Pass the soy sauce packet please."

"Here you go." *This is going to be fun.*

* * *

Guilt nagged him as Preston knocked on the door the next morning. *I hope she got some sleep. I'd die wearing that huge cast.* Hearing her call for him, he came in sounding as cheery as he could muster. "Hi. I was just wondering if you had any ideas for today?" He sat next to her on the edge of the bed.

"You must've read my mind. These poor gray sweatpants with one leg cut off are getting a little ratty looking and my top is kind of dirty. But at least my nurse was kind enough to pass it on from the unclaimed Lost and Found and she said the clothes had been washed. I hope so! I can't believe that motel I was in 'lost' my bag. Someone

35

probably took it. Some of my favorite breeches were in there." She grabbed her hair and a scrunchie and pulled it into a messy bun. Some strands fell around her face. "Can you put up with pushing a wheelchair-bound charity victim through a clothing store?"

He tried not to stare or reach out and stroke her hair. *I love that blond shiny hair of hers. Stop it! Control yourself.* "No problem. I wanted to get you a few things anyway."

"Seriously?"

"Yeah. I thought you'd like that."

"Thank you. I'm sorry I'll be so underdressed for shopping, but hopefully my wardrobe will benefit from this excursion."

"Need a few minutes, or are you ready?"

She laughed. "I'm ready."

He sat on the sofa. *God, she's cute no matter what she's wearing, cast included.* "Come to think of it, I need new clothes too. I only have a duffle bag with a couple of tee shirts and jeans."

"Dumping the coveralls?"

"For now." He grinned.

* * *

Arriving at the mall, June transferred from the car into her wheelchair and Preston elevated her cast. June tossed her hair. "Does my hair look okay?"

"Looks long, blonde, and beautiful." *And I could just run my fingers through it and then…*

"I couldn't see much in the mirror. It has to be better than helmet hair, right?"

"Helmet hair? Never heard of it. But yours is pretty. Your blonde ponytail was shining that day and caught my eye."

"Oh, you. I don't have any makeup on or even with me."

"You don't need it." *That's no lie.*

"I know, but at least I can get a few things, like lip gloss, mascara, an eyelash curler, eyeshadow, and some blush and …."

"We'll get whatever you want."

"Wow."

"Got it." He pushed her. "Hang on. We're rolling, literally." *I can't believe it feels so nice to be needed, but I hate being expected to do things. Eh, she'll never know.*

"This feels so weird."

"I agree."

* * *

They returned home three hours later, loaded with bags. Preston put the bags in their rooms and came back to hers.

"Preston, I'm too tired to move."

"Here, I'll help you lie down in bed. You should rest."

"Want to rest next to me?" *I can't believe I just invited him to bed. Okay, well, not bed, bed, but still, he's a hot guy.* "We can turn on the TV."

"I can go to my own room, June. You don't have to feel obligated to spend more time with me." His eyes lit up. "Unless you want to. I would like to."

"I don't want to be alone. Preston, I've had months of being alone. That's what riding and training horses is all about. Me and them. You're not D," she patted the bed, "but come on."

"Got it. I'm no horse, but I'll do in the meantime. Alright. I'm tired too, plus, we can just talk." He gently got into the bed and looked over at her. "Hmmm …. Pretty nice."

"Uh huh. Pillow talk." She smiled and eyed the ceiling. Taking a few deep breaths, she let her body relax.

Pillow talk? Girl talk. He looked at her. *No doubt about it, she's all girl.* Heads down on the pillow, they looked at each other. "June, I let you have the right side because of your leg. But for the record, that's my side of the bed."

"Very nice of you. Your side too, huh? What else do you want me to know about you before I close my eyes?"

"I got the best side."

"No, you didn't. You just said …"

"I did. I got the side next to you."

She swallowed hard. "You're a considerate and nice person, Preston."

"Just nice?" *What are you doing? You're her caregiver after you almost got her killed.*

Her cheeks got hot. "No, not 'just'… You're cute too. Hard to believe you don't have a girlfriend."

"I don't. I told you, I'm into being free and able to travel. Guess that's why I'm alone."

"I understand. That's how I felt about riding. I rode several horses a day and that was about six days a week. I know what it's like to have a commitment to following your desire. I'm usually alone, but never lonely."

"I'm glad you get it. Not many other women think like that. That's how it is for me with the cars. I like working alone." *That's it. Stay back. She's getting to you like a torque wrench on a stubborn bolt.*

"So do I. But for now, I like your company. We're uhm …"

"Inseparable." *I've never said or thought that before. God. Am I crazy for committing to this girl?*

They closed their eyes. The room was peaceful, and they napped.

* * *

June opened her eyes and saw her arm draped across Preston's stomach. She pulled it off as lightly as she could. He stirred and grinned when he opened his eyes and saw her watching him. "Spying on me?"

"Yes. It's fun watching you. You looked so comfortable."

"I could say the same with your arm draped over me. Feel better?" *Her sweet, warm breath. I could kiss that mouth of hers. She'd boot me out of here if she could read my mind.*

"Yes. Oh my gosh. It's almost dinner time."

"How about pizza?"

"Sounds good. What kind?"

"You pick. There's no such thing as a kind I don't like."

What? Not picky either? "Okay. I'll go get one. Want some beer or wine?"

"Either."

"You're my kind of girl. I'll be back in less than an hour. Do you need anything before I go?"

"No, thanks for asking." *He's too good to be true, but I need his help. I am really stuck.*

* * *

Pushing his chair back, Preston stood. "I'm so full. Want to move to the couch and watch TV?"

"Sure."

"Okay. Let's get you over to the couch and comfortable. Here's some extra pillows for your leg. I'll get the remote." Opening the curtains, Preston peered outside. "The end of the day."

"Preston, it's getting kind of late. I think my leg needs to rest in bed. Shall we call it a night?"

"Okay. I'll go to my place, and I'll be back early in the morning."

"Sure." She reached out. "Let me give you a hug. This has been an amazing day. Thank you for everything." *He is so opposite and so much more considerate than Tanner ever was, and Tanner was my boyfriend! But, like Tanner, this one will be gone too. Only this time, I know about it. It has to be that way. I miss horses. I could bury my face in a horse's neck and hug it out. At least I wouldn't end up heartbroken again.*

"I had fun too. See you in the morning. I'm thinking tomorrow night we can go out for dinner. You got some cute clothes."

"Yeah. I'll just have to modify my wardrobe a little for the cast, but I'm game. Tomorrow though; right now, I'm exhausted. Good night. Will you lock the door on your way out?" *This is so much better than being in the hospital. He's right next door.*

"I will. Your cell phone's on the nightstand. If you need anything, just call."

* * *

How had this happened? A stranger had come into her life, and he was treating her like a princess? A wounded princess, but still. Her breakup with Tanner had almost devastated her and derailed her riding focus from the aftermath. And now her reality was a broken leg and a drifter unable to commit to anyone and stay in one place? Had her horse dreams gone by the wayside forever? The right horse required lessons and hard work to earn them. All she had to bank on were her skills to take her to the end of the tests, so to speak, and those were gone and so was a suitable horse. Face it. This relationship spelled trouble without—pardon, the pun, a break in sight.

8

Knocking on the door the next morning, Preston waited for her to respond. Hearing nothing, he used his key and poked his head in the doorway. "June! Are you okay?"

Yelling, she responded. "I'm fine. Just brushing my teeth. Come in."

"Good morning. Let's get out of here. There's a nice breakfast buffet in a downtown hotel lobby. It's a beautiful hotel. I almost got our rooms there, but they just didn't have the access I was looking for the day you were being discharged and I was in a hurry. We could move there if you want."

"No! This is just fine. Sorry, I'm still in my same clothes. I was going to shower and change." *I've never looked so crappy in my life!*

"You look fine to me."

"Are you sure?"

"I'd like to see anyone say you don't."

"Fine. To the black SUV, then. I like the color."

"Glad you approve. Let's go."

* * *

Walking to the restaurant check-in desk, the attendant smiled. "Hello, sir. It's so nice to see you again. Breakfast for two?" She

42

glanced down at June as she unfolded and placed the cloth napkins in their laps with a flair.

"Yes, please."

Seated at their table, within seconds the attendant returned with a red rose. She placed it on the table in the center of Preston's space. "This rose's for you, sir. It's my way of welcoming you back." She winked and walked off.

June looked at Preston. "Do you come here often?" *God. I'm out of place here! Underdressed and quite haggard looking as a matter of fact. I hope I don't embarrass him.*

Preston fidgeted. "I've been here a couple of times. Not often. When I'm passing through." Picking up the rose, he handed it to June. "To you, from me." He reached out and touched her hand.

"Oh. Thank you. Wow. Such a deep red. It's lovely." She looked around and flattened the wrinkles from her napkin. *Wish it was a blanket and could hide me. Geez. Fancy. And he's not batting an eye. He's used to this.* "What if she sees that you gave it to me?"

"I don't care."

"Anyway, this is such a nice place. I bet the rooms are too."

"They are. They're not on ground level though and I thought our place would be easier for you."

June's cheeks pinked. "I'm not complaining about where we are. Our place is nice, it's just this is a type of luxury I'm not used to. I don't need to stay here. I'm glad we're here for breakfast though. Nice choice, Preston."

"Good."

The server brought menus. "Hello and welcome. We have menu options, or our champagne buffet." Smiling, she held out menus and they both reached for one. "Nice to see you back, sir."

Preston gulped. "Thanks." He glanced and pointed to the

main dishes. "These have potential, we'll start with coffee and OJ…I'm sorry. June, would you like champagne instead or we could have mimosas and have both that way."

"What a great way to start the day. I'd like a mimosa. Can't say I've ever had any champagne at breakfast before. Fun!"

"Make that two please." The server left the table.

After deciding what to order, June quizzed him. "Alright, she knew you too. You must be very memorable."

"Some people have good memories." He chuckled.

The server returned. "Two coffees and two mimosas. Ready to order?"

"We are. My lovely lady will have the corned beef and eggs, scrambled. And I'll have the same. She has good ideas."

"Yes sir, she does. Be right back."

She left and Preston reached for June's glass to hand it to her. *He even talks different here. 'Lovely lady?' Hmm…* "Here, let's toast…." The glass slipped out of his grasp and spilled all over the table and splashed on June's white shirt. "Oh my gosh. I'm so sorry."

Looking down, orange spots splattered across her shirt, and she gasped. "Oh no. That's okay. Just an accident, but God this looks awful."

"It's not that bad, here comes our server. We'll get you another one right away." He wiped the tablecloth near June. "This will stop the drips from heading to your lap."

She looked down and then back up. "Not quite. But thanks. I'll cover my lap with the napkin."

The server finished cleaning up the spill and brought June a new drink. Their white tablecloth was now half orange, but ignoring it, June teased. "Good distraction, but I was going to ask about your flaws besides driving so fast you pop your car tires."

Preston cleared his throat. "I didn't drive that fast that day, but I'll admit I had a good pace going. I had to rev that car a little bit." He grinned. "Anyway, to answer your question, I'm an only child and I had everything handed to me. So, when it comes to relationships, I put zero effort into meeting the right woman."

"So, you're a zero-effort guy. Uh huh. Go on."

"Secondly, I don't trust people—women, right off the bat. They're not what they act like they are, and I can see that very soon. They're not authentic. They always have an angle. They're into trapping a guy."

And he thinks men are 'authentic' and don't have an 'angle'? Ha! "Alright, you're a confirmed bachelor and want to stay that way. Go on." *Keep talkin' bud. Tell it like it is. At least he's spillin' the beans. I've got to figure him out!*

The server returned with their food. "Would you like ketchup for your potatoes?"

June replied. "Yes, please."

"I have it right here for you." She set a mini-sized one-inch-high bottle of ketchup on the table.

"Thank you." June reached for it and started opening it. "Gosh this plastic seal is hard to get off this tiny lid. My nails are too short to lift the edge. Oh! Here it is." She dropped it on the floor. "Oops. Can you reach it?"

Preston stood. "Got it. I'll open it for you." Struggling, he worked to get the plastic off. "You're right. They've got this sealed tight. Here let me give it a good twist." He moved closer and ripped the lid open. The ketchup flew out and the little bottle dropped onto June's top and straight down to her pants. "Oh no. Not again. I'm really sorry." His entire face was as red as the ketchup.

The middle of her top had a huge red vertical stain and looking down at her sweats was no different. Her cheeks burned. "Well, this shirt's a mess. I think I need a bib for this wardrobe disaster."

"It's okay. No one's looking."

She glanced around in horror, and her eyes met the other patrons' stares. "Uh … not sure about that, but at least we're out of town and no one will know us."

"True. You're a good sport. Anyway, back to my flaws … I don't know how to flirt."

"Because you don't put any effort into pursuing someone. Go on."

"I'm guarded."

"That doesn't count. That's a repeat of not trusting people. So, let me ask you point blank. Are you honest?"

"Well, yes. To a point."

"To a 'point'?" *A red flag answer if I ever heard one!* "What does that mean?"

"I'm sensitive about sharing personal details about my childhood, and all that. That's all."

Her cheeks burned. *Oh my. I hit a nerve. What happened in his childhood that traumatized him?* "Sen …?" her words stopped when a buff, jaw-dropping, muscle-bound guy came up to the table. "Hey man. I didn't expect to see you in town. Good to see you."

"Oh hey, David. I didn't expect to be in town."

"I see you have a dining companion."

"Yes. This is June."

June smiled. "Hi." She squirmed. *Okay. So, who's this? I thought we were going to be unnoticed in here. This is turning into a reunion.*

"Are you in town for long?"

"No. Actually, we're just here for breakfast, Good to see you, but our food's getting cold."

"Oh. Sure. I see. I had some tickets to a NASCAR race in the Sonoma area that I thought you might be interested in. The race isn't until early next year, but they are reserved prime box seats. I uhm…know a couple of ladies that wanted to join us, but never mind. I'll shoot you a text and catch up with you later."

"You got it." Preston's forehead glistened with sweat. He took a deep breath.

David turned and came back. "Hey, uhm…. is it okay if I say you're looking forward to the event? There's a chartered jet for VIPs and that could be a sweet ride, you know? For you. I mean you and your date and a buddy and his date. Know what I mean? Tryin' not to namedrop but, you know how it is…."

Clearing his throat, Preston coughed. "Oh, uh, yeah sure. You want a ride in a jet. Whatever. Use my name. See ya around, ok?"

June sat taller and her ears perked as though she had radar capability. *'Use my name?' I peeked at social media and his name didn't bring up anything. Why'd that guy say that? Another red flag.*

Randy's smile stretched from ear to ear. "Thanks, R…"

Preston interrupted before he could finish. "Hey, it's okay. Our food's here…"

"Gotcha. I'll be in touch." He walked off, turning back once to give Preston a thumbs up. Preston nodded.

June touched Preston's arm. "Are you alright? You seemed edgy about that guy seeing you. Oh. It's me…."

"No, June. It's not you. I told you, you're beautiful. Yeah, a little messy at the moment, but no big deal. I just wanted him to leave. I've worked out with him a couple of times at the gym, but

he's not my best friend. He's always trying to hang out with me."
He took a sip of his drink.

"I could see that. I've known a few people like that. They
wanted to have me watch them ride without paying for a lesson."
She shook her head. "Or they like to talk about horses, riding
clinics, and shows more than they ride."

"Ah, so you understand. But hey, if he does send me the tickets, would that be something you'd like to go to?"

"To a race in the beautiful area of Sonoma? Wine tasting and
everything else great in that quaint area? I've never been there.
Yes, I'd like to go. But if it never happens, don't worry about it.
The thought was nice." *What an offer. Who wouldn't?*

"Oh, June. That's a nice thing for you to say."

"I mean it. Thank you for thinking of me." She reached over
and put her hand on his. *Something's not adding up here. Car mechanic? He's nice and apparently, even other people think he is, but
things aren't painting a clear picture of him. The truth will come out
one day. I wonder when.*

"I'm not worried about you either and I'm not even going
to ask about your flaws. You are injured and in pain. That alone
brings out the truth about people. Right now, you are transparent."

"And over the next ten weeks … We … ."

"Are going to both be absolutely transparent."

*I will be, but you? Don't know about that. He's seems so wonderful
though.* "Transparent? I can go for that. My boyfriend lied and
cheated on me and then dumped me. But that's because he had
wants I could never afford. So, I guess from that perspective, he
was better off with her."

"That's mean. He should have broken up with you in an honest way and then went on to the other woman. You would've still been madder than a wet hen, but at least…"

"It would have been the truth. All I ask, Preston, is for you to tell me the truth. I do not expect one other thing from you. And no, I don't want to trap you. We are going to get through this and be on our merry way. Promise." *Be realistic, June. You are maimed, can't walk or drive, don't want to tell Mom and Dad and face the fact they were right about not having a backup plan. And, after this is over, you'll be flat broke and starting from scratch. Impossible? No! Just get through this and get back to your real life. He won't care.*

He gulped. "Point taken."

The server returned. "No hurry, sir but here is your ticket."

"Thanks, here's my card."

Reaching out with a big smile, she took the debit card. "Be right back!" She sauntered off.

June gasped. "Whoa. When I get to walking again, I hope I have that sort of spring in my step. Preston, your face is red. What are you thinking?" She giggled. *Another one? I don't think he planned on encountering all these people.*

"I'm thinking you're funny."

The server returned. "Here you are, sir. Your card and your receipt."

"Thank you." Looking at the receipt, Preston's cheeks turned bright red.

"What's on the receipt?"

He put his hand over his face and shook his head. "She drew a caricature of me and included her phone number with hearts above it. Oh man. And a gift coupon for dinner for two here along with a bottle of wine or champagne. I'm going to put this in your wallet. That way, you'll always have a fancy dinner ready and waiting for you and someone special whenever you want." He looked around. "Anybody else coming out of the woodwork? What's with this place today?"

"They're all about you, aren't they?" *Wonder what his explanation is!*

"Nah. It's all because I have my cute dining companion here. Let's get out of here."

* * *

Driving back to the room, Preston needed a transition from that craziness back to their reality. He spotted a park. "Want to take a drive over to the park back there? The one we just passed." *I hope this works as the perfect distraction. The restaurant was a scene I didn't need.*

"Sure. We can walk off our huge breakfast." She giggled. "Well, one of us can!"

"I'll turn back." *Good plan.*

"I just wanted to say thank you for sharing one of your favorite places with me. I know it is since you've been there more than once. That was so much fun dining in an elegant atmosphere. Very thoughtful of you."

"You make it fun for me to do things for you because you don't expect anything from me. After the spills, any other girl would have been mad and the whole breakfast would've been ruined. But not you. You're a good sport."

"I've been on my own for a couple of years with only myself to rely on. I set the bar high, but only for me. I've learned if you don't expect too much, you won't be disappointed."

"Good advice. Hey. I just remembered something. I'll show it to you when we get there."

"I'm excited to see it."

"It's for you. You'll never guess what it is. I call it destiny now that I know you."

"Seriously, now I'm dying of curiosity. Hurry and park."

* * *

He parked and helped June into her wheelchair. "Okay. Let's elevate that foot. Your toes are a little swollen."

"Good call. Okay."

Coming around to her side of the chair, he pulled her closer to a bench. He sat next to her and reached in his pocket and holding out a closed fist. "Go ahead. Open my fingers and see what it is. I call it destiny."

9

Lifting his fingers one by one, she looked at his palm and took a deep breath. "My bracelet! 'Reach for the Stars.' Oh my gosh." She took it and pressed it to her chest. "I thought it was lost in the arena sand forever. Thank you. Please put it on me. How did you find it?"

Buckling the bracelet, Preston looked into her eyes. "The EMT gave it to me. I'm sorry it took me so long to think about giving it back to you. We've been busy and I left it in my coverall's pocket."

June swallowed. "I'm just happy to have it back. It was the first piece of jewelry that I bought in California. I always wear it for luck. I call it lucky. Why do you call it destiny?"

"Because of it, the EMT thought you had an allergy, and it was one of the main reasons he let me go with you in the helicopter; so I could search your purse for allergy info."

"Which I don't have ..."

"Right, but ..."

"It brought us together. Wow, Preston. That is destiny." She shook her head. "I feel energized. Let's explore the park."

"Let's go."

* * *

"I love it here and being in the fresh air. I would give anything to hike around here and explore this park in every corner.

Even better if we were on horses ...." She sighed. "I miss two working legs as much as I miss horses. Would you mind getting me my crutches? I'd like to walk around the best I can."

"Sure. I'll be right back." *Poor June. I'm glad I've gotten to know her. Just wish it hadn't been because of the accident.*

Returning with the crutches, Preston handed them to June. She got out of her chair and stood. Preston pushed the empty chair. "We better keep this close by."

"I am such an invalid. Gosh. Let's go to the bridge. We can look over the rail and throw stones in the water."

They walked a miniscule number of steps to the bridge and stopped in the middle. "Look down, Preston. I love how the light moves on the water. It has such a gentle flow. Reminds me of how calm it would be to be in a sailboat."

"You like sailing? This is something I didn't expect to hear." *Something else in common?*

"Oh no. Something I always wanted to do but never have. Not even in Florida. A little too rich for my blood. All my money went toward riding lessons, and all my time went toward working, cleaning stalls, and exercising horses to earn it. Dry ground only. How about you?" She looked at his blue eyes and his tanned arms.

"I never wanted to sail. Probably because it's what my dad wanted me to do."

"Why?"

"I don't know. He was so insistent. Made me finish college and I did. But right after graduation, I left home for good. I've always had access to cars and my business was easy to develop once I was free." *No way am I living his desired life for me.*

"I didn't go past my A.A. degree in college. I would've, but my time and energy weren't there for it. I couldn't continue wasting some teacher's time or take up space in a classroom that belonged to someone all about being in school when my heart wasn't in it at all. My parents weren't happy about that, but they couldn't stop me. If they hear all the gory details about my leg, they'll probably be over here, or worse yet insist I go there, and my two months of seclusion are over. Glad I totally downplayed, err…more like, lied about the extent.

Well, what's done is done. My recovery must be quiet and just let the time go by. Thank goodness Florida is far away from California and no one in San Diego really cared what my trip up north was all about anyway. As far as they knew, it was just another trial ride on a potential horse to train and show. It sounds awful, but I'm too busy riding to make time for friends. I mean, I talk to a million people every day, but I don't hang out with any of them."

Preston reached in his pocket. "I have two shiny pennies. One for you and one for me. Shall we make a wish?" *I hope your recovery is perfect. Then, I can go my own way without feeling guilty and you can go back to riding your horses.*

"Okay, but no telling what we're wishing for. It's the only way to make your wish come true."

"You got it." The coins splashed.

"Preston, I hope my wish comes true. I made it for you."

"You would." His face came close to hers and he took her chin in his hand. "You're the nicest person, June.

"Mister, you're hard to resist." She touched his cheek and let her finger drift down his face. His skin had a slight shadow, and the stubble slowed her finger. She paused. "I like your aftershave. I can smell bay and rum. It's kind of a light scent, right?"

"It is. Glad you like it." Her hand touched his face.

"I should've shaved."

"No. Your face is perfect."

His skin got clammy. It was hot from the sun, or maybe just hot. Her fingers were so soft and cool. *They could just stay there.* He stood motionless. Neither spoke. He scolded himself, but couldn't pull away. He moved closer. He could hear her breathing getting a little jagged.

She let her fingers glide through his hair. "You're a lone mechanic. Why?"

"I don't want a girlfriend." *You seem perfect, but we're not a match in real life.*

"I'm lucky you don't. We wouldn't be standing here making wishes."

"True. You're my little sweet project. Yes, a project better than any other project I've ever had. Making me put my tools down and stay out of hot cars. You're quite the woman, June." *I would've never told anyone else that. I couldn't trust they wouldn't be pressuring me. They all do, but I don't think she's like them. Face it. I'm slipping, and I shouldn't . . . for her sake.*

"I've never been someone's project, but I like being yours."

He moved a little closer. "You getting tired standing here? You can rest your head on my arm, or should we go? It's getting hotter out here, isn't it?"

She moved closer and let her head and body rest against him. She closed her eyes and lifted her face to the sun. "I love being outdoors, but it is hot now and yes, I'm getting a little tired. Let's go back to the room. I think these crutches are getting heavier. My poor armpits. Ouch."

He looked down at her face. *I'm heating up too and it's not just the weather. This can't be happenin'.* "Here, June. Sit in the chair and give me those crutches. That's enough for you."

"Okay, nurse." She giggled.

* * *

They arrived at her door. "Preston. Come in, okay?" Their eyes locked. *You know where this could lead, June.*

He pushed her chair all the way in—next to the small sofa and sat on the arm. "I was heading that way. Special invitation?" He let his eyes continue to meet with hers. "Something on your mind, ma'am?" He took her hand.

"I want to take a shower." She bit her lip. "Could you help me?"

"I can." He looked around. "Where's that cast protector that the doctor gave you?"

"It's still in my hospital bag in the closet."

"I'll get it. Yep, here it is." He took it out. "I'll go turn on the shower. Thank goodness it's made for you."

"Boy, I'll never underestimate the importance of accessibility for people. You never know when something like this will happen."

"I know. Out of the blue. Alright, the water's running."

They looked at each other. She tapped her fingers on the armrest. "I'm not sure what to say. You don't have to leave." *You're walking right into this, aren't you? This is vacation, kind of. Stop kidding yourself.* "I don't want you to leave."

"Are you saying you want to take a shower together?"

She looked deep into his eyes and held her gaze. Her thoughts raced. *Should I, or shouldn't I?*

"Because I would love to join you—in a heartbeat, June."

His words stopped her doubt.

He continued. "Or I can keep my eyes closed and let my skilled mechanic's hands undress you without looking. I mean, if I can take an engine apart by feel…" A sly smile lifted the corners of his lips.

"I see…Well, I can catch and halter a horse; tack it up, bridle it, and ride in the dark." She reached out and held his hands.

"I'm sure you can." Letting go, he put his hands on the arm-rests and pulled her a little closer. "I saw your skills in the few seconds I watched you riding. You looked like a vision or something. If that tire didn't blow, I would have pulled over and watched."

"You liked watching me ride? Mister, you know the way to my heart. Would you ever video my ride if I ever ride again?"

"I don't see why not. You're going to be well again, one day. I know it seems impossible right now. Yeah, I would video you."

"Oh my gosh. You do know what to say. I know what. Let's play a little game and see if you know what to do. After every piece of clothing comes off, we kiss. My shirt's first." She grabbed the bottom and lifted it one inch. "Want to finish it for me?"

"I do." He swiftly got the shirt off and they kissed.

"Your turn. Shirt, right? Come closer and lean down a little so I can reach the top button." She unbuttoned all of them and pulled his shirt open and off. His chest had just enough blonde chest hair to accentuate his defined muscles. She ran both hands across his chest. "I love your muscles. Wow. They're ripped."

Her fingers traced them across his chest. "I want my kiss. Can you help me stand?" They stood together in a close hug. He ran his fingers up and down her back. She swept her hair back and he kissed her neck. She let his fingers find her waistband and, with ease, her pants fell to the floor. Without words they kissed and pressed in close. The small lower part of his back led to tight muscles that ran up his spine and connected with his broad shoulders. Her hands grazed his back in a firm rub as the edges of her nails skimmed the surface. With a solid grasp on him, she unbuckled his belt and buttons so that his pants fell into a heap. Another kiss lingered.

He reached around her back. "Silky little garment…but not as soft as you are though." He pulled her into him and gently held her while he ran his fingers through her hair. Skin to skin, they lingered.

She tugged at the waist band of his boxers and ran her hands down his thighs. The briefs were snug to his skin but slid and ended on top of the growing pile on his feet.

"Okay, June. What little is left is coming off next and I'm putting on your cast protector. You're about to get squeaky clean."

"Don't forget my kiss."

"Never."

* * *

The bathroom was steamed up and the hot water running. They stopped in front of the fogged-up mirror, and he drew a heart. They kissed until the image fogged back over. They entered the shower and sat on the tiled bench shower seat. He washed her body with a gentle touch. He watched as she washed her hair and indulged in the hot water, the steam and the feel of the water running down her skin. "Let me wash you, Preston."

"Alright. But then we're going to get wrapped up in towels and go to bed. Forget the crutches. I'll carry you."

"I'll do anything and go anywhere with you right now." Their embrace brought them even closer, and she melted into his touch. "Don't stop, Preston. I don't want you to stop, okay?"

"Not stopping's easy."

"I wish I didn't have this cast on."

He put his finger on her lips. "Listen, your leg's only a small percentage of your body. I can work around it." He turned off the water.

She kissed him. True to his word, he carried her to bed.

* * *

Talking quietly, she ran her fingers along his chest. "Gosh darn cast. Only half of me gets to be next to you."

"No problem. It won't be there forever. We're doing just fine. Hey, something to look forward to."

"Yeah, and I just remembered that I have a cast change in a few weeks. It'll be below my knee and it's going to be a walking cast."

"See there? Told ya. You're making progress every day. Like your doctor said, you're young and strong."

"If only he included that I'd be able to ride again. I've never had so much time off from riding. It's scary."

"What's unknown can be. That's how I felt when I started my business. I didn't want to fail and let my dad know. There was a quote I came across that I've never forgotten. Not sure who said it, but it goes, 'The unknown is where you can grow into the person you will truly be.' Ever since then, my business has worked for me.

"Such a positive spin on my situation. Aw…so sweet." She reached for his hand and held it. *I've never known anyone like him.*

* * *

Hours later, they entered the restaurant. "Oh my gosh, Preston. I'd forgotten how nice it is to go out for a steak dinner. I'm usually so wiped out at the end of the day, it's all I can do to get out of my breeches, take a quick shower, eat, and crash. Usually, early because I'm back up before dawn."

"I'm a night owl and like to sleep in when I can, but I don't go out much either. Used to, but not inspired to until now. Shall we toast the occasion?"

"With our water glasses."

"No, in a minute with the champagne I'm going to order."

"Ooh la la, mister. Sounds like fun."

* * *

They raised their glasses as soon as the waiter left. "Hey. No spills. To our first and special time together, June." Their glasses clinked and they sipped. "Ah … I haven't enjoyed one-on-one company in a long time."

"Me either. My 'one-on-one' has been me and the horse I was riding since you know who left the picture."

"I think his priorities were messed up."

"I agree, but then again, you want kind of what he wanted and what I want—our own thing. It's just that he used a scheming way to get what he wanted, and I got dumped. You and I just want it by hard work."

"True. Wonder why it sounds good when you say it, yet when my father did, it sounded like I was a failure or a moron for not following his footsteps."

"Was your mother supportive?"

"They divorced and she hasn't been part of my life. She's got another family life going and lives on the east coast. It's okay. They split up when I was young; I'm used to it, I don't hold any grudges against her. I see her from time to time—whenever I have a client on the east coast."

"Gosh. Your clients are all over."

"They are. Multiple states—California, duh. Then there's Washington, Oregon, New Hampshire, Rhode Island, Connecticut. I've got some new clients lined up. I'd like to get some southern states too. Cars are everywhere, June."

"I see. And so are horses!"

"Ah. The possibilities of work, work, and more work. Shall we toast again?" He raised his glass.

"Why certainly, sir." She raised her glass and then clinked and sipped.

The waiter came back over. "Ahem … I saw that you two toasted. Are you celebrating a special occasion?"

June looked at Preston and her eyes sparkled. "Should we tell?"

Preston's cheeks turned bright red. "That's up to you." He cleared his throat.

"We're celebrating our first, uhm … fancy dinner out together."

The waiter beamed. "Then congratulations and we are ecstatic you picked our restaurant. Are you ready to order?"

Dinner ended with a complimentary dessert tray that was promptly devoured. "Preston, it's a good thing you don't have to carry me after all that food."

"Hey, I can carry you across the threshold to your room. I might have skipped a few days of working out but you're not too heavy for me."

"I can see where this is going."
"Me too. Like it?"
"Sometimes actions speak louder than words."
"Show me."

10

"Wake up, Preston. My appointment's at 10 o'clock. Best Tuesday ever! I can't believe I'm getting my new cast today. Below the knee! I'll be able to bend my leg and the doctor said it was going to be a walking cast. I'll still have crutches, but they'll only be for balance. I'm so excited." *Halfway to having my legs again. Yes!*

"Good morning, sunshine. I can see that you are. Let me get the coffee going. Should we have a quick stop for breakfast or eat breakfast bars here."

"Breakfast bars. I'm too excited to eat!"

"Okay. I'll get moving." He grinned. "Coffee and a shower?"

"Deal." She laughed.

* * *

Waiting in the reception area of the doctor's office, June and Preston whispered back and forth about the upcoming process.

"Are you scared, June?"

"Heck no. Give me a hacksaw and I'll cut it off myself."

"Whoa. Alrighty then. I'll be a fan of your bravery."

The door opened. The attendant called out, "June?"

"Right here." She stood, got her crutches and they took off for the cast changing room.

* * *

The process looked scarier and more painful than it turned out to be as the cast cutting saw made its way down the full length of her leg. June kept it as still as a rock. The cast pieces peeled away. She looked at her leg. "Well, my leg is still there! Kind of white and hairy, yuck. But at least it's not deformed."

"No way is it deformed." He started cleaning her leg. "It looks good. You're doing good, June. What color cast would you like? White again?"

"Oh no. I'm a lot happier now. How about that hot pink color?"

"Absolutely. Great choice." Within minutes, the technician applied the new cast and commended June's stoic behavior. "Wow. You are my most impressive patient of the month! You'll be out of this one in six weeks. You should like this one much better."

"I already do! It feels so light on my leg compared to the other concrete block." She giggled.

Dr. Carson came in. "Hello, June. Let me see your new cast." He looked it over. "Uh huh. I see Billy's got you all fixed up again." He turned and nodded at Billy who, taking his cue, left the room. "According to your x-ray, your healing is progressing as expected. You're a good patient. Keep it up, June and in six weeks this one will come off. I like the color! Very zippy. Take care and see you in about three weeks for another x-ray to keep an eye on your progress. Preston, keep taking excellent care of our girl."

"I certainly will, sir."

* * *

"Preston, I just remembered that there's a recognized show not too far from here. It's this coming weekend. God, I've been so distracted and in another world. How could I have forgotten about it? Have you ever been to a dressage show?" She took a bite of her sandwich.

"No, but I'd like to see one after hearing all your horse talk. Want some of my chips?"

"Yes, please." She offered her Cheetos bag. "Want some? I wonder how that is going to feel being a spectator at the show instead of a rider?" Her eyes looked downward. "I'm wondering if that will ever happen for me again. I should send Mary a text and tell her about my new cast. I'll make sure she understands my recovery has been and is staying in California." She took a big bite and chewed looking at him.

"Yeah. Good plan so she knows you're around and keeps you in mind." *I'll text my next clients and give them an update too. Work is looming…*

"I agree. If you hadn't been there for me, I'm thinking I might have had to go back to Florida. How was I going to get around? I'm sure other people manage, but I didn't know how I was going to deal with it."

"I think things worked out. What do you think about getting back to riding now? Does it seem more possible?" He reached out and took her hand. *She's going to be tough to leave when all this is over. Wonder if she feels the same? I'm not going there.*

"I still don't know for sure, but I'm feeling more optimistic. I'm healing, but I still have six long weeks left to go. The main issue is what about after the cast. I wouldn't say I'm scared to ride, I'm just worried about my skill level if I decided to go for it again."

"Oh. I think you'll be fine. The doctor seems to think so."

She smiled. "Yeah. He did say that. Anyway, now that I have crutches and a smaller cast, I think we could go to the show for a couple of hours. It'll be fun to share my past life's obsession with you. Glad you're interested. We'll get to see some good rides."

"I'd like that since I saw a few seconds of your ride and I can tell you; it was eye catching. That blonde ponytail of yours. It's shiny and cute, just like you."

She squeezed his hand. "You're always on my side. Maybe you can see the test I was riding. It's the last one before Grand Prix. And maybe I can introduce you to some people that I know if anyone from down south is signed up. I doubt it since there's lots of other shows at home going on. But this is a qualifying show, so you never know."

"What's a qualifying show? I mean, for what?"

"The annual championships. Each class competes. Only certain scores that are high enough count for qualifying, that is. You have to have a certain number of them by the time the Championships come around."

"Sounds interesting. Let's plan on going. What do you want to do before then? How about a trip to Tahoe and we can stay one night and be back in time for the show?"

"Tahoe? A mini vacation? Sounds great! South Lake Tahoe or North?"

"I don't care."

"I don't either. Let's google it and see which one we want. I would love to take a cruise out on the lake. I know I would love it. Being out on the water…sailing along. Sounds like a dream."

He gulped. "You really love boats and the water?"

"Gosh, yes. I would love, love, love to take a cruise on the ocean one day. I'll put that on my bucket list."

"You do have quite the sense of adventure, don't you?"

"Guess so. How about the boat shows at the convention center at home? Don't you just drool over those yachts? Some of them are magnificent. I went to one, once. You never said what kind of boats your father builds."

Oh no. Not going there either! Coughing, along with feigned choking, Preston laughed. "My lord, where do you get all this enthusiasm? We don't need to bog down our conversation about what he builds, do we? Think parts and pieces for now. Engines, June, engines."

"Okay. Let's change the subject. Talking about your dad's never your favorite topic. No problem. I don't want to talk about my parents either!" She laughed. "Yes, I have enthusiasm and love being busy. Let's find out what Tahoe has to offer. I'm excited and can't wait to go. Sorry, but I have to look on my phone. Oh, look at this! I googled South Lake Tahoe." June handed him her phone.

"Let's see. Top ten things to do. Cool. That's quite a list of choices. We're only going to be there one night though so we can make it to the horse show. How about getting there early on Thursday and coming back Friday? Then we'll have Saturday for the show."

She took the phone back. "We could leave super early on Thursday. That's sounds like enough time there. Short, but that's fine. Let me see the phone again." Reaching for it, she looked up. "Aw … They have a horseback ride tour with view of the lake and mountains."

"I haven't ridden a horse and uhm, excuse me … your leg, June. Remember?" He laughed.

"Oops. Minor detail. Okay. That's off the list, for now and maybe forever. The old June just popped out for a minute."

"You're going to be on your two feet in a few weeks."

"Yeah, I'll be independent, and you'll be dumping me. We're even." She tickled him.

"Not dumping you. You'll be running off to ride as soon as you can, and you know it."

"And you'll be running off to your business and workout schedule. Ah. Reality will set in quickly and that's not a bad thing, but I'm going to miss you."

"I'm not going anywhere for a month and a half. Let's not wreck our time thinking about something that hasn't happened yet." He leaned over and kissed her. *At least she's still not putting pressure on me—hard to believe. Maybe she's saving it for the end. I hope not. But she's right, things will change when her cast comes off.*

"Good point. I would've signed up for the Tahoe ride…. Dumb cast. But here's an interesting link." She clicked it. "Cruise the largest alpine lake…luxury yacht…Sunset cruise? That's one thing. We can do that at the end of the day. How beautiful. Sailing at sunset. I've never been on a yacht. Can we?"

He ran his fingers through his hair. "You have to ride something, don't you? Okay. It's your speed and something you can do. At the end of the day, you're going to be tired and that will work out with our schedule."

"We don't have to go. You don't sound excited. Uh oh. You've been on a yacht, haven't you?"

"But I've never been on one in an alpine lake. Let's do it. That's only one thing. Okay, what else is there?" *We'll go and that's it. She'll be happy.*

"Back to my list. Hmm…water ski school, lakeside marina

boat rentals…stay in a cabin near the lake." She cracked up. "I'm kidding! Oh, here is one other thing beside a Tahoe Trout Farm." She snorted. "Kayak rentals."

"June!"

"Sorry. I can't do any of those things. Rats! How about Emerald Bay Underwater State Park with scuba diving in clear water to explore historic artifacts? Oh my gosh. Endless ways to torture you."

"Hilarious, aren't you? Can you find one thing without water? Or else give me your phone and that list, and I'll pick."

She moved the phone out of his reach and read from far away. "Final choice. Drum roll please. How about Lake Tahoe Balloon? Uh oh, it says…"It is retrieved from the lake."This is crazy or some sort of plot. Here we go. A gondola ride at Heavenly Mountain. Spring weather and a gondola ride. What a combo and I can do it."

"Sold. Then we'll have time to put a few coins in the casino machines. We will be busy. Let me see that phone again. Aha! New idea!"

"What did you see?"

"Not telling."

I can't believe we're going." She leaned over and kissed him.

"We are." *Maybe I should've picked a spot with water nowhere close by.*

It couldn't be argued that things were going well. Maybe a little too well. This woman was winning him over and he found it unsettling. But then again, not too worrisome because, as they said, separation was imminent when she was well. Perfect, if everything went according to plan.

11

Leaving early Thursday morning, they ate breakfast along the way in the car while driving. Passing by scenery that drew attention from the fact neither one of them had ever seen it before, June pointed. "Look what's ahead. A casino! Should we stop and try our luck?"

"It's early in the day, but why not. We can stretch a little before heading into town. I have an idea where we should have lunch. You'll see the place when we get there. But as soon as we have lunch, we should check in at the hotel for a quick rest before the Sunset cruise."

"I wish I could help with the driving. This is quite the trip for such a short stay."

He parked the car and opened the door for her. "No problem. I can handle it. Here you go. Crutches instead of a chair. Glad we have it though, just in case. You might be exhausted, and I'll have to carry you around."

She held her hands out. "It's a walking cast, but I don't know how it's going to feel. Crutches it is. Let's go in. I want to be vertical."

He laughed.

"What?"

"I want to be horizontal."

"Oh you. Let's go in. I hope we win big! We might end up rich!"

"Keep dreaming, June. You're so cute."

* * *

They entered the casino. Preston stopped in front of a long row. "How about those machines? Penny machines…we can max out our spins."

"Spoken like a pro."

"Far from it."

A soft voice called out. "Hello! Is that really you?" Preston's head turned and they spotted a gorgeous, tall, shapely woman with long red hair coming their way. Preston stammered. "Sheila? Uh, hi." He reached out to shake her hand.

"A handshake? Really?" She licked her lips and batted her long eyelashes. Emerald green sparkling eyes lit up as a naughty smile lifted the edges of her lips. She wagged her finger. "I waited for you to call and that never happened. Oh, I'm sorry. You have your sister with you?"

Preston shoved his hand in his pocket. "Sister? I don't have a sister and you know that. This is my friend, June."

June reached out. "Hi. Nice to meet you."

Sheila stammered. "Oh. I just thought with your blonde hair and all…"

Preston coughed. *Yeah, right. Oh God.* "Nice seeing you, Sheila. We need to make our visit short. June's ability to stand is a little compromised for now." *Go away, would you?*

"I see that. So, pardon my assumption that you were his sister, I get it. You're his girl."

June stood a little taller. "Uhm…we're just friends. I had, uhm…an accident and he's kind enough to entertain me while I'm recovering."

"Lucky you, girlfriend. He," she cleared her throat," is very entertaining." Her fingers flew to her chest, and she turned to Preston. "Okay, heartbreaker, I'll leave you two to enjoy. Take my advice, June. Hang on to him while you can. The ride's going to be short and sweet." She turned and walked off in a super slow, taunting, and maddening lethargic pace. She swayed with each step and ran her fingers through her curls, letting the ends of the strands drop on her shoulders. She then turned and flashed a smile before entering a row of slot machines.

Jill looked at Preston's red face. "Jilted lover? Thank God I didn't get clawed."

"She's harmless. I never made her any promises." *Good thing she didn't say too much.*

"Hmm … Back to our machines?

"Yes."

They put coins in and lost in minutes. Preston laughed. "Well, I guess that's as far as that goes."

"Boy the money sure did go fast. But then again, we didn't lose much. That's a good thing. It's getting close to lunch time."

"Let's go."

* * *

June chuckled softly to herself as they sped along the road. Preston looked over. "What are you thinking about?"

"I'm sorry, but that Sheila girl was a character, asking if I was your sister. I have one sister and you're nothing like her!"

"That woman," his voice escalated, "feels like she was scorned and burned by the way she put on her little act."

June laughed. "Uh, yes. She must have been into you big time, mister. Was she?"

Oh God. She was trouble with the potential for a whole lot more if she had blabbed on. "Let's not go there. Tell me more about your sister. I'd forgotten about Sheila, and I'd like to keep it that way."

"Okay, my sister is my hero. She fell in love with a British guy. He's a lawyer. She teaches little kids, and they live in bliss in England. They're not married, but my parents don't criticize her because she's my big sister and has a bachelor's degree in education. But, my point is, she is living successfully on her own."

"Would you like to go and visit her, err … them, one day?"

"I would, when I can afford it."

"So, you like traveling?" *Let's see what she says about this.*

"Never thought about it before, but …" looking at her cast and shifting her leg, "I would have to say I would. This cast is affecting more than my leg bone, it's got me thinkin' there's a big world out there and I'd like to see it, along with stickin' to my horses, of course."

Good answer. "I could see you seeing the world, June."

Giggling, she reached for her phone and pretended to start dialing. "I'll call her and tell her I might show up on her doorstep one day."

"If your cast is still on, I'd show up with you." He laughed. *I'm not kidding. You are fun to be with.*

* * *

They parked and walked down the sidewalk. "Where are we heading, Preston?"

"Over to the Heavenly chair lift. I hope they can stop it long enough for you to maneuver getting in. You can't afford to fall. Let's fill out the release forms and get our tickets. Don't worry, if it isn't safe for you to get on, we won't."

"Thanks. I'm not worried, but I'm going to be squeezing your biceps and hanging on for dear life. That lift is moving kind of fast."

"June Tarlin, you're a character. Don't be scared. Squeeze away, here we go." *I like her. She's fun to be with. Don't ever change, June. Women always change. Maybe she'll be the exception. I shouldn't care if she is or isn't.*

* * *

Safely onboard the enclosed lift, they took off with a jolt. "Oh, my goodness, Preston. Look down. What a sight. Seems like we're miles high in the sky. Look at the panoramic view of the lake and the mountains. Wow. I've never been snow skiing. Have you?"

"Just a few times. See those trails that are wide. That's where I spent most of my time. But not here. I skied in Utah."

At every pole there was a small bump and June squeezed his hand. "Oh wow. There sure are lots of sports to choose from. At least I'm expanding my repertoire. I'm considering things I wouldn't have given a second look. I think learning to ski would be fun. It's just that from San Diego, that would mean a bit of travel to get to a ski mountain."

"Yeah. But most people take vacations."

"Vacations? Duh. Where have I been all my life?"

"Well, I haven't been exactly trotting the globe either. Maybe we've limited ourselves."

"Limiting, for me was also intentional. I was saving up money for a barn or a top-of-the-line horse. A horse can cost as much as someone's home. Maybe I could've started with a youngster. But the only bad thing about that is then it's a long hard haul to get them show ready. And you don't know how capable they are or what their gaits are going to be like. I like horses with a lot of impulsion."

"The horse you were on had impulsion, alright. He was the equivalent of a sportscar. Whew."

"Yeah, he's got a lot under the hood, but that was just a spook. All horses spook. Look up there." She pointed. "We're almost at the top."

The lift cabin slowed, and they continued to the top rather than the halfway stop. Arriving at the top, they stopped for her departure. They took off looking around. "Preston, this view is so great. Wow. Love it."

He put his arm around her. "I think anything's more fun when I'm seeing it with you. It's almost like I'm seeing things for the first time too, even if I've been there, done that."

"I guess being out of the box is good for people. I think it'd be fun to do some exploring. Still save money and ride of course, one day, but you know what I mean."

"I've had many missed opportunities too, June. Speaking of seeing, want to go see what's on the lunch menu?"

"Let's go to lunch. More my speed. Hey. Try to keep up with me."

Preston shook his finger. "Race? Wait for me. Don't leave me behind." He pleaded and laughed. *How does she do this? I wouldn't have committed to or done half these things without someone holding a gun on me.*

* * *

"Preston, look over there. They're serving a barbeque. Aw, I like the red and white checkered tablecloths on the picnic tables. Quite a breathtaking setting for lunch."

"I know. We can see for miles up here. We should come back here…" He stopped short and looked at her.

"When? I would be up for coming back. In the winter or in the summer?" She looked him in the eye. "What's the matter? Oh. I see…changing your mind about what you just said. Well, no worries. There are no horses up here, so you won't find me up here again. Come on, let's go eat."

"June, I didn't mean it that way. I was just thinking that we only have a few weeks left together and I'm having a lot of fun."

"Me too. So just because we say stuff like 'come back here,' we don't have to take it as a binding agreement. To me, it just means this is an awesome place that would be a good place to visit again in our lives. There! How's that? Pressure off now?"

"Well said. You've never put any pressure on me, and I appreciate that. You're the only one in the whole world that's never tried to force me into anything—even when you were in your worst condition, and I was feeling as guilty as a thief stealing Christmas stockings from little kids' houses on Christmas eve."

"I knew you felt awful for my accident. You haven't seen my true self because I do, I mean did, ride 24/7 but that was all I had going. My barn, my horse dreams. But I guess you understand because you've had to work all on your own too." She looked at him. "Okay, now what did I say? You look a little embarrassed or something."

"It's just that you accept me as I am. I could say you haven't seen my true self either. I only had my own plans to worry about. Hmm. Think two people that don't put any pressure on each other could go through life that way?" He swallowed hard. *What! Have I lost it? 'Go through life…' Zip it.*

Her eyebrows raised. "These are all new thoughts for me. I guess it just depends on the two people. Before this cast held me back, you would've had to shoot me or something to keep me off horses. But I can see that life is good at throwing curve balls. I can't believe I'm saying this, but it's nice to see that life can take different directions and still be fun."

"So, since we've solved all the world problems with relationships, my appetite is ready for that barbeque. You?" *I'm ready for a beer.*

"Yes. Watch these crutches go." She turned back. "You giving me a head start?"

"Yes. But I'll catch up in two seconds. I want you to stay close."

"You're so protective. Come here so I can give you a kiss."

He came to her side. "I can't say no to you."

"Good."

* * *

It took a broken leg to get her to see the world. How could the restriction of a cast cause her to find more freedom than ever? Instead of bringing her down, she was flying high and opening her mind. But was she falling in like or falling in love? Was he a knight in shining armor or a heartbreaker extraordinaire? When her leg healed, would her heart break? Was she doomed to being broken? Oh geez. Knock it off, drama queen.

* * *

Preston returned and sat next to her on the bench. He scooted closer. "That's better. You were too far away." He swept her hair back and kissed her cheek. Your blue eyes are sparkling in the sun."

"Flattery will get you everywhere. I think I'm tired." She feigned a yawn. "Naptime? We should go to the room before it's time for our sunset cruise."

"You read my mind."

"Oh really?"

"Yes indeed." He put his arm around her and kissed her neck. She batted her eyelashes. "Let me copy Sheila."

He laughed. "Oh my God. No need to. Believe me, I don't miss her."

"You're such a handsome flirt and impossible to say no to."

"Well, who says you ever have to say no to me?"

They ate and observed the surroundings. June crumpled her napkin and put it on her plate. "I'm liking it up here, but I'm stuffed and ready to go. Kiss for me?"

He swung his leg over the picnic bench and straddled it. "I can sit a little closer to you this way."

"Why certainly."

He planted a long kiss on her lips. "Your lips are luscious and as sweet as strawberry Crush. They're my dessert. Let me take this trash and we'll head to the lift. Give me a big send off for my efforts, darling."

She wrapped her arms around his neck. "This is just a preview of what's to come." They laughed and kissed a couple of more times. He nuzzled her neck and she giggled. "You know how to get me going, don't you?"

"I've been practicing. One last kiss and then we go." They kissed. "That was pure Heavenly. Ha. Ha. Pun intended." He stood, looked up and froze. Redness flooded his face.

June touched his hand. "Are you okay? Look," she stared straight ahead. "That man is coming over to us."

Preston cleared his throat. His words choked out. "He is." *Oh no. I'm busted. No way to run or hide.*

12

Dressed in a sporty long-sleeved button-down shirt, sleeves rolled up, pricey sunglasses, chino pants, and loafers, he was the image of casual business attire and stood out amongst the jeans and tee shirts that were everywhere around him. "Hello, son."

"Hello, Dad." Preston dropped the trash on the table and braced.

"I must say I thought my eyes were deceiving me. But at least they can still be trusted. It's been a while, but now I see why." His eyes glanced down. "Hello there, young lady."

"Hello, sir." June attempted to stand up. "Now for the tricky part. Pardon my climb over this bench. It's a little awkward."

"Dad, this is June." Preston's hand shot out to her. "Here, take my hand. Be careful, don't twist your leg." He helped her stand.

"Young lady, that cast must be a challenge."

"It is. This is cast number two though. It's a lot smaller than the first one. And it's coming off in about five weeks, right?" She locked eyes with Preston.

"Yes. We're in the home stretch."

Preston's dad cleared his throat. "'We?' My son's part of your cast journey?"

"He is, sir. Ever since the accident, he's been great support."

"Ahem … I saw, I mean see that. Pardon my lack of introduction. I'm Robert Wa— …."

Preston cut him off. "Just call him Bob, June. All his friends do. Right, Dad?"

"They do." He looked puzzled and hesitated for a second. "Bob is just fine, June. So, tell me, you had an accident and he has been, uhm … helping you?"

June nodded.

He turned to Preston. "That's nice to hear but I'm not surprised. When he commits to a cause, he commits. But you're a long way from Portland, aren't you? How did you end up here?"

"We're just here for a short visit. Then we're heading back."

"To Portland?"

"No. Back to Elk Grove. I had a new client in Elk Grove, and I was driving a car for him and well, that's when I met June. Anyway, she was in an accident and that's about it. This is just a little outing while she's on the mend."

"So, you haven't been working since?"

"No. What about you? How'd you end up here?"

Bob coughed. "No work? Uh … at all? So, you're saying you took time off? Now that's a first. But uhm … I'm here with Liv. She wanted to see her daughter and Cassie invited us up here because she couldn't get away from work. We rented a little cabin on the lake. Cassie's firm just acquired the resort's accounts. I told you CPAs get to travel, son."

"Dad. Cassie can travel whenever she wants. Whatever. Glad this worked out for you."

"Cassie, I mean Liv and Cassie would love to see you."

"We won't have time, but thanks." *No plans on doing that anytime soon. Leave, Dad. God.* He took a deep breath.

Smiling, June interrupted. "How nice to have a cabin on the lake. We're going out on the lake tonight."

Bob's eyebrows shot up. "You two are going out on a boat?"

Without a second's hesitation, June blurted out. "We are. I'm so excited. I love boats."

"Dad, she loves lots of things. It's just an evening ride."

"Hey. It's not just a ride. It's a sunset cruise." She wagged her finger.

Bob adjusted his sunglasses. "A cruise? Sounds like a big boat. I'm sure he could tell you a lot about…."

"I don't know much about the boat, Dad."

"But we know it's an 80-foot yacht, according to the internet." She laughed. "I'm sure they got it right."

"Young lady, if you're getting him out on the water, then it makes perfect sense to be here. Call me, son. Nice meeting you, June. Good luck with your recovery. Injuries can be quite devastating and derail a person's plans."

"Thank you, Bob. As horrible as the accident was, meeting your son made it one of the best things in my…Well, he's been helpful and kind. Nice meeting you too."

Preston tensed. *June, no. He doesn't need to know details.*

Bob shot a quick response. "Car accidents can…"

Preston jumped in. "Don't blame cars Dad, uhm…I mean, June fell off a horse." *Some things never change. Always ready to blame me and my cars.*

"A horse? Now I know there must be more to this story. A horse…okay. I should get back to Liv. Come see me when you're back in San Diego. Do you live in northern California, June?"

"No, sir. I live in San Diego. I was just up here riding a horse I was training for the owner. I'm into dressage. A little sidelined now but hoping to get the future straightened out and see if the centerline comes back to me soon. Sorry! If I say dressage, I get all excited. Show ring talk still gets me. I mean getting back to being in the arena competing."

"June, I'm sure you are quite the rider. Not sure how 'he's' in on all this," his hand gestured toward Preston, "but let's finish this story on another visit, shall we?"

"Say hi to Liv, Dad." *Thank God, he's leaving.*

"I will." He walked off.

Preston sat on the bench and wiped beads of sweat from his forehead. "That was exhausting." *At least he didn't push me into too much talk. Not his usual interrogation.*

"Why? He seems so nice."

"Nice? He was on his best behavior. Anyway, let me throw this trash and we're out of here. I need a nap." He kissed her on the cheek. "You?"

"Me too. Exhausted. I'm glad I got to meet your dad though. I'm sure he's got lots of boat talk he could share. It would be interesting to hear some of his stories."

Preston grimaced. "I'm sure. He's got stories, alright."

"Preston, do you think we're too hard on our parents? I mean your dad doesn't seem as pushy as mine."

"Without a doubt, he can be downright 'pushy' too. And no, we're not hard on our parents. They're hard on us." *Quick to judge and quick to blame.*

"Okay. I agree. That's enough of parent talk. Eek. Something we have in common."

13

The yacht pulled away from the dock. The low voices of the couples on board could be heard as the shoreline vanished. The boat rocked smoothly and rhythmically. The evening air was fresh and cool. The flapping of the small waves hitting the boat was the only noise outside of the hum of the engines. June and Preston sat in the front to watch the direction of travel.

June held tight to Preston's arm. "This takes my breath away. The float and movement are the closest thing to a sitting trot that I've had in weeks. Close your eyes and feel the motion of each new wave. It's similar, of course not the same, but very much like riding the trot stride of a horse with suspension or a slow collected canter. You know, kind of a swaying, lilting float?"

"Hmm…if you say so."

"I do. Of course, I'm a little riding deprived. Forget it. Look at the surrounding view. The sun is going down and the sky is a little red. The tree line is starting to look beautiful. Dark and mysterious." She moved closer to him.

"I'm glad you're enjoying the scenery, that's the whole point. Looks like we're going to tour the lake. They have snacks and drinks on board. Want a drink?"

"I'll take a glass of wine if they have it. Wine would pair well with the lake don't you think?" She reached out and tickled him. "I'll take whatever they have."

"You got it."

He returned in minutes. "Wine it is!"

"Very nice. Let's toast and sip as we go." She closed her eyes. "Feel the breeze. Not too strong and just so fresh. Clean air. No smog, right? I wonder what it's going to be like going back home to San Diego?"

"I'm hardly ever there. I haven't been there in a long time."

"Oh. I forgot. You're in Portland and other cities. Sounds like quite a few businesses."

"My clients live in various places, so I have places to stay in most all of them. I try to avoid hotels."

"Like the one in Sacramento?"

He threw his head back laughing. "Exactly. I mean sometimes I must stay in one, but not if I can help it."

He's a traveler, just like he said. Hmm… "Anyway, this is nice and then we have the horse show. After that, how about a life of leisure until my cast is off and I am a free woman!"

"I think you're going to be very happy. I don't want you to be sad."

"I won't be. I love riding but I must say, I love being out on the water."

Preston's eyes darted around. "Don't let my dad hear that. He's just beginning to accept that I don't want anything to do with his static operations."

"Relax. He's not here. Besides, I think he's nice."

Preston scoffed. "Even when he tried to pair me up with Liv's daughter?"

"Oh, come now. You evaded that quite easily." She leaned over and kissed his neck.

"Aren't you glad I did?"

I didn't know my opinion mattered! "Of course. Oh hey, look at the shoreline now. Some of those trees must be gigantic. On the ocean, we would see waves. It would be very scenic too."

"It's pretty and peaceful here. Very much a couple's thing. Glad we came out. Look at the setting sun. It's almost down."

"Oh yeah. Gorgeous. What a spectacular sight."

* * *

The boat ride ended and all disembarked. June stopped and tapped Preston's arm. "Look at that couple sitting on the bench. She's crying and the guy's arm is around her. Should we ask if they need help?"

What now? "I don't want to interfere." Preston whispered. "But it's getting dark and no one's around." He hesitated. "Okay. Let's walk over."

June called out. "Hi." They looked up and the woman wiped a tear. She looked at June's crutches. "Oh, are you okay?"

"Thanks, I am but we were just stopping to ask you the same thing. We just got off the sunset cruise. Do you guys need help?"

The guy responded. "Well, unless you're a boat mechanic, I think we're out of luck."

"Preston. I mean, him," June pointed, "he's a great mechanic."

Preston raised his hands up. "Only a car mechanic." *She believes in me just from what I've told her. Not something I'm used to, and she has no proof.*

"Well, I have no clue about anything mechanical." The guy shook his head. "This is our yacht. She's small, only 40 feet. A wedding gift from my parents. This is our honeymoon night and we're sitting on a boat dock." He shrugged his shoulders. "I wanted to take my bride, and the yacht, on a sunset cruise too."

The dock lights turned on. Preston delayed answering and felt a thick cloak of disappointment smothering the moment. "Well, it's past that time now, but maybe I can take a quick look and see if maybe it's just an electrical connection or something that got loose in transit. Did you just have her transported? Maybe I can get her started and you can have a sunrise cruise in the morning."

"That would be appreciated. Come on board you two. I'm Andrew and this is Alicia. For our wedding gift, shipping was included. And the dock hands tested her out and said all was fine."

"Hmm. Okay, no promises but I'll try. Oh, I'm Preston and this is June. Come on, June. Let's get you on board."

June exclaimed. "Your yacht is amazing. What a wonderful gift."

The yacht was gleaming. Its white pristine exterior contrasted with shiny black adorning the port and starboard sides and dark tinted windows caught June's eye. "My favorite colors. Don't get me started." She chuckled.

Alicia added. "It is gorgeous. Thank you. I feel bad acting like a baby."

June added. "Hey, I understand missing out on something important. No worries. Preston's an experienced mechanic. Let's hope for the best." Her eyes looked ahead at the classy interior. Wood paneling, lavish seating everywhere, and chrome! Lots of it. Shining like brand new horse tack. "Takes my breath away, Alicia. Wow."

Andrew stepped in and stretched his hand out for Alicia. Preston took hold of June's arm and steadied her balance while she boarded, with Andrew holding her crutches in one hand with his other hand outstretched.

June beamed. "Made it! Whew. Forget about having sea legs, I would settle for having balance." Everyone filed along to find a spot for June to sit on the white leather seating.

Preston spoke up. "Andrew, I should take a look in the lazarette to start with."

Andrew's cheeks pinked. "Uh … Oh yeah. I remember. We head to the stern."

"Very good. Yes. It's probably a good-sized area for this ship."

"Yes. Hey, you do know boats."

June interrupted. "His father builds …."

Preston spoke over her. "No matter, June. It's okay. No getting Andrew's hopes up. We'll be right back." They took off.

"Okay, Andrew. Batteries and all your safety gear look okay. Let's go to the cockpit and see the controls." Preston muttered and inspected all that he could access. "Hey, Andrew. Got a flashlight and small screwdriver? I have an idea what's wrong."

"I do. There's a toolkit in the lazarette. I'll go back and get it." He returned with the tools and Preston got to work. "This is such a nice yacht. From down south?" *As if I didn't know.*

"Yes, it is. My dad's friends with Robert Wahlberg. His company manufactured it."

Is this a small world or what? Wahlberg …. Say no more. "I saw that. Just chit chatting while I get this panel off." He bit his lip. *Suddenly, the need to stand up for the boat's qualities overwhelmed him. But out of nowhere, his father's words taunted him … 'Run Preston.' No! I'm going to step up to the plate again. I helped June out of the blue too. For Christ sakes, he'll never approve of anything I do that's not his idea. I don't care. I got this.* "I know the company and the line. She's a fine vessel. Waveflames II is all power. Let me just check a few things. Okay! She should be a fine sail for you guys. Can you start her?"

"Yes. At least I know how to do that." He laughed. "I've had all my boater safety and I can handle the key."

Andrew turned the key to the first position and not to a full start.

Preston clucked his tongue. "Aha. It's simple. See that little red light? Did you have the boat techs here test her?"

"I did and they said she was ready to sail."

"Really?" He scratched his chin. "Let's go back to the ladies. I'll give you a full report."

Andrew's face was tight with concern. "Okay. I'm nervous, but we should all hear what you have to say."

Preston began speaking and everyone perked up. "Well, Andrew. There are many things to consider and that need to be inspected. Things such as ground tackle that includes the bow roller, and cracks in the surrounding structure. Is the anchor shackle wired shut and the swivel to make sure it turns? And then there's the windlass. That involves checking the pawls, lubricating points, and eyeballing your wire connection. A stern anchor is probably in the lazarette, and it should be checked."

Continuing, Preston's hand went to his waist, and he stood taller with authority. "Furthermore, boats are built of pumps. Like fresh water, saltwater, engine, A/C and more but none of these is more than the bilge pump. Do you have a portable manual pump or even buckets? You might need them. The engine room with its numerous systems should be inspected and then last, but not least, filing a float plan—much like a flight plan can save your life! Shall I go on?"

Sweat poured off Andrew's forehead. "I don't know what to say."

Preston chuckled. "I'm just trying to put your boat's issue in perspective, that's all. Because what they must have done, accidentally, is run the boat on reserve. She won't start full up and run without a reserve. It's a safety feature that my, err…I mean the Wahlberg company builds into their newest models. You must know the exact gallons in the tank to know how long to sail. Of course, you've got your fiberglass dinghy and outboard motor, but out on the ocean, that's mandatory equipment for a true emergency."

Andrew coughed. "I agree. So, if I get some gas brought over and flip the switch to main, all problems are solved?"

"Yep. June and I could even come by in the morning after you get your tank filled and watch you guys set sail across the lake. Bring your champagne and orange juice because I'm predicting a great voyage across the lake."

Andrew reached his hand out to shake Preston's. "You had me going!" He roared laughing. "I'll admit I have a lot to learn but at least for now, I'm relieved knowing everything is okay, and I can be confident in my boat. Thank you so much."

"You got it! Wahlberg boats are well built. Congrats on yours. Sorry, I couldn't resist having a little fun. Boats in proximity are getting to me." *See, Dad? You were wrong again. Axel would've appreciated all this. Philip was a jokester too. This one's for you, Philip.*

Alicia, just as excited, leaned down to hug June. "You two are invited if you'd like…

Interrupting, June held up her hand. "Thank you, Alicia, but we can't barge in on you two! Not on this special occasion. But I promise we'll be here to see you set sail. Wow. What a wonderful gift. Lucky you. I just fell deeper in love with boats."

Preston cleared his throat. "June, darlin', you ready to go find dinner?"

"I am." She stood up. "Bye, guys. Congratulations on your marriage. We'll be back here at…? Uhm…what time, Alicia?"

"Ten, right Andrew?"

"Ten o'clock should be perfect."

June and Preston took off. June stopped and looked at Preston. "You're good at helping people in distress. Know that? You calmed Andrew down and solved the problem. What about me? I would've thought being alone with a broken leg was pure disaster, but here you are, making my whole recovery happy and I have a chance of getting back in the saddle thanks to you. If I think I can that is…"

"You're the only one that's ever said that about me. It's cute when you're so dramatic. I'm thankful I helped those guys out. At least my boat background helped more than any mechanical ability. But I must admit, seeing my father out of the blue today and then this episode makes me realize I've been kind of hard on the old man. He did teach me a lot and I just thought he was always talking and not listening to what I had to say. Hmm…Let's eat dinner and go to the room. We've got a big day tomorrow."

She reached out and squeezed his hand. "Let's go."

14

At ten o'clock, Preston and June walked down the deck and waved at Andrew and Alicia.

Andrew came hurrying over and shook Preston's hand. "Good morning. I can't say thank you enough for your help."

Sincere appreciation. Nice. "That's okay. You better start it up first and check it out."

Alicia hugged June. "You said you guys live down south too, right?"

Clearing her throat, June explained. "We really met, uhm … not long ago, so I'm not sure about where Preston calls home in San Diego. He lives in Portland."

Preston's shoulders raised and shoved his hands in his pockets. "Call me a nomad." Everyone laughed. *That worked.*

Alicia continued. "I'd like to stay in touch. With both of you."

June pulled her cell phone out. "Me too. Let me add you as a contact. I'll be going back home in a couple of weeks."

"Just you?" Alicia's eyes narrowed.

Preston's arm went around June's shoulders. "That's her plan. My plan is a little off kilter since we met. I've got clients in other cities to take care of. But with June's number, you won't lose track of us."

"That's good to hear. I mean we must know how June's leg is doing after her cast is off."

June added. "Boy, I'll say, Alicia. That's my million-dollar question too. I have a good doctor. So, you guys don't worry. Have fun on the rest of your honeymoon."

Andrew added. "That's the plan. Time to set sail my love," and hugged Alicia.

With smiles and waves, they boarded. Andrew and Alicia headed for the cockpit and disappeared into the helm station.

Preston and June let out a happy whoop when the boat started and watched until it was out of sight.

June took Preston's hand. "Cute couple, huh?"

"Yep. Ready for the drive back home? I mean to our place?" His cheeks burned and he looked away. *I should explain some things to her on the drive home, but I like things the way they are. Later. Maybe.*

"I'm ready."

* * *

Saturday morning, June's cell phone buzzed, and she reached out to answer it. She sat up and Preston stirred. "Preston, it's my mom calling. I better answer." She put her finger to her lips for quiet.

He mumbled, "You should."

"Hi, Mom."

"How are you doing, honey?"

"Oh! Hi, Dad. I saw Mom's number. I'm doing fine. Guess what? I'm healing and my leg is doing fine. I have a brace, it's solid, but I can walk on it. I get it off in about five weeks."

"A brace? Solid? June, you must've had a bad injury a month ago. Unless you fell off again. We really didn't understand your leg was so hurt. We would've flown out right away. Those horses!

I wish you would give them up. The odds finally caught up with you…"

Oh my gosh. I knew it. I would've had weeks of lectures. "I'll be fine and no; I didn't fall off again." *Good God, I'm a professional! Well, used to be.* "Same leg issue. It's just that my doctor thought this brace would be better for me to have. Anyway, I know you guys would've come out here, but my leg just needed time. No one could really do anything about it." Sweat broke out on her forehead.

"When you first told us you just needed time, we were thinking it was a bad sprain or strain. Well, it's too late now, but at least it sounds good so far. So, you're staying close to your doctor?"

"Yes. He's good. We're…I mean I'm still in the Sacramento area. You know, Northern California—close to the riding area I told you about."

Her mother's voice chimed in. "Are you managing okay without riding? You could never be off a horse for more than a day."

"Oh! Hi, Mom. Well. I guess that had to change for a while. But I'm going to a show today with my uhm…caregiver, Preston. He's never seen one. A dressage show, I mean." She giggled. "I know. My world, right? How are you guys? Life in Florida good?"

"It is. You never said your caregiver was a boy. We miss you and we've decided to make the trip over to see you."

She sat up straighter. "You are? Okay. When?" She covered the phone and whispered to Preston. "They're going to come for a visit."

"When you're back in San Diego."

"That'll be nice. I'll be in the same apartment, and I'll be working at the barn, if my leg is okay. Maybe cleaning stalls more than riding, but I hope to get back to work." She swallowed hard.

"We're anxious to see you." Her dad interrupted. "Your mom wants to keep talking. Bye for my part."

"I'm here! I want to tell her something too. Love you, Dad." She paused. "Mom, I just want to say that Preston's been very responsible and helpful. Don't worry about him. I can't wait to see you guys. I'm glad you're flying out. I have a couch that makes into a bed. I'll sleep there so you guys can sleep on my bed."

"Thank you, honey. We miss you."

"Aw, that's sweet to hear. I'll be looking forward to your visit. Big day ahead for me, Mom. Horses…. I'll only be a spectator at the show, so don't worry."

"Good to know everything's alright, but I'm concerned about how much longer you have with the brace. Your injury was extensive. Sounds like you needed much more than a little healing time.' What do you know about this boy that's been helping you? Is he safe?"

"Yes, he's safe, Mom. I checked him out before I let him take care of me." She scrunched her face and put her left hand over her mouth. *He was a stranger!*

"So, the young man stayed with you and didn't go to his job? Or he is unemployed and taking money from you?"

"No, Mom. He owns his own business and he's not taking any money from me." *Little does she know I'll be broke at the end of all this.* Her left hand flew to her mouth again and Preston turned over and put the pillow over his head. The bed shook with his muffled laughter.

"Well, that's good, but listen, honey. This young man hasn't made any promises to you, has he?"

"Promises? Like what?" Preston removed the pillow, turned over, and tuned in.

"Like just how long he's going to be there since you said, you have five weeks left to go wearing the brace. Right?"

"Right."

"And you can't drive at all?"

"No. He's been doing the driving."

"And you've depended on him this past month for everything? Transportation, living expenses, food, and everything?"

June gulped. "Well, yes, but he offered …."

"And that's my point. June, he 'offered' but he has no commitment to you or to be there. You've been lucky so far, but what if he just ups and leaves? He can, you know. I think you should come back to Florida for at least the next five weeks."

"Mom, I'm fine here. Preston's staying until my brace is off." *Good thing I hid as many details as possible from them as long as I could.*

"Sounds like a temporary situation and you don't know anything really about this boy, err…young man. Do you?"

"No. But he's very reliable and helpful." *Nothing on social media. OMG. I knew, err… nothing about him. Well, at least I met his dad and he looked respectable. Oh geez. Face it. The lies are flying out of my mouth like a flock of birds.*

"So was Tanner, at first. June, you need to have your guard up. Think about coming home. If you're going to continue riding, what if another accident happens and this boy, err…man, is nowhere in sight and long gone? Coming back to Florida is safer…just in case, God forbid."

June coughed. *Never does think much of my judgment.* "I'll think about it, Mom. Well, I better get moving to get ready to go to the show. Don't worry. I'll be far away from the horses. And, who knows, maybe I'll stay away from them forever." Her voice cracked and she brushed a tear off her cheek. *They will never change. Ugh!*

"Honey, please don't be upset. We're here. Think it over. I'll let you go. Love you."

"Love you too, Mom." She hung up. *At least I have weeks to prepare for their visit.*

"Well, Preston, you heard all that."

"Poor you. I can't imagine being upfront with my dad. I avoid getting into those kinds of conversations." He sighed. "That's why I like my independence. My dad doesn't hesitate making me feel bad about my choices either."

"Enough of all this." She sighed. "Exhausting and not a fun conversation. I'm glad they're going to visit me, but at least it's not happening for a few weeks. I have to call Brianna and share my happy news! She'll get a kick out of my misery. Just kiddin'. She's on my side. But I don't want my parents here yet. I'd rather have a plan than have my mom casting more doubts. It's hard enough not knowing how my leg is going to be after all this." She tapped her cast. "Oh well, let's get ready and head to the show grounds. I can't wait to see the horses! I never thought I'd still be in Northern California for a horse show! I would've been home long ago. I had planned on competing down south, not up here. So, it'll be exciting to see these show grounds. Upper-level rides come first so the horses are pumped and ready. Hurry!"

"Okay, we'll stop at Starbucks on the way and get more coffee and some food to go."

"It's getting late. Let's move it."

* * *

Staring out the window, June's view of the passing ranches was familiar, and here she was again? The same country roads that she had traveled a few weeks ago. What was so different now besides everything? Hadn't she turned into a passenger in a car instead of the driver? Not so bad if you eliminated the cast on her leg that blocked her driving capability. And what about a handsome guy sitting close that didn't belong to her but was 'borrowed'? Again, thanks to the cast. What would have happened to her if Preston didn't have a heart and hadn't been the good Samaritan? What if he left her earlier than expected as her mom said? Why had she put herself into some many threadbare situations? Tanner dumped her. What if Preston bailed? Maybe she should take precautions and protect herself.

Ten years of nothing but horses had left her sidelined with a shaky future and no safety net. *I never thought anything like this would happen to me. What an idiot. I'm human. Too late to make up for lost time? Maybe. But maybe not.*

15

They pulled into the visitor parking area located close to the office. June's crutches crunched in the fine gravel as they made their way to the bulletin board to see ride times and show rings for the rides.

"Preston, look. Tanner was signed up for a Grand Prix ride. He scratched? Even though he's the most competitive person I know, I don't believe he would come this far north for this show." *He wouldn't be here unless he has a good reason. His good reasons can be bad—for other people.*

Preston scratched his chin. "There's his name again for tomorrow, and that ride is lined out too. He's here."

"I'm sure. His horse would only be shown in one ride today. It takes a lot of warm up and a lot out of them. I would never ride two rides on the same horse at that level. I would want the horse to have all its power. I'd give it a little walk or light ride or two in the afternoon or evening. Okay, let's keep going. I'm glad he's not here. He's probably down south wooing some rich woman owner anyway. That's Tanner for you."

Scanning the other ride sheets, she studied the entries. "Look, there are two other Grand Prix rides, two Intermediate and then on to other levels. Let's go watch the first rides. We don't have much time. At least the main show ring is the closest. Crutches…Can't wait to ditch 'em. My underarms have had it."

Preston hugged her. "Want me to get your wheelchair?"

"No. Thank you. I'll be okay. At least they have chairs in a covered area for spectators."

"Let's go. I want to see this. All I remember is your horse skipping across the sand."

"Those were flying changes. They're so much fun. Come on. I'll give you a blow-by-blow personal commentary on my former dream ride. I still know the test by heart." *This is my zone. I've got to make it back to the show ring.*

* * *

Who could miss the morning atmosphere on the show grounds or the buzzed-up hype despite this quiet and cool time of the day? How was it possible that nerves could be at such far ends of the spectrum here? Onlookers casually sipped coffee while riders filled the warm-up rings in preparation for their ride and strived for calm when butterflies that should be flying in formation were most likely flying out of control. Trainers had earpieces connected to their students and feverishly watched and coached in the final minutes before their pair would enter the ring. Was it too late to accomplish anything new at this point? Or could this be the pinnacle of success after hours, months, and even years of training?

For some, the warmup went well. For others, struggles with unruly horses wreaked havoc with the plans to shine and get qualifying scores. Some trainers held show jackets and towels for a last-minute spruce up and shine of their rider's boots and a bottle of water, sports drink, or what not. Eek! To each their own? The support system was a well-oiled machine, at all levels, to get riders ready to enter the ring.

* * *

"You know, Preston," June sipped her coffee, "looking at this show from a spectator's point of view is so different. If I wasn't a rider, I'm not sure I'd appreciate the tension and the pressure of it all. But this is my life. I'm not supposed to be a spectator." *My God. I'd do anything to be out there warming up.*

"I can feel your sadness, June, and I'm sorry you're missing out. It won't be forever."

"I hope you're right." *This is frustrating. I feel like a trapped rabbit in a snare.*

* * *

June and Preston took their seats. The horse and rider entered the show ring for the first ride of the day. "I'll try to explain, but we can't talk loud during the ride. As soon as the whistle blows or the bell rings, the rider will have less than a minute to enter the court. She will enter and halt in the middle and salute. Then her test begins."

"Got it."

June held her breath as the whistle blew and watched the horse and rider entering in a collected canter.

Preston leaned closer. "I'm surprised that horse is moving so big and galloping so slow. It's opposite of horses racing."

"Because it's a collected canter. Power and lift from the hindquarters, minus speed." She bit her lips. "Watch the trot. You'll be blown away." The horse's legs reached forward and extended out.

"That saddle doesn't have anything to hold onto. How does she stay in the saddle without holding on?"

"She knows how to use her legs, core, and reins to prepare and releasing the horse rather than forcing the horse forward with strong driving aids. Then, she follows the movement with her seat and holds her core firm."

"Huh? Like pushing on the accelerator and holding the clutch in and letting it out slowly so that the car moves without a jerk, but more like a plane taking off from the runway?"

"That's a good analogy," she laughed. "I'll have to remember that one for my students. Look, now it's a half pass at the trot…"

"What? Sideways instead of straight ahead?"

"Yes, with good flexion of the neck and bend of the body. Now, watch her ride in a diagonal straight line across the arena from the letters M to V. It will be passage. It will look slow, powerful, and cadenced."

"I was wondering why all those white tall cones have random letters on them."

"The big letters mean the letter is on the edge while the little letter means there's an invisible letter on the centerline. And the centerline is invisible too." She elbowed him and grinned. "It's all to get the rider from point A to point B, literally."

"Oh, so the whole ride is scripted."

"Scripted?" She chuckled. "I'm keeping that description too. Yes, for every ride at every level, unless it's a freestyle. Watch now."

"That horse is trotting in place. How does she do that? I thought all horses just went forward."

"No." June held her breath as the horse began flying changes.

Preston grabbed her arm, "That's what I saw you doing, just before…amazing."

June kissed his cheek and glanced at her cast. "Thank you for appreciating my riding." *I can't believe I'm sitting next to the guy that caused it all. I'm not angry anymore. Just worried.*

The ride ended on the centerline with a final salute to the judge. June gazed at the duo. "This was a gorgeous ride. I'm salivating."

"Want to walk around some after a little bit?"

"Yeah. A couple more rides and then we'll check out the place. I hope I don't spook any horses with these crutches. I might have to stay a bit away."

"No problem there. I don't want to get too close to them. They're big. I don't want to get run over."

He knows nothing about horses and he's here with me? I used to think I could never date a guy like him. June patted his back. "I'll make sure we stay a safe distance. Gotta take care of my caregiver." She leaned over and kissed his cheek again. "Oh, the rider just entered. The whistle will blow soon. This is a guy, they're going to announce his…" Her words ended and her mouth dropped.

The announcer's voice boomed on the loudspeaker. "Our next rider is Tanner Harmon, riding Delphina's Delight, a 13-year-old Hanoverian mare owned by Sally Greenborough from Fresno, California.

June squeezed Preston's hand. "Tanner? Oh my God." *Our dream… my dream, now he's riding Grand Prix.* Her eyes bored into him as she evaluated what she'd missed out on during the past year. *He dumped me. I survived it and this temporary setback is not going to stop me either. There has to be a reason he's here. Does he want me back?* Her stomach knotted.

* * *

Was it possible the sight of this pair could take your breath away? Minus an ounce of fat, his lean, muscular frame opposed that of a body builder. Yet, the strength evidenced by long lean legs in white breeches matched by equally tall black leather boots with silver spurs highlighted the grey mare's gleaming coat and hind legs with white stockings up to her hocks. His body was squarely positioned in the saddle with a bit of white fluff from a half pad buffering against pressure onto the white saddle pad. The presentation provided a cushy sight of comfort for this mare's back as Tanner's black shadbelly coat, tucked in at the waist, and serving as confirmation of his upper-level status with coat tails resembling a tuxedo's tails, flapped against his white breeches at the walk.

He passed the judge's booth and nodded a greeting as he continued around the outside of the court. A gentle breeze stirred the air. Against the morning sun, the juxtaposition of formal attire in an arena surrounded by tall cypress trees and white sand was eye candy and as refined as a piece of equestrian art. A pretty picture? June's mind screeched as though a DJ had just scratched a vinyl record on a turntable for a frenzied crowd—and Tanner always played to the crowd. *He's a hot guy on a fancy horse. No wonder I fell for him.*

* * *

The whistle blew. June squeezed Preston's hand, then dropped it, and clutched his arm. "He's got her collected and ready for the depart. There they go." Her eyes followed his cues to the horse. "He's gotten so much better. Quieter and steadier."

"I wouldn't know."

"Well, it's true. He used to be strong and clumsy. Huh. Must have had some top-notch coaching. And this mare? Close to, if not more than six figures."

"For a horse?"

"You wouldn't believe the dollars that can be spent for these equine pets."

"Well, cars appreciate with age, can't really say that about horses can you? I mean, they're on a clock."

"Don't be mean."

"It's the truth. I liked the first ride." He moved his arm away.

"I'm sorry. I didn't expect this at all." *Preston's jealous? After I've been meeting all his former sidekicks and put up graciously, I must say, with all of them? Well, well. Interesting.* "I don't think I would've wanted to come to this show. I just wanted to show you the horses."

"I know. I'm sorry. This guy is making me a little crazy. He's your ex. You wouldn't like bumping into mine either."

"True. I already did." She muttered under her breath. "But Preston, we're going to be moving on soon anyway. Let's just forget this ex- stuff. Besides. He would never think I'm here so we can just sit back and enjoy the pleasure of the day." *I'm pretty sure that's not true. Tanner must know I'm here.*

"Good point."

Out of the blue, a large hare darted across the arena right in the middle Tanner's extended canter across the diagonal from M to X to K. The mare, moving out with top power and impulsion, bolted left, and turned. Tanner kept control and turned her back to the letter K. Though he lost points for going off course, he continued his ride as though nothing happened.

June shook her head. "If the mare would have bolted right and leaped over the rail, he would have been disqualified. He rode that big spook so well. I wish I ...." She shut her mouth and looked at Preston.

Preston reached over and hugged her. "If a huge piece of big black tire rubber would have been sailing at that horse, I think the spook would have been every bit as disastrous as what happened to you. Sorry, but a rabbit on the ground is not the same as a flying object."

"Thank you. I like to think, well, I have to think that I'm capable of riding through spooks. I always was."

"And you will again, when you're ready. His ride's over. He just saluted."

"Hey. You got this. Want to go get some coffee and come back for the next class? It's going to be Intermediate II. My last ride."

"Let's hurry so we can see all three rides and compare them."

"Oh my gosh. You really are getting this. Let's go."

* * *

Coffee in hand, they sank into their seats. June put her cup down on the table. She let her head relax back onto Preston's arm and shut her eyes. A man's voice called her name, and her eyes flew open. She sat straight and turned her head.

"I thought that was you. I figured it had to be."

"Tanner? How would you think that?"

"Sally told me about your accident."

"Sally? The mare's owner? I don't even know her."

"Yeah, but June, people talk, and Sarah told a few people, and you know how the rumor mill goes. Anyway, sorry to hear about your leg."

Yeah, right. "Uh huh. That's why you called, right? Just kidding. Ha ha. I'm getting close to getting my cast off."

"It's been over a month. Hasn't it?"

"Yeah. A couple of weeks to go."

"I see you have company here. Hi, I'm Tanner." He stretched his hand out.

"I'm Preston. Nice to meet you."

"How'd you meet June? Were you the guy that caused her fall?"

Preston laughed. "Let's just get to the point, right man?"

June interrupted. "For God's sake. It was a car tire that spooked D, not him." *Go away, Tanner. It's enough just watching you in the ring.*

Tanner stood taller. "Calm down, June bug."

June sputtered. "Don't call me that. You know I hate that nickname."

Preston stood and the chair legs scraped back. "Listen, buddy, we're just going to enjoy our coffee. Why don't you maybe come around after these next couple of rides and talk later. Okay?"

Tanner moved away. "Oh, uh, sure man. Whatever. Sorry, June. I gotta little wound up for a minute. Talk to you later." He turned and walked off.

June tugged on Preston's shirt. "It's okay. He's gone. I'm glad you got him to leave. Let's go back to the ring." *I haven't missed him — I've missed what we had. There's a difference. He looks good on the outside, but he's rotten on the inside.*

Making it back just in time, June pointed. "Look, here comes the first rider."

The next rider entered the ring wearing the same formal show attire. Her white gloves and black velvet helmet were spotless. She was announced. "Jessica Trindale from Sacramento, California riding Romano's Resolution. A 10-year-old Hanoverian gelding." The rider and bay horse entered down centerline.

June blew her breath out in a long exhale. "She looks like an awesome rider. Look how quiet her hands are. She's got him relaxed but charged up and ready. Now that's an art. You need the power, but you need the control, too."

"June, you should take the announcer's mic and be the show commentator. The audience would appreciate these details."

"Are you teasing me?"

"No. I'm not. I bet half the people here watching are like me and don't have a clue as to all this behind-the-scene knowledge."

"Okay. I'll take that as a compliment." *He's never sarcastic. Complete opposite of Tanner.*

"It is."

They watched all three rides and reviewed each privately.

Preston pushed his chair back. "Want to walk around?"

"Sure. Let's go over to the main barn. We should take it slow in case a horse is being tacked up and gets spooky looking at me."

"Awe. That's very considerate. Okay. Like I said. We can stay w-a-a-y back. No problem."

* * *

Arriving at the barn, Preston stared at the surroundings. "Gosh, everyone around here has just as many tools as a mechanic." *Different world from mine, no doubt about it.*

Grooming with speed and purpose, a rider had her horse cross-tied at the stall opening. Her box of supplies was overflowing with spays, rags, and an assortment of picks, curries, combs, brushes, and sponges. Around her apron was a braiding toolbelt stuffed with even more banding supplies so that the mane braids and forelock would turn out their best.

"You're so right. It takes a lot of gear. Just think, all this had to be packed and brought here and packed up again at the end of the show. Like those trunks, mounting blocks, muck carts, and rakes. Then there's horse blankets, coolers, fly sheets, boots, wraps. You got it. Tons of work. The truth is most riders are just dreaming about hanging their ribbons on their horse's stall. I admit it. My dream too. Winning isn't everything, but who honestly, wants to lose?"

"Truthful observation."

"It's because within the classes is one thing, your own personal scores and then there's high points for the entire show. Everyone here is competing in more than one way."

"Glad I'm not into car racing. Although some of the car owners are into car show competition."

"What about your dad's boats? Are they shown or raced?"

She always manages to bring up my dad. I wonder if the two of them would get along. What am I saying? He'll never get to know her. No chance of that. "If so, not by him, necessarily. But just like these fancy horses, they're a trophy on their own for their owners."

"I'd like to see where he builds boats. Sounds fascinating. Kind of like going to a breeding farm in Germany. Maybe one day…"

Even horses can't get her off topic. She's drawn to him and boats. Unbelievable. Never known anyone like her, that's for sure, and she doesn't know a thing about my family. Preston coughed. "We're far from that up here. Or even from the east coast. Anyway, hey. Look at that horse. It's braided and shiny. Must be going in soon."

"Yep. If we sit in the middle, we can watch a bunch of people coming and going."

"Okay. Change of scenery." After a couple of minutes, Preston watched a horse led out. Tacked up and ready, the rider's clothes were pristine and show ring ready. The rider stepped to the top of a mounting block and got in the saddle. A trainer walked alongside them talking nonstop. The horse's hooves clopped on the gravel aisleway.

June tapped Preston's arm. "Want to follow them to the warm-up ring? Might be kind of fun to see what level she's going to show."

"Okay. Looks like they turned to the outside area."

"Let's see. Maybe it's for the next levels. Not FEI."

"What's FEI?" *I like being with her, but our lives and interests are too far apart.*

"It means Fédération Equestre Internationale (FEI) for international events as opposed to the National organization United States Equestrian Federation or USEF. But the two organizations work together at events and other equestrian disciplines besides dressage, like jumping, venting, vaulting, and more. It's an amazing web of systems."

"Looks like a web alright, or a beehive of activity." He laughed. *She's far from being a stick-in-the-mud.*

* * *

They went to a table to watch the warmup. Tanner spotted them and came back over.

"Looks like a little picnic here. You two sure are having a good time. Especially you, June. I've never seen you sitting around for more than a minute."

June choked. "Well, have you tried walking around with an anchor? Geez, Tanner. Don't you have any other rides to get ready for?"

"Not right now. I'm riding a youngster a little later."

"Oh, God. Don't tell me. It's first show?"

"Yep. Another one of Sally's. It's a four-year old Dutch Warmblood."

"Young. Good luck with that. You sure traveled a long way to come to this show. I didn't expect that. Anyway, mare?"

Answering, he put his hand on top of the back of her chair. "Nah. Took ya by surprise being here, huh? It's a gelding. I'm anticipating Sally sending me more of her horses for training. Hey, Preston. Sorry to be talking over your head."

Preston cocked his head. "Far from it."

Tanner stepped back. "Okay. I'm sure your weeks of time with June have made up for never having been around horses."

"Who says I've never been around horses?"

"Social media. Ever hear of that?" He sneered. "Boats and cars right, Preston?" His ridiculing tone hovered on Preston's name.

"Whatever. I think your young horse needs a little warmup. Bring it out and give us a preview."

"Whoa. Talking the talk, aren't we?"

Preston's fingers fisted. *This guy's big mouth is leading to trouble. I wish he'd disappear and if he doesn't on his own soon, I'll help him.*

June scoffed. "That's enough, Tanner. I don't need your company. And neither does Preston."

"Interesting…"

June shook her head. "What's 'interesting' pray tell?"

"Who you're with."

Preston shoved his chair back from the table and put his hands on top of his thighs and looked him in the eye. "Is that all you've got to say, Tanner?" *Face it. Tanner knows more and he wants June to find out. That's why he's here in the first place. He planned on seeing her. Never was just about business. Good ruse.*

"For now, man. But you know," he paused with a devilish grin and a smirk in his voice, "I just thought of something."

16

Tanner continued. "Hmm…you, going by Preston rather than Robert. I wonder why?" His eyebrows raised. "I'll leave you two at that. Goodbye, Robert. Or is it, Bob?" He strode off.

"What in the world was he talking about?"

Preston squirmed. "He was referring to my dad's name. It's true. I avoid it even though my name is the same as his."

June gulped. "Your dad? What? Your name isn't Preston James?"

Preston's cheeks were on fire. "Some of it is. I just shortened it, kind of. It's really Robert Preston James Wahlberg, IV."

June sputtered. "That's your dad? The man I met?"

"Yes."

"My God. Even I know that name! The Wahlberg that built Andrew and Alicia's boat? The boat multimillionaire or billionaire, whatever, is your father? The one that lives in San Diego? Are you kidding me? You're not a poor guy making it all on your own like you told me?" She crumpled her half-eaten bagel and cream cheese in its wrapper and pushed it away. "You led me to believe we had that in common, Preston." Tears came to her eyes. "I feel like a fool."

Preston reached out for her arm. She pulled it away and he reached out again. "June, look at me. I never said I was poor. I said I've been on my own and I have been." *She's mad, I'm rich? Now this really is a first.* "I ran from that. You heard my dad say it. Why do you think I've been living away from him and San Diego? You saw how people treated me at the hotel? I'm sick of that phony baloney stuff. I wanted to make it on my own with my own business. No lie!"

"But you're, you're..." she stammered. "Phony too because you're rich. And you, err...hide it. Well, hid it. From me anyway."

Because I have had nothing but phony people in my life who were after the prestige and not into the real me. Because if you knew who I was and had, it probably would've changed you. It always does. "Okay, so I have assets in the bank, but I've been earning all my own money that I've been living on for years now. Sure, there's a bankroll for me invested, and inheritance, one day. For God's sake, I'm his only son. But I've stayed away on purpose. His expectations were too much, and he wouldn't, couldn't back off me. That's not his nature."

"I don't know what to say. Why do men lie?" She dropped her head into her folded arms.

His mind raced. "My feelings for you...all the care I've given you...none of that's a lie. I can't help that I have a background that's a, a high level. My father worked for that too. I don't fault him for that. I only have a beef with his pressure on me. I won't interfere with who you are or your real life. No pressure, June. You'll be free as a bird once that cast is gone."

Lifting her head, she looked him in the eye. "Well, I'm far from free right now. I can't drive yet or anything. I'm so stuck. I hate it." She hung her head and wiped tears that dripped on the table.

"Nothing's changed. You are you and I am me. We're still together in this." *She's not wanting anything more from me so far. Huh. Unbelievable.*

She sniffed. "Are you sure this is all you've been hiding? I never felt stupid even though I never finished college, but you're making me feel so dumb. Even Tanner knew. He always, always made a fool of me and you're no different." She scooted her chair further away.

That's enough. Now I'm insulted. "Hey. I'm completely different from that jerk of a guy and don't tell me I'm not. I resent that, June. No one can change the family they were born into. Because of all the wealth, I've had nothing but doubt and unrealistic expectations dumped on me from day one. I told you my dad wanted me to be with Cassie, Liv's daughter. No deal. I didn't need or want a set up. With her it would have been more of a corporate merger."

He reached to touch June's hair, and she moved her head out of reach. *I've never seen her mad. She's not after money and I was too mistrusting to tell her the truth. She has not misrepresented herself like I did. But I didn't owe her any more than I've done.* "I wanted to be by your side from the moment I saw you hurt, and nothing has changed. Haven't I been there for you every second since the accident, June?"

"Yes, but because you had fun living in a fantasy world. I was just a little dumb, hurt person. Don't get me wrong. I appreciate everything you've done, but I am so mad that once again, Tanner has one-upped me. That darn man. You helped him make a fool of me."

"I did not." *She's honest about him too? Yeah, because she doesn't see he wants her back. What then? He's working those horses alright, to get them and her! Why should I care?*

"Oh, so I did it on my own? Don't answer that. I was stupid to trust you without really knowing who you were. No worries. I won't be using you for your money. I just need someone who can drive a car. If I had enough money, I'd use uber instead." Tears welled in her eyes.

"Stop, June." He touched her arm. "I can give you the money for all the uber rides you want and more. Just tell me. I don't think so but also, I'm no hit-and-run type of a guy. I stepped up to the plate—out of my comfort zone, and I intend to follow through for once in my life. You can doubt me all day long and so can my dad—the person you seem to always mention, I must add. I don't care. Go ahead and choose, June. Me and my care or the money to get you through this? I've had a lifetime of mistrusting people myself. Just because someone came along that was honest didn't mean I could change my beliefs overnight. Could you?" *I don't think so because she knows what she wants and no one and nothing is standing in the way. I like that!*

Brushing the tears with anger, she sat up. "I guess not. Horses are part of my being. I can't be without them." June's head slumped. "No. I don't want uber." She whispered. "Or money. Let's stick to our plan and go our separate ways when the cast is off, if you still want to help me." Her eyes focused on his.

She doesn't want the money. Huh. "Sure I do, but since we're being honest, let me add something. I don't want you to take this the wrong way. Looking at it physically or logistically—and not with the heart, you need me more than I need you." *Test. Now what?*

She bit her lip.

"But this, June, is about the heart, and the heart is not ruled by physical issues or by money. I'm here because of my heart and my own free will. Don't forget it when things come up."

"I won't. Even if I had known who you were, it wouldn't have changed anything for me. I had a broken leg, no horses, and ten weeks of recovery. No money could fix that."

"True." He shook his head. *Horses. My God. Her true love. That's where her heart is.*

"Alright, Preston. Officially, I still need you."

Smart girl. "I know that's hard for you to admit." Preston wiped his forehead. "But I'm glad. It's settled?" *I hope so. I am not ready to leave her side. For her sake, that is.*

"Settled." She sniffed.

"Good." He reached for her hand and gave it a little squeeze. *She's letting me hold her hand again.* Then let's watch some of the warmup over in that covered area. Looks like it's getting a lot more crowded."

"It's because the lower-level rides are starting soon. There's more riders than at the highest levels. Let's see if I can point some things out."

"If Tanner comes back, I'll share my knowledge." They looked at each other and laughed. Preston added. "He tried to pull one over on us, didn't he? I wonder what else he's got up his sleeve?" *If I'm right, and I think so, he'll come up with more underhanded moves.*

"I don't want to find out."

"I do. I want to see for myself what he's all about. I'm glad he got second place in his class."

"Class? Wow. That's right. He did."

"I've been listening, June. That's what the announcer's said a few times. He said 'class.'"

"I've created a monster. Now you're talkin' the talk. Okay, now look over there."

Pointing, she took in the full arena scene. "See that horse's head getting a little higher. That's not good. It's got a red ribbon in its tail. That's a warning to the other riders that the horse kicks out. I try to stay away from those."

"Yikes. Now look, someone just passed them because they suddenly stopped, and the horse flattened his ears. I think he's mad."

"Yeah. He is."

Suddenly the horse stopped and started backing up and going sideways. The rider was helpless to get it to move forward. One kick from the rider and the horse gave it's answer with a buck. Off went the rider and the trainer rushed in. The horse was caught and led over to the rider. The rider was okay and stood brushing the sand off her breeches and coat. They left the arena but were still in view. The trainer got into the saddle and took the horse back into the warmup ring. Suddenly, the horse acted completely different, and the trainer climbed down, and the rider got back on. No further scuffles happened. In a few minutes, the trainer motioned the rider to come close and offered her a drink. The rider shook her head no. They left the arena and headed for the show ring.

June tapped her fingers on the table. "I hope everything goes well for her. If it was the championships, the trainer wouldn't have been allowed to help like that."

Preston shook his head. "I'd be scared. I think riding's hard enough without a scary horse to deal with." *June, you're gonna have enough on your plate without having an albatross like Tanner hanging around when you're back to riding. He needs a red bow pinned on him.*

"Well, sometimes horses can change into beings you would never expect at a show. You can't let them win or you'll always be at their mercy. Seems like the trainer did the right thing. Riders need to get back on whenever they can. It can blow your confidence if you don't."

"Are you scared to ride now?" His eyes were wide.

"No. I'm not. I have every reason to be, but I think this fall was just a freak thing. I've fallen off before and it was no big deal. But it's just that I'm starting to think about the future in a different way than I ever used to."

"Good. This sport isn't for me, but it's fun to watch."

"I'm glad you're not bored. Some people think watching dressage is as exciting as watching grass grow."

He scoffed. "It's not that peaceful." *God. That's an understatement. Our first fight and we're still here. Another first for me, but this isn't over. Tanner is scheming to get June back and she can't see it. Because of him, I'm starting to think things will be harder for her on the sidelines than on the centerline after her cast is off.*

17

Tanner entered the warm-up ring on the young horse. The horse was 17'1 hands high and its size was a great fit for Tanner. The horse's black tail swished and swung with the impulsion and steady rhythm of the trot. Tanner's handling was impressive and made the horse look like a piece of cake to ride.

June chirped. "How does he get so lucky that this newbie of a horse is behaving like that?" *He always gets lucky. I should know.*

"He does make it look easy out there. That horse has its head down and it looks like it's doing what it's supposed to."

She bit her lip. "Let's go get a seat next to the ring he's going to be in. Will you go check the board to see what ring number they'll be in? My curiosity is killing me over this ride."

"Alright."

* * *

Preston returned. "He's going to be in Ring 2. That's a bit far for you to go. Should we go now?"

June stood and got her crutches underneath her arms. "Okay. Let's go. His ride's in a few minutes."

They made it to the entrance of the warmup and Tanner came out on his horse. June took a step with her crutches and her bright pink cast swung as she moved her crutches. The horse's eye caught her and suddenly he spooked sideways and would not stop. He took off at a dead gallop throwing bucks as he went. Tanner moved into a two-point position and rode the bucks until the horse stopped hundreds of yards away down the decomposed granite road base leading to the stalls for nonboarder horses.

June gasped. "Oh my God. I knew some horse would get spooked by the sight of me. I feel bad about that."

"That horse was out of control. I'm glad you weren't on it."

"I can relate to the run, but at least that's all I knew before I blacked out."

"Oh my gosh, June. I am so, so, so sorry."

"It wasn't your fault."

"And neither was this. You tried to stay back from the horses."

"I did."

* * *

June and Preston took their seats at the ring. June's crutches were propped against the picnic table. Tanner and the horse came walking back.

June tugged on Preston's sleeve. "Tanner looks calm, but look at the horse. He's still too pumped. Look how sweaty his neck is, let alone his hind with white foam all over. He must've given Tanner a hard time after he quit bucking. Two of his braids are loose and ready to come unbraided."

Minutes later, Tanner reappeared on deck and was ready to enter the ring for his second ride.

June whispered. "Here comes Wild Child." Her eyes twinkled. "Any bets how it's going to go?"

* * *

June spoke as soon as the ride was over. "Well, that was a success. His score is going to be high." *Like I said, he always gets lucky.*

"Let's watch the next few rides and go see the scores."

* * *

They walked over to the posted scores. June turned to Preston. "Tanner probably won his class. That guy can ride. If only he was as nice as his riding is. But he's not." She took a deep breath. "I don't know about you, but I'm tired now."

"Good call. I've seen plenty today. We can always come back tomorrow if you want."

"Oh, I don't know. This is kind of bittersweet being here. I love the ambience, but then again, I've seen enough as a spectator. I miss the real deal and don't know if it's meant to be mine again."

Preston ran his fingers through his hair and turned her chin to him. "You'll be in the game again soon, June. You're getting your cast off in thirty-five days, give or take a day or two."

"That's right. The beginning of next month. Oh, I hope my leg's going to be okay."

"I think it'll be a little weak at first. But so far, the doctor hasn't said you'll need physical therapy. That's a good sign."

"I'm lucky. Okay, here's his class. Wow. Even with all that trouble on his first ride, he got a 69.75 percent, second place. Anything over 60 percent is good to excellent. Up into the 70s is great. Oh, here's his second ride, first place with a 75.4 percent. Geez…Lucky guy."

"I can't agree with you this time."

"Why not?"

"Because I'm the one sitting next to you, not him."

"Aw…thank you." *Hold onto your heart, June. You've got trouble brewing with this guy.*

* * *

Tanner came up behind them and spoke low into the back of June's neck. "Whatcha think there, June? That youngster gave me a hard time, but I got him to listen."

June leaned on her crutch and her shoulders scrunched up to her earlobes. She put her hand up to her neck and felt a hot spot. She rubbed the sweat beads and swept the back of her hand across her forehead. "True, but then I would've..." She bit her lower lip.

"Say it. This is our world, June. Face the reality. 'You would've'...."

18

Tanner continued, "…done the same thing. You need to get back in. You could've ridden through that little runaway scene no problem. You belong here in our world, and you know it. Not everyone does." His eyebrows arched and his eyes looked at Preston.

She stood taller and clinched her fist. *Presumptuous man. How dare you say "our" when all you did was leave me?* "That's a ways off. Preston and I…"

He cut her off. "It's a different day job than other people have, June. People like us aren't made for the sidelines. Don't let people talk you into being content on the sidelines. Other people don't understand."

Preston cleared his throat and stood taller. "Who said she's being talked into 'being content on the sidelines.' I haven't heard that from anyone except you."

Tanner sneered. "Okay, big guy. I didn't exactly mean her." His eyes darted to June, and he shook his head. "But I got your message and I'll be leaving now. See ya." He turned and walked off. He turned back and called out. "I meant what I said, June."

Preston shook his head. "That guy…"

June interrupted. "He's arrogant and cocky. This is a glimpse of him and how he thought it was okay to dump me and move on at uh…opportunity. An opportunity in the form of another woman with money. Don't kid yourself, he's not jealous of your money. He wouldn't keep circling back at us. Until this show, I haven't heard from him in over a year. He's just super competitive. He plays to win."

"Are you sorry he saw you today?"

"Only sorry that I'm down with a cast at a moment. Before this, I would have loved to be riding against him. I'm not afraid of seeing him."

"Hey. A cast is temporary. His outlook and personality aren't. You're too good of a person for someone like him."

"Although, there's no denying he's moved into being a top pro now." She bit her lip and her eyes looked away.

"A pro? Pro butthead?"

June laughed so hard her arms shook and her crutches wobbled. "I need to sit down." She giggled. "I'm going to fall over and break something."

"Oh no you're not." Preston put his arm around her waist and took the crutch. "Let's go to the bench, rest, and then head for the car."

"Okay." She shook with laughter. "What's next? Your past people, my past boyfriend. Our past is not far away from us."

"You know my answer."

"What?"

"Let's run."

"Geez, Preston. Maybe you haven't been wrong after all."

* * *

Preston opened their suite door and took a deep breath. "Here you go, June. Have a seat. Nice comfy place on the couch and I'm just gonna squeeze in next to you. Know why?"

"Because it's a beautiful evening and we should celebrate the fact that we spent another day together?"

He caressed her face and lifted her chin. "I'm so glad you said that. I'm sorry we had that little fight." His lips found hers, parted, and enjoyed the softness. Her arm reached over for him to come closer.

"How about this?" He slid her onto his lap, and she wrapped her arms around his neck.

Nose to nose, she pulled away just a little and held his face. "You said I needed you physically."

"Yes." His eyes looked deep into hers.

"More than you need me?"

"Now, June. Don't use my own words against me."

"Well? That is what you said, right?"

"Correct. However, I must add that," his fingers played with her hair, and he kissed her neck, "I also said logistically. True?"

"True."

"So, once again I'm going to live up to my end of the bargain." He picked her up and she laughed.

"I should know you would have a comeback." She kissed his mouth.

"Oh, I do. You must be a mind reader. And logistically speaking, I'm moving you."

"Now you're the mind reader." *I wonder what your real life is like, but I could care less right now.*

He carried her off and the rest of the evening was all theirs.

* * *

Moving quietly, Preston opened the curtains, and the sunshine

126

poured in. "Good morning, June. I made your coffee." He came and sat on her side of the bed.

"I feel like I had a great night's sleep."

"Me, too. Want to have some toaster waffles and head out for the last day of the show?"

"Your call. I'm hungry. It's late. We better hurry if we want to see the first class." She sipped her coffee. "Oh. So good…Nothing like a dark roast."

"Alright. Waffles it is. I'll put them in the toaster."

"Okay, I'll help."

The waffles popped up. Preston laughed. "That was quick!"

"I agree. I barely got the plates and utensils out."

"This toaster is supercharged. I'd like to take it apart and see how it's made."

"No one called for a mechanic, mister. Come on, sit down. Let's enjoy." She picked up her knife and buttered her waffle. "Lots of butter. Gooey. Now for the syrup…Watch my style." She poured it on with deliberation and sat back to admire it. "Perfect! Good thing we bought a big bottle. Yum. The first bite's the best. Sorry for talking with my mouth full…" She chewed and licked her lips. "Y–u–m–m–y…."

"You're so funny. What happened to being in a hurry?"

"Well, syrup and butter make even these instant waffles taste good. I love the smell of waffles. Kind of sweet and nutty, right? I haven't had a Belgium waffle in forever. Let's have some soon." She took a sip of coffee.

"Me either. Reminds me of eating at home. Sometimes I miss those days. Sunday morning waffles were one of the few times that my dad and I spent together, and I looked forward to that time when it was just the two of us—just like this, sitting together. Although we didn't cook them, our chef did." He looked into her eyes. "But that counts, they were homemade."

June laughed. "Technically, it does." *Gosh. He never would have said something as revealing. I had no idea he wasn't able or hadn't been telling me things that were on his mind this whole time. This is nice. We can be open now. Unless he's hiding something else…*

"Being a bachelor and cooking on my own can't compare to Sunday mornings with him. We can't carve out time like that anymore."

"You don't have to give all that up, you know. He seems like he misses you."

"Nah. He's got a full life. He's in his own world, June. He's surrounded by Yes People, and he's used to getting his way. He's bossy, opinionated, and snobby. I mean it. Spend any time with him and you'll see and hear it all. He doesn't hide his feelings either."

"Gosh, I think you needed to say those things. Feel better airing your thoughts?"

"I do. I'm surprised you could tell."

"Oh yes. I can tell what horses are thinking too." She grinned.

"I knew there had to be a way for you to work in the word 'horse.' I'm sure you can. Now, if you can read people that well, no one will ever be able to fool you."

"Right back at me, huh, Preston. You and I can really talk."

"I wish I would have told you about my background long ago, June."

"Me too. It hasn't changed a thing." *Geez. He said he was 'sensitive' about his past, and I know that was no lie.*

* * *

They pulled into the visitor parking at the horse show. Preston opened her door and held her crutches. "Thank you, sir. Let's go see the ride times. You're going to like the rides around lunch time. I spotted them the day we got here. I think there's going to be three at least. I hope none of them scratch. Three different levels. First, Third and a Prix St. Georges."

"Something I haven't seen?"

"Yep." Her crutches crunched in the fine gravel. "Come on. Now I'm all excited. I'm glad we didn't miss this after all. I love the last day. And there's also going to be one other thing that this show will have. I've never been here to see it, but today's the day."

"Good grief. You are a horsey person. I'm walking fast to keep up with you."

"Okay, here's the board and here's what I was talking about." She reached up and pointed to a list at the far right. "See that?"

Preston scratched his chin. "Freestyles. What's that all about?"

"Rides to music."

"Really?"

"Yep. They're awesome. Haven't you seen the Olympic rides? Those are Grand Prix rides. My God I would have loved to ride Grand Prix…" *I have to get back out there. Please leg, get well and strong.*

* * *

The time came for the Freestyles to begin, and June took Preston's hand. First up was a First Level Freestyle. June clutched Preston's hand. "I know this rider! Isabel Sheffield. I'm surprised she's up north too." What were the chances of seeing her here too?

The rider took her place and raised her hand. The announcer

stated, "Your music is playing." The horse and rider began moving in harmony to a lively entrance at A with a flowing working trot down centerline. Timed to the music, the gelding's trot appeared almost as big as an extended trot of an upper-level ride. Progressing from trotting straight ahead to 10-meter trot circles, the music progressed into more dramatic beats and soon the horse was moving sideways and showing classic leg yields to the right and left. With another change in song, the horse began to canter onto 15-meter circles with changes of directions through the trot onto a new circle to accomplish both right and left.

June whispered. "In dressage, we always show both directions for every movement. Not sure if I told you that."

"I think you did, but here it looks different. It's hard to keep track of all the rules, but this does look pretty good. Oh, look she's got a big run, uhm … I mean, gallop, going across the sand, uhm … diagonal."

You are so cute trying to talk dressage. "Very good. Yes. At this level it's called a lengthened stride at canter. I really like her music. Good job matching the gait changes to the music."

The ride ended with a medium walk turning down onto centerline and halting at X with a salute.

"For First Level, Preston, I would give that ride a top score. Isabel's a good rider. She's doing great with Zephyr Starr. He's her own horse; lucky duck. Wish I could've shown D. He was solid at his level. Mary still might … nah, I'm sure Sarah's got him by now." Her voice faded and came back up. "For an Amateur, Isabel's a rider that will go far and probably turn pro. Her family's farm has good horses. She was raised with the best horses. Years of lessons and, now look, she's the real deal. Can we go talk to her?"

"Sure. What about your crutches? I can go up to her and tell her to come meet us at the picnic tables near the barn if you want."

"Oh yeah. Oh my gosh, I just remembered Tanner's take off ride! Yikes. I felt bad about that. That's okay. I'll be in touch with her another time. I don't want to cause another spook. God, I've never scared a horse before. Oh, look. Here comes the Third Level ride. I can't wait 'til you see it and then the last ride of the day. You're gonna love 'em."

* * *

June sat back and looked at the empty show ring. "It's over. Wow. Another good ride. What a show. The competition rides are over. Next up is going to be even better. It's a demonstration ride and won't be scored, but I think we'll be impressed. Fingers crossed for the riders, especially Isabel. I would love to see her and be able to congratulate her if she wins her class, and I think she will. This is going to be a nail biter." My God. Tanner's right about one thing for sure. I do belong here. Or, used to…Weeks to go until I know for sure if I will have a comeback or not.

19

Twenty minutes later, the show announcer called attention to the next and final ride of the day. The crowd gathered and was delighted by the appearance of two bay horses with white blazes on their heads that came close to being an exact match—almost as if the horses were identical twins.

June sat taller and moved to the edge of her seat. *I can hardly wait for this.* "This is going to be a–m–a–z–i–n–g. Pas de Deux. It means two horses. A Pas de Trois would be three. Can you imagine the sight, Preston?"

The horses stood as still as statues. Braided black manes in white bands, long flowing black tails, dark chocolate brown legs with a hint of black and wrapped from hoof to knee in white polo leg wraps, completed their quintessential appearance of elegance and the majestic presence of horsepower at its finest. Dressed in formal show attire, the man and lady rider gathered their reins and proceeded to canter around the outside of the court. They both halted in opposition from each other, facing each other, and prepared to enter the arena simultaneously. The entrance railing was opened wider to accommodate the pair.

"This is cool, June. What can I say?" He swallowed hard and stared.

The music began and the horses cantered into the arena and went from canter to halt. The riders saluted. From there the music was symphonic and traditional. Harmonic and rhythm changes flowed as classical tunes matched the precision gaits. The crowd hushed as the riders rode flying changes alongside each other and turned in harmony to follow the diagonal line across with another set.

Preston whispered. "I'll never forget how you looked when your horse was skipping."

June gripped his hand, her eyes glued on the horse duo. "I'm glad you got to see my ride. It was one of my best. I miss D. I'll have to check on him. I told Mary about my new cast, but she never mentioned D. I wonder why … Oh look, those are pirouettes in canter. Look how they're making a complete circle and they'll do one each direction. I wonder who choreographed their ride?"

"That was cool too. Look at that trot. Whoa. That's big."

Glancing at Preston, June smiled and nodded. "Yes. They're both big movers. Look how the power is coming from the hind and pushing the front legs to extend out. That's dressage. Gorgeous."

"They're not moving fast, it's more like … uhm …"

"Ground covering with a float?"

"Good words. That must be another rider thing."

"It is. It's a treat to ride that too. The float and the feel is exhilarating." *I wish it was me and D.*

Minutes later, the ride ended with a reunion of the two horses back at centerline and a halt at X. The riders saluted and everyone clapped. June gripped Preston's hand. "Thank you so much for bringing me here today. This is the best recovery I could have ever had. Whether I ever compete again or not, this has been spectacular, and I've loved sharing horses with you." She wiped a tear from her eye.

Preston leaned over and whispered. "Aw … You deserve the best, June."

June put her hand up to her eye and brushed the start of another tear. "I better quit getting so emotional. Geez. One more thing to watch that you're also going to like." *Money can't buy this! This experience is priceless, well, to me. I should let Mom know the show was great!*

"How long do we have to wait?"

"About twenty minutes."

* * *

"Preston, this is where the winners and awards are shown off by a victory lap. Look," she pointed. "Tanner's out there with riders from the upper-level classes." *Figures he'd do well. He certainly can ride.* Well, this is all about the classes of competition, not the class of the riders. "Ha. I can only imagine his ego now. Pumped to the sky." *He's a confirmed top rider. Will I be able to reach the top? And, what if I don't get D back? I'm going to need a horse with good breeding, conformation, and talent. He's got access to many horses now. Just what he wanted all along. What else could the man want?*

All the horses were back with braided manes and white leg wraps. Ribbons won were hooked to the bridles, and if they had a sash, it was on. Only those comfortable with their horse's ability to remain calm at the group gallop were going in. Seven horses were ready. The announcer called for attention and the riders proceeded to the entry point and circled the perimeter of the largest outdoor arena for this ride. To the crowd it was a grand spectacle and a lovely picture of what it meant to ride a winner. The riders galloped and waved and amazingly, all of the horses were in control and pulled off the end of the show with class and conformation.

***

Preston stretched. "Whew, June. This has been a day. You would have missed all this."

"I know. But I didn't, thanks to you."

"That's good. I love my motors and I love my mechanical challenges. We both love horsepower, that's a fact."

"So true, but I'm ready to go."

"Me too."

They headed back to the car and were almost at the parking area when a female voice called out. "June!"

June turned around. "Isabel! Hi. I wanted to see you. We watched your ride. You did great!"

"It's so good to see you, June. I heard about your accident, and I heard you were here. The crutches helped me spot you. Let me hug you."

The two girls hugged. June reached from Preston's arm. "This is Preston. He's been my caregiver and companion during my recovery. I get my cast off in five weeks. I'm getting excited."

"I bet. Nice to meet you, Preston." Smiling, they shook hands. "Well, I won't keep you, June. You should sit in the car. But let's call each other when you're back home. I want to hear how everything goes for you. I might be going to school near you."

"School? You mean college? San Diego State University?" June swallowed hard. *What? She's doing great in her riding and starting college?*

"Yes. My parents are encouraging me. I should say pressuring me. You know how that goes. But I think they're right."

Oh, my God. I would've never said that about mine. "Wow."

"I figure, I could take classes and work in horses. We're capable of long hard days, maybe a little bookwork and studying wouldn't be too much. Hey. Maybe you could enroll and work on your degree too."

"Just like that, Isabel? You make it sound so simple. And you're so energetic. You're nineteen and I'm twenty-seven." *What a girl with it all going on.* "Okay," she dragged the word out and caught a glimpse of her toes sticking out from the cast. She wiggled them. *They still work.* She let out a deep breath. *I can't tell her I'm the complete opposite. She'll think I'm a total washup standing here maimed and against making progress in life? Yikes. Even I sound bad to myself thinking it!*

"We'll talk. I have so much to think about my head is going to burst. I have to get back to my old self first and that's number one. But school—aw, tempting hearing you say it. Don't tell my parents I said that." She looked around. "Any spies close by?"

Isabel's arms stretched out. "You're so funny. Promise, I won't tell. Nice to meet you, Preston. Take care, June. Bye."

June got in the car. Preston got in and looked at her. "There is way more to you than I ever imagined, June Tarlin."

"What about you, Robert Preston James Wahlberg, IV?"

"It's complicated?" He grinned.

"Let's go home. I mean back to our place. We better rest up."

"Nap time?"

"Drive, Preston."

* * *

What happened to the safety of seclusion? The days were flying by, and reality was creeping to a picture of an unknown future. How could dressage have developed into a relationship that had a clock ticking and now parents on the horizon and a possible inkling of a return to college? Was an existence without pressure all it took for her to take a break and think things through? One thing was for sure, Tanner was out of her life forever. No way would he pursue her again and if he did? Why? Wasn't she potentially less than she was before he dumped her?

*   *   *

Days later, driving back to the suite from the store, June looked over at Preston. "I just remembered my car. What is wrong with me? I don't believe I haven't given it much thought until now. My gosh. Where is it?"

He cleared his throat. "I contacted your apartment's manager, and they said you had a designated parking space. I explained your situation and the manager put it in a secure location since I told him you wouldn't be back for several months."

June gulped. "You did? Yes. Oh my God. That was nice, but I haven't paid my rent. What if…"

He turned his head quickly and gave her a glance. "I paid your rent for the next four months."

June gasped. "My goodness. That is so nice of you. Thank you, but I'm going to pay you back. That's a lot."

"June, please. It's okay. I can handle it. Besides, I already did. You'll be home in a few weeks and so will I."

Reminder and alert for my heart…just in case I start fantasizing this is anything more than a planned arrangement. "I know you can 'handle' it, Preston. But I do earn money."

"That's obvious. You were fine before my tire blew."

"True. Almost back to my old self again." *Not until I have a saddle underneath me and make a little money from giving lessons, at least.* "Speaking of old self, tell me about your first car. The one I'm driving is my first car in California. It's kind of a beater, huh? But it gets me from point A to point B. I bought my real first car in Florida. I waited tables at a pancake house to earn the money. I could work practically any time of the day or night. It was a great set up for a first job. But this one came from giving lessons and training horses. I was pretty proud of myself for qualifying for the loan! What was yours?"

"That was quite a while ago. I've driven a lot of cars since then."

"Oh, come on. You can remember! Everybody remembers their first car. What was it?"

"A BMW."

"I love little BMWs. Was it a 318 or 328 model? How could you fit in it? Kind of small for you."

"It was a 7 series."

"Oh, I forgot. You had a fancy car!" She took her hand and mockingly fanned it at him. "So ritzy!"

"Knock it off, June." He glanced over.

"Oopsy! Sorry, Preston. Just couldn't resist." She giggled.

"Yeah, well. Please resist. I'm driving and this topic is …"

"Alright." She sighed. "How did you earn the money for it? Those are so expensive!"

"I didn't have to. My Dad bought it for me on my sixteenth birthday. I never had a job until I graduated from school."

"Oh. High school?"

"College."

"Wow." *Oh my God. No wonder he never said anything. Some people hold things against rich people. Not me. If they have money, and a horse, and want lessons, they are welcome in the arena*! "Alrighty then. Let's change the subject. Tell me about your dad."

Preston squirmed in his seat and stretched out a little. "Only if you tell me about your family. I know you have a sister."

"I do. It's just the two of us, and I know you don't have any. Remember Sheila at the casino and how you confirmed that little fact?"

Grimacing and shaking his head, Preston faked a cough. "Woman, you know too much about me."

"Ah, and that was never in your plan. Funny, ha ha, it's okay for you to know all about me. So, tell me more about your dad." Her hair hung past her shoulders, loose and shining, and June played with a strand.

"Gosh your hair is pretty. You're distracting me. Anyway, 'Bob' is quite the dad. Never shy about sharing his opinions. Runs his business with a solid set of rules. Everything seems to work out for him. He has manufacturing shops in multiple coastal locations. He builds 'em and sells 'em. And he always wants me to get involved. I like mechanics. But like you, I like to do what I like to do."

"You know my address in San Diego. Is his factory or shop close by?"

"It is."

"Can we go to it? I'm sure it's an impressive business."

"You always bring up topics that have to do with him."

"Something wrong with that? I'm sorry."

"I don't mean it that way. It's just that somehow the subject seems to involve him. I'm wondering if you have a connection to him in a past life," he laughed.

"Too funny! Past life…what about this one?"

"June, if you want to see him again and see the shop, that is just fine with me. Take heed, he is not a warm and fuzzy guy, to say the least."

"I don't know why he seems to come to mind when I talk to you. I have no idea where that comes from." *His dad's probably not that bad! I've dealt with lots of rich horse owners. They needed me. I was their trainer. I could handle Bob, no problem. He might even like me!*

"I'll accept that. He's as supportive of me as your parents are with you and making a living riding. Can I meet your parents? You're making me curious about them."

"You can meet them if you want to. I would like you to, but 'take heed' yourself, Preston, they are not supportive of anything I do. I'm not Brianna my sweet sister and their little idolized daughter with a great career and a safe job! So, do you still want to?"

He laughed. "Put it that way, I want to meet them even more…I think. If I'm around, that is. I hope so! But what will they say about me living with you for the past month?"

"I won't wave it in their face, but I won't hide it either." *They'll think he's using me to get out of going back to his real job.* "In their own way, they're as opinionated as your dad."

"Huh. Well, my dad met you. So, I suppose I should make it a point to meet your parents. You should know that he not only expected me to date Cassie, but he also expected me to marry her. It's not like he and Liv are married, so Cassie's no relation. I'm not sure you'd like him if you got to know him."

"Okay. I'll have to take your word for it. What is it about her that's so compelling for him to want you to marry her?"

"Her wealth. Or her mom's wealth, I should say. Liv's almost as rich as he is and Cassie's an only child too. He wanted me to marry money. Cassie's nice and works hard but she's a businesswoman all the way. She's a CPA and the CEO of her own accounting firm. She's two years older than me. I'll say one thing, she's super smart. I've always admired that about her."

"Oh. I think after all our talks, we're both just curious to meet up with the parents. No big deal, right? I can handle it." *So, I am out classed by this Cassie woman, and he doesn't want to say it.* "No problem." *We will be going our separate ways for sure.*

"Bring on the parents!"

Oh God. I know my parents. Trouble ahead once they're in the picture!

* * *

After putting their purchases away, they went outside and found a bench on the grounds of their suite and watched the birds and squirrels. June closed her eyes and took a deep breath. Beautiful and peaceful. We look like a couple in love. So not true. I can't let that happen!

"You went to college? Right?"

"Yeah. It was an okay experience, but I wanted to work with engines and motors more than paper or computers. I like working with my hands."

"Maybe so. But you've got the cleanest mechanic's hands I've ever seen."

"I don't mind getting them dirty if I need to. Mostly I like figuring out the problem and then I find it and get down to fixin' it. The challenge is analyzing the issue."

"Whoa. You sound as smart as you say Cassie is. I get it. I

know what I want too. But what if I'm missing out by not getting a bachelor's degree?"

"It took Isabel to make you say this?"

"No. She just gave me something to think about. There's not that much time left until my cast comes off. Seems like forever sometimes, but not always."

"When doesn't it?"

"When we're having fun and talking about stuff. I really appreciate how you're making the days pass by so quickly. Aren't you excited to see my leg without the cast?"

Preston's shoulders shook as he laughed. "Does it still match your other leg?"

June burst into laughter. "It used to. We saw it at the four-week mark!"

"You're making me laugh."

"Okay. But what if my leg is shriveled up and useless." *Nightmare.*

"Then, I guess I'll stick around for a little while longer."

"What if it never comes back to what it was? Think about that. You could be stuck with me forever then."

"I'm not worried."

"Not worried about my leg or not worried about being stuck with me?"

"June, neither."

"Would you want to be stuck with me?"

"I don't think that's an issue to worry about."

"You're right. We have an exit plan." She looked at him. "No comment?"

"Nope."

June bit her lip. *At least he's being honest about the final count-*

down to freedom. How is this going to work? I'll pretend I can wing it. I need to cut the cord sometime soon.

20

Days passed until, two weeks later, Tuesday morning came with a dose of welcomed sunshine on a summer day. Fall weather was on the horizon, but it wasn't here yet and lounging around made the days peaceful from sunup to sundown. Some TV shows were entertaining, others questionable. June laughed. "I think going back to school would be okay after all. My brain is turning to mush after all this TV."

"Well, no harm with a little motivation. But remember, homework piles up and gets old. It's probably easy to think about going back since you're stuck on this couch so much." *I think the school thing is going to get old fast too! Wait until she gets busy with horses. I don't think she sees herself as capable of being fully back in her world, as I do.*

June laughed. "Yeah, but I like being busy. Or are you trying to tell me, you don't think I'm cut out for school."

"Not cut out? How can you think that? You've already got one degree. You just need more credits, and you'll have a bachelor's degree. It's not rocket science."

"Well, well. Aren't we mister educated? Excuse me, but a bachelor's degree in business is not going to be a walk in the park for me. I'll have to study a lot to pass!"

"I didn't mean to belittle it. Just trying to encourage you."

"Okay, thank you. Maybe the class difference between us makes your words sound a little different to me."

"Thanks for being so honest. Just what I wanted to hear. I knew it. Every woman I ever knew can't handle the real me. See? That's why I was afraid to tell you." *'Class difference'? I knew it. The start of the end of it all. How many times have I been through misconceptions, misinformation, and misgivings over getting involved? Been there, done that.*

"You were afraid?"

"Yes, because, believe it or not, I really like you and I didn't want to mess it up." *Our time together has been the best, but no woman, June included, is going to put up with my constant absences. Even clingy Sheila couldn't!*

"I thought you were questioning my ability to handle school."

"No. Don't jump to conclusions."

June looked across the room. "Oh! My phone's buzzing, can you just see who it is? It's in my purse on the counter.

Preston checked it. "It's a text message from…Tanner." He watched her reaction.

June groaned. "Eh, put the phone down. I'll read it later. I need a breath of fresh air. I'm going to step outside for a second."

"Okay. I want to see the end of this game show." He returned to the couch.

June got up and went outside and closed the door behind her.

Preston looked at the TV and looked back at her phone, now on the counter and in easy reach. *Just a quick peek.* He walked with quick steps and picked it up.

—Hi, can't quit thinking about you since the show. Do you feel the same? Call me. Let's talk, T.

Preston slammed the phone on the counter and quickly returned to his seat. *The nerve of him. He knows I'm with her and sent the text anyway. He doesn't see me as any competition because I'm not into horses. He made that clear and now he wants her back! Devious, conniving guy.*

Seconds later, June opened the door. "Oh, fresh air. Sure cleared my head. Thought about homework. I'm ready! Let me see what old Tanner had to say." She picked up the phone. "Preston!"

"What?" He muttered.

"I can't believe this. This is great news!"

Preston pursed his lips and tried not to explode. "What!" His face started to burn.

June looked at him. "Hey. Relax. It's all good. I just saw a message I missed."

"Oh. Who's it from?"

"Isabel!"

Didn't expect to hear that! Preston came over and looked at the phone with her. "Yeah, you missed it. Good thing you saw it." *Huh. No interest in Tanner's message? Maybe she doesn't want me to know what his message is. Or maybe she thinks so little of him that she doesn't care what he has to say? But what if she thinks he's just being nice and wants to know how she's feeling? No way! She can't be that naïve!*

"She ..." June read on and looked up. "She wants to know if I can go back to the showgrounds. Zephyr Starr's boarded there, and she wants to know if I could help her with a couple of things. Uh oh. She sent the text yesterday."

"Things? Like what?"

"I think she needs help with her riding. You know, a mini lesson. Might be kind of fun to watch her ride and give her a commentary that you say I'm so good at." Her hand went to his thigh. "What do you think?"

"I'd be up for that. I'd like to see your work."

"Maybe one day I can watch you work on a car."

"I was thinking you might want to see my place."

June swallowed. "Your place? As in where you live?"

"Yeah."

Her jaw dropped. "In Portland?"

"Why not? We could go after you get your cast off—the day after your appointment? Want to? One last trip together before you ditch me?"

June coughed. "I'd love to see your place, but I thought we'd be going our separate ways."

He shifted his stance and ran his hand through his hair. "I'm not sure I can handle letting you go cold turkey, June. I mean, you've been my main concern for weeks and months and all of a sudden, we'll be saying goodbye. I know. That's the big plan and that's okay, but how about if we keep our last week as our final time together and enjoy your return to health for a few days. Then, whatever works for you, works for me."

"Really? Okay. I can live with that. But what about you meeting my parents and me seeing your dad's place and business."

"You're into my dad, aren't you?" *What would he say if he heard her? He would flip. His world, my world. She doesn't understand I haven't been there in a very long time. And he's not happy about that at all. Maybe she'll change her mind. I don't want to deal with him. Tahoe was nothing, but when he's in his element ... God.*

"I'm into seeing what your family business is all about and yes, more about your dad means more about you. Besides, he might be proud that you took such good care of me all this time. You know, his son, being a caring person? How about you and my parents? Same thing. Why are you 'into' my parents?"

No changing her mind. Him? 'Proud' of me for 'caring'? No, he won't be. She's never known anyone like him. "Okay, okay. Fair enough. We're both curious and I'm sure our parents are too. Let's go up to Portland and come back in time for me to meet your parents and you'll see my dad's place. I mean, my home that I left and his boat business. Happy?" June flopped on the bed, and he plopped down next to her.

June's casted leg bounced up. "Whoa, Preston! Yes. That plan works. You have more energy than D. Speaking of which, I'm going to give Mary a call. I haven't heard much about him, or Mary, in a l–o–n–g time. I should let her know I'll be coming home soon. Anyway, should I text Isabel and confirm a time to meet? I'm glad she stayed up north. She must've been working with a trainer in the area. Lucky me, for once! Well, I shouldn't say once." She leaned over and kissed him on the cheek.

Returning her kiss, his lips lingered on hers and she left them. Their velvety softness, so familiar now, calmed him. *She's cast a spell on me.* "Hey, I'm the lucky one, I've got you next to me. But it's a plan." He rested his hand on her thigh while she typed the message. He looked at her fingers. *So slender and delicate. She's cute from head to toe.*

June sent the text and got an immediate answer. "Preston, Isabel said 11:30 a.m. Is that okay with you?"

He stroked her thigh. "Yeah." He kissed her again. "If you want to." He kissed her again and pulled her close. He kissed her neck and let his hands feel her lean body. He looked into her sparkling blue eyes. Her smile made it impossible to let go of her. "When?"

She touched his face and let her fingers play with his hair and her hand drifted without boundaries. "I give up. How about in a little while?"

"Works for me, June."

* * *

"Look at the time! Now we're almost late. Hurry, Preston. I'm getting excited about another horse day! I'm starting to feel like my old self. It's great!"

June picked up her phone and scrolled the messages. "Oh God. Here's Tanner's message…"

Preston watched her read the message. *I'd like to punch that guy.*

She deleted it and plugged her phone into the charger.

"What did his text say?" He studied her reaction. "Hey. Well?"

She came over and took his face in both of her hands and planted a big kiss on his lips. "Nothing I care about, especially now. Let's hurry and get ready." Scrambling to find the clothes they wanted, they bumped elbows digging in the drawers. "Look at this cute top. I love it!" She put it on.

His eyes followed her. *It's a spell…*

"How does it look?"

"Nice, but better if it was off."

She laughed. "After the lesson." She put on a little perfume. "No time to shower. Keep going! We can't be late!"

"Aw…now you smell good too—like flowers…Just tell her we'll be a few minutes late."

"No way. We just…Men! Good grief." She started brushing her hair and put on lip gloss. Her blond hair glistened as she gathered it into a high pony and flicked it at him, giving him a naughty grin.

He groaned. "We better get outta here, now or else."

* * *

The drive didn't take long and soon the grounds were in sight. Preston turned onto the gravel road. "I'm sure learning my way to this place. Same parking spot. Then, to the barn to Isabel."

What a sweet guy. In real life he would make the perfect boyfriend. Loving, attentive, fun to be with, and good lookin' but—in this case, sadly, gone. He will be disappearing—like a rabbit in a magic show. Poof!

"Preston, to save me steps, can you please go and look for her? Tell her I'll be at warm up ring five. There's a table close to it with a good view of the arena."

"I'll let her know. Be right back." His eyes darted to the left and right.

"What are you looking for?"

"Tanner!" He laughed.

"Not funny! Oh my God. That would ruin the day. Now go, and we'll keep our fingers crossed he's not even in California." *The thought of Tanner is like a black, bulging rain cloud hanging above an outdoor wedding! He had nerve texting me. He's so self-centered he probably thinks I'll rush to text him back. I am a little curious to find out what he has to say though. He might be the perfect kickstart to my career!*

21

Preston returned. "I found her and look what she sent you. A little speaker."

"Smart girl. She has a headset for me so I can talk to her in a normal voice while she's riding. And she'll be able to talk too. Nice! I wonder what's going on with Zephyr. He's only been shown at First Level. She must want to work on something Second or Third Level. Can't wait to try riding again. Enough with this spectator stuff." She scoffed. *I would kill to be in a saddle.*

"Try to be patient. Couple of weeks away now. That's all."

Soon Isabel came riding into the arena. "Hi, June. Thank you so much for helping me out. I'm trying too hard with this boy." She reached down and patted his mane. "Stubborn little cuss. But I really like his suspension. He's got a lot going for him, that's for sure."

"Okay, that's a plus. He sure looks good. You've been doing a good job with him." *She is a rider I could work with on a consistent basis. Can't say that for all of them in the barn!*

"Thanks. I needed your positivity!"

"We all need positivity. I mean it. You're a good rider, Isabel. So, start warming up and take your time. Don't pressure him too much. Let him come to you. Legs quiet and on. He'll respond."

Isabel patted the horse again. "Come on, Zeph. Let's do this."

June watched. She squeezed Preston's thigh. "I'm so glad I'm

151

here today. Watching her ride is as sweet as candy." *So much potential here. I could bring her along to the next level. I know I could.*

"I get it, June. I work with my hands too and feel satisfied when the engine and car's body are together as it should be. Probably is a lot like a horse and rider."

"I'm glad you understand." She pressed her mic button so Isabel could hear her comments. "Good job, Isabel, with your trot work and canter. Good basics. I don't see anything wrong yet."

"Just wait." Isabel transitioned to a walk and came over to talk. "What's going on is that he has his simple changes down so nicely he doesn't want to move into the flying change. He's not slow behind, he's just resistant to my aids, or I'm just not cueing him right."

Preston whispered, "What's an aid?"

"She means leg or rein to help tell the horse what to do. Alright, Isabel. Canter and then show me a simple change for both the right and left leads."

Preston tapped her on the arm. "What's the difference between a simple change and a flying change?"

"A simple change is where you canter and come to a walk and pick up a new leading leg for the canter. A flying change is what you called it when you said my horse looked like it was 'skipping.'"

"Oh, I get it." Isabel rode as directed.

"Great job, Isabel. You're right, no issues. Now, let's try a flying change."

Preston cocked his head. "She's ready to try?"

June whispered, "Yes, he's got the basics, and she's got him balanced with a good canter cadence."

Isabel's voice came through. "Here we go!"

"Pick up the left lead counter-canter, collected please, and go down the long side to P. At P prepare him for the corner and the new lead … June's instructions continued until Isabel was two or three strides away from the corner, June had her ask for the change while his leading foreleg was still in the air.

June coached. "Easy, not too much leg, you've got time and a balanced counter. Prepare …. And … Done! There you go, missy. One flying change!"

Isabel laughed. "Oh my gosh. It worked. Thank you! That was his first." She patted the horse.

June clapped. "And it won't be his last. Good job!" She reached up and high fived Preston. "She nailed it! Whoa. That was so much fun."

Preston leaned over and covered her mouthpiece with his hand. "You are an incredible teacher. I would love to hear you while you're riding."

June's head turned to look at him. "Are you a bit gaga over this riding thing or what?" She pretended to punch him on the arm.

"Probably just gaga about how much you know. No cast is weighing that part of you down."

June covered the mouthpiece. "If only everyone shared your opinion. I have owners to impress if I'm going to get back in the game. Oh, look. She's trying again."

Her eyes followed Isabel. "Oh now, she's trying the other lead and … Geez. She did it again. Great job, Isabel! Way to go!"

Minutes later, Isabel stopped in front of June. "I appreciate your help. Now if we can just ride and study together in college."

"That might be a little tougher, but not impossible. Have you finalized your choice of colleges to go to?" *What if she names an impossible one for me to go to? I can't uproot myself from Mary's barn. That is if I can still ride and give lessons there!*

"No, I just need to be close to a barn. I've done some prep work, and I have choices. Good thing we bumped into each other. Let's talk a little more while I cool this horse down." She leaned down and patted him with her whole arm and stroked his neck. "What a good boy today."

June watched as the horse stretched down and moved on with a big, relaxed walk. "You know, this is a possibility." *Maybe I was too quick to rule out school a couple of years ago. Probably just because I was being lectured about it. I'm beyond that at my age!*

"Maybe we could be partners and if one of us needs to study, the other one could take care of horse stuff. Whatever that would be. I'll need to give lessons to make some money, unless my parents chip in. They might faint from hearing about all this. Thanks for making my life a little more complicated, Isabel." June laughed.

"Hey. Isn't that what friends are for? That's exactly my same thoughts. Let's stay in touch. We have a few months until the fall classes start anyway. I say getting your leg back is number one, then horses, and then classes."

"Well, at least you've got the order right. Take care, Isabel. I'm going to head out of here. Preston will carry my mic back for you. If you don't mind?" She slipped the mic off. "I'll meet you at the car."

"Sounds good. See you soon." Preston walked off, following Isabel and the horse.

June's mouth dropped. If someone could only get a picture. Wouldn't this be a sight she would never believe if she hadn't seen it with her own eyes. *Two people in my life just when I need them the most? Others? Just a revolving door of students and people bringing in horses for training. Seems lonely. But it wasn't. I was alone, but not lonely. Big difference. And now? Too good to be true? Maybe for her and what she was used to, but wasn't it worth a shot finding out which path is the right one to take? Horses or college, that is. Preston — out of the picture. He'll be gone soon.* She sighed. *I know how to teach, but can I still ride?*

22

June rolled over in bed and forced one eye open. "Hey, Preston. Happy Wednesday! In two days, this cast is hasta la bye bye!" She flopped both arms on the mattress and stared at the ceiling, then sat up with a burst of energy. "I can't wait. Hey, who are you texting?"

"It's a surprise. You'll see this afternoon." *Tanner would never believe I'm capable of arranging this little outing. He screwed up his chances with June and I'm going to keep it that way. Not that I can be around, but she just recovered from a broken leg, she doesn't need a broken heart!*

"For me? I can hardly wait! You're the best! How should I dress? Casual or dressed up?"

He laughed. "Whatever makes you feel cute. We'll be spending the afternoon and evening outside. Something kind of dressy and sporty. You won't be the only one with a leg 'wrapped' if I may quote you." *Our last days together should be great and something to remember—as though I could ever forget her.*

"Oh my. I'm as curious as a cat!"

* * *

En route, June's cell phone buzzed. "Oh. It's Tanner again. I never texted him back. Hmm…He wants me to call him. Says we need to talk."

Preston's knuckles gripped the steering wheel tighter. *Yeah, right. About how he wants her back? What else? He's a schemer.* "Talk? About what?"

June giggled. "I'm not a mind reader, Preston. I won't know unless I call him."

"Call him now if you want to. We have a few minutes until we get there."

June hesitated.

"Well, why not? Right, June?" *She probably wants to talk in private.*

"Okay. Here goes."

Huh. Didn't expect that. "I hope he answers so you can find out what he wants, and he can quit texting you."

June laughed. "Preston! Geez. He's just bein' nice." June dialed and her call went straight to voicemail. Leaving a brief message for him to call her back, she laughed about playing phone tag and hung up.

"Well, that's that. The ball's in his court. I bet he just wants to talk about horse issues. I have no clue why he needs to talk about anything really."

"What if it's more than 'horse issues,' June?" He looked over and scowled.

"Preston, he's a jerk, but he's got a lot of potential going on. Hot action, really. He had some great rides on some great horses at the show. What if there's an opportunity for me that I'll need down the road after this cast is off? I might not have anything else depending on how my leg has recovered. I shouldn't rule out at least finding out what he has to say. Me and Preston, as a couple, are over, okay? At least, that's how I see it. I hope he calls soon. But not during our special outing. I don't want to be bothered there!"

"If you say so." *Tanner is up to no good. He is bad and she thinks he has an 'opportunity' for her? More like another chance to do her wrong.*

* * *

They arrived at a field on the outskirts of Sacramento. A huge white tent was set up and designated parking as well as horse trailers occupied the grounds. The grounds were buzzing with hype and activity. Preston grinned. *Just as I imagined. She'll like this.*

"Preston, there are horses all over the place here." She stared at the horses. "Oh my god. All their legs are wrapped in white leg wraps. This is awesome. And riders wearing …. Oh my gosh! Polo attire! You brought me to a polo match! This is so wonderful. I've never been to one."

Preston grinned. "Didn't think I had any horse connections, did you?"

"How did you find out about this?"

"Friends in San Diego. They have connections up here. My friend Jeff was always into polo, and he took care of the details. So, we're going to watch the match and then attend the catered buffet. It's a fundraiser for a good cause—whatever that is, I'm happy to donate. Later, there'll be another little surprise." *The smile on her face is all I wanted.*

"I never thought about polo in San Diego. A new horse sport … You're spoiling me, Preston."

"It was my intention." *She's going to be hard to let go of, but my money has to be earned—not a handout from Dad. He's persuasive and doesn't back off, but I won't let him play me like a puppet on a string, even if it means I have to sacrifice seeing her sweet face every day. I've got to get back to work.*

* * *

The match began. June squeezed his arm. "The horses are amazing. Look how they switch out the ponies. Those are great horses. Sport horses, just like dressage horses. Different breeds, but all have a purpose."

He watched her head following the action on the field. They held hands and tried to figure out the strategy and the techniques. Thundering hooves and horseflesh so close was exhilarating and first-rate entertainment. The turf was kicked up and the divots flew across the ground. The sound of the whacks from the mallets as they connected with the ball and the smell of horses added to the ambience.

"You love all of them, don't you, June?" He laughed. "You're drooling. Should I go to the tent and find a napkin for you?" *She can't be without them. This is her thing and school, well, good for her, I guess. I'm still not completely convinced it's for her right now or, more importantly, if she thinks it's for her. But this? This is her passion. I can never expect her not to be with horses.*

"Ha, ha. This match is amazing! I love these horses." She reached for his hand and brought it to her lips and kissed it. Just then, her cell phone buzzed. "Incoming call…Glad it's on silent. It's Tanner—lousy timing. I'm going to answer. But I'll make it quick."

"Hi, Tanner." She pressed the phone to her ear.

"You what?"

"I said I have a horse coming in at San Diego in a while. I think it might be a good training prospect."

"It can't be for me. I still have a cast on and I'm right in the middle of a polo match, believe it or not."

"Okay. I figured you'd be getting the cast off soon. I've still got some planning to do. You're distracted. I can tell. And I can hear a lot going on in the background. Don't tell me, Richie Rich is strainin' to hear every word you're sayin'."

"Don't call him that! I hate the nicknames you're always giving people."

"Okay, June. I'm sorry."

"You don't sound sorry."

"Whatever. Call me when you've had a chance to think about what I just said and the possibilities. It's me, June. Thinkin' of ya, just like you used to like me to. A horse like this one doesn't come along every day!"

"What you're talking about seems far off to me. Thanks though. I'll keep it in mind. Gotta go. Talk later." She hung up and squeezed Preston's arm. "Thank you for arranging this. I love it. I wonder what the after party is going to be like."

"What did he say?"

"What? Oh, You mean Tanner? He told me he has a horse coming for training that he thinks might be good for me. Maybe. I guess."

She looked over at the tent. "Getting busier over there." She reached out and held his hand.

Scheming to get her back. I knew it. He thinks he'll be good for her, not the horse! "Well, considering the 'donation,' I would guess a nice hot, fancy meal, champagne, a bar, and dessert."

"Whoa. Even out here. And look, there are white cloth tablecloths and musicians under the tent now. They have it all. Sure is fancy. What a treat."

"That's nice." *Hmm … She just likes life and having fun. Cool.*

"Will you dance with me if there's a dance floor? I know I have a cast…"

"If you can dance, then I can shuffle around out there. I'm not used to dancing." *That's an understatement. I hope I don't look like a fool. I don't see anyone I know.*

"Me either, but live musicians. Uhm … Romantic, right?"

"Quite." *We'll be dancing. Eat your heart out, Tanner.*

* * *

The match ended. Preston reached for June's hand. "Wow, that was exciting." *Wonder when my next 'surprise' for her will happen?*

All of a sudden, four riders galloped over to Preston and June. "Hello!" They called out. "Hey, Preston. We spotted you two. And we saw a cast peeking out from your pant leg and figured it must be you, June."

Preston grinned when June's cheeks turned bright red. "You guessed right! I'm June. Love your polo ponies."

One rider spoke. "We heard you're recovering and just wanted to wish you well. We hope to hear you're back in the saddle soon. Preston, Jeff sends his greetings to you too!"

Preston grinned. "Thanks, guys. We're enjoying the event."

"Glad to hear it! See you in the tent. Gotta go take care of our ponies. Glad you enjoyed the match." They waved and rode off.

Preston turned and gave June a kiss. "Like that?"

"Of course. How special. Thank you for all that too." She leaned over and kissed him.

"Nothing's too good for you, June." *Burn, Tanner, burn.*

23

Preston sat on the arm of the couch. "That was a fun evening last night. Never knew watching horses could be so much fun, June. But hey, let's go shopping today. The stores will be opening soon. We can make a whole day of it."

"A guy that wants to go shopping? Unheard of! You offered; I'm taking you up on it. Right now!" She giggled. *I'm having a hard time believing my old life will be back soon. I'll be trying to work hard and make up for all this lost time.*

"Yeah. I'm on another mission. Shopping and one last excursion before your cast removal appointment tomorrow!"

"Be still my beating heart. Let's get moving. This is gonna be fun!"

* * *

Pulling into the shopping mall's parking lot, Preston gave June a little smile. "I want you to have something you can touch and remember me when I'm far away and working somewhere." I never knew 'stepping up to the plate' would get me this involved. I never expected any of this and wish I could have known she was a sincere person from the very beginning…Too late now. It just wasn't in my experience. Of course, we haven't parted ways yet. Maybe that will bring out a different side of her. Look at Sheila. Nice at first, then a total…Ugh.

"That's so sweet of you."

"And after shopping, one other place to go visit."

"Visit? As if we're tourists?"

"Yep." *So what if I'm spoiling her?*

* * *

After going into a few stores, they ended up at an upscale department store and stopped in front of a glass case.

"June. Do you like perfume? This display has a purse and a perfume deal combo. Like it?"

"A Gucci bag and perfume. Yes, my goodness. I'm not a fool." She reached for the tester. "Smell this. Like it?"

Preston inhaled. "Oh. That's so rich. Like a field of flowers, with a breath of fresh air and a hint of musk or something exotic. I do like it. Want that set?"

"That is a great gift, Preston. Thanks. I will always think of you rifling through my purse to find my I.D. to give to the EMTs when I'm searching through this purse. You were so great about all that."

She is the most appreciative person ever. "This isn't your memento. This is just a little something. Come on. Look, there's a jewelry counter." He pointed. "I see you don't have any jewelry on besides your bracelet. Don't you like jewelry?"

"Yes. I like it. Mine is at my apartment. Well, I own a little bit. I don't usually wear any rings or bracelets when I'm riding or working with the horses. The gloves catch on rings. I don't know. Just a habit."

They looked at the counter. "Here are some nice things, June. Like diamonds? How about some diamond earrings? Could you wear those while you ride?" *I might be gone, but I don't want to be forgotten. Not like you can forget a guy that broke your leg! Need a little positive memento.*

June's hand touched her forehead and wiped a small bead of sweat. "Those are nice, but they're probably expensive."

Preston swallowed. "It's not the price. It's if you like them. They need to be special."

"This pair is so pretty. Here comes a salesclerk."

A smiling clerk approached. "Hello. May I show you some?"

Preston cleared his throat. "Sounds good. She can have what she wants."

June tried on various earrings. "You know what," pointing to the case, "I think these look beautiful."

Preston looked at them. "Can you tell us about them?"

The clerk brought them out. "These are Italian 18kt white gold Love Knot earrings. They're beautiful and I personally think you can wear them with casual or dressy clothes."

June reached out. "They are lovely, Preston. I mean, I love diamonds, but these are basic and beautiful."

"Are you sure?"

"Yes. I could wear them right now."

Preston looked at the clerk. "We'll take them. She can wear them now if she wants." *Leave it to her to choose something elegant and practical. So unpretentious. A woman like her is as rare as the Hope diamond. Most would pick the most expensive. Although that's a guess because I've never bought anyone jewelry before. They would've expected a proposal!*

June's hands shook. "I'm not going to take them off. I love them. Do you happen to have the earring backs that lock and won't slide off unless you squeeze the tabs?"

"I know what you mean. Let me check. Those are usually a special order, but I believe we just might."

"Preston, they might cost a little more, but I don't want to lose them. If I go back to riding, my helmet chin strap..."

Putting his finger on her lips, he smiled. "No problem. I'm glad you're so excited about them. That's fine. I hope they have them for you."

Returning with a big smile, the clerk brought two packages. "Let's try them out and then hopefully, one pair will fit them." Putting them back on, she exclaimed. "This pair fits!"

June was excited and reached for them. "Thank you. This mirror is just what I need." She put the earrings on. "There! All done. What do you think, Preston?"

"They're great. With your hair tucked behind your ear, they really show." Smiling, he waited for the clerk to finish up. "Let's go have lunch and celebrate. But are you sure you don't want diamonds instead?"

June gulped. "I'm sure."

"But you do like diamonds?"

"No. I love diamonds!"

"You're so funny. Let's go eat. My breakfast bar is long gone."

"Mine too."

* * *

"Preston, I'm glad we ate a quick lunch. I can't believe you have something else planned for today. You're scoring points, my man!" She came up behind him sitting in the dining room chair and put her arms around his neck and leaned down to kiss him. "My goodness. At this time tomorrow, my cast will be off." *What if my leg is messed up? I'll die.*

"I know. That's why today has to be a big day. Because tomorrow, we start the final leg, ha, ha, of our journey."

She tousled his hair. "Funny! Speaking of journey, where are we going now? I hope people will be there to admire my new earrings and, little do they know, wish my cast farewell."

Preston looked at the time. "Oh my God. We're gonna be late. Let's get out of here."

She dug through the drawer, came across his coveralls, and holding them with both hands, brought them to her heart. *He said he'd be needing them again. Aw … that's the old him. I remember him sitting in the hospital chair wearing them. I've never really seen that side of him.* Putting them down, she grabbed a new top. *Love this little, black-laced trimmed one. V-neck and fitted. It's going to be super cute with dark-wash jeans and my new earrings. If I could ditch the cast this second, it'd be a perfect outfit. Will tomorrow ever come?*

Preston's voice pierced her thoughts. "Almost ready?"

Am I getting sentimental? I better brace myself. "Am I wearing the right clothes?"

"You look great. Come on. We can't be late!"

* * *

Preston talked as he drove. "Are you sure you want to go back to college? That's going to add quite a lot of hours to your workday, won't it?"

"It does sound hard to me. I'm no Isabel, but I think it's a good move."

"Speaking of her, Isabel comes along out of the blue, says a couple of things, and suddenly you're back in college. And you don't even have a college picked out. Just seems so spontaneous, that's all."

She stared out the window. "It seems spontaneous to me, to

be honest. And you're right. I do plan many things, but I also have learned to deal with being in an unstable state of life.

"Like?"

"Like having to keep going when Tanner left me high and dry without a horse. I scrambled and found Mary, D, and some new clients. Broke my leg and found, guess who?" She reached over and squeezed his thigh. "I'm capable of handling challenges."

"Do you think you'll go for San Diego State?"

"Yes. It's at the top of my list. Don't know about Isabel's list. But at least it's close enough to commute and juggle riding and school."

"Okay. Sounds like you want to." He took the exit. "We're getting close."

"Can't wait to see where we're going. But anyway, yeah, I need to secure my future. I'm not rich like you." *He is, but he never flaunts it. Tanner would have blown through every dime! Ew.*

"I'll ignore that comment."

"I didn't mean any harm, Preston. What's wrong?" She looked at his glum expression.

"Things were calm and now they're getting crazy. I have to start sharing the hours in the day with other people and other things. This is the most settled I've been. Sorry, June. I'm a little upside down, too, right now."

"What other people?"

"I mean people that I work for and the fact I'll be traveling again. The gyms, and all my past life too. I haven't missed any of that, to tell you the truth, but we can't do this forever."

She reached for his hand. "I think we'll figure out what to do. Let's change the subject. I have no idea what my parents' visit is going to be like, but they'll be here in less than a week. I'm getting worried about their visit. What if my leg isn't well enough to ride that soon and I have nothing to show them but failure on my part? They're going to lecture me like no other! Hearing all that negative stuff won't be a nice ending for all your help during my recovery. Still want to meet them?"

"I do. Their comments won't bother me. I'm on your side. Do you still want to see my dad's place? I mean my old home and his work?"

"Both. And yes, I want to see your dad again, too. Think he'll recognize me without a cast? Since he wanted you to go to college, maybe I should share that I'm going to go back to school."

"Don't worry about impressing him, June. Seriously, don't. He's harsh with his opinions."

They turned down a city street in Sacramento. "I'm going to tell him anyway. Where'd you go to school and what did you study?" *Geez. I really don't know much about the person I've been living with. What would Brianna say? She'd freak out! Her and her safe choices…*

"Yale. I have a bachelor's degree in mechanical engineering and a minor in business."

June choked. "Excuse me. I'm blown away. Yale? Hiding anything else from me? Are you really twenty-nine years old? You don't have a secret wife and kids, do you? This is a lot to take in."

"I made the most of school since I had to go. I developed business contacts and that's how I built my businesses. Lots of my classmates had prestigious fathers and most had cars. Car collections, and that's the whole truth. I have businesses in different locations. I watched how my father managed his businesses in different locations, and I figured I could too. It's just that he didn't travel much, but I wanted to. I've escaped being tied down by him or anyone, and I've enjoyed my work."

"Well, I guess I've been quite a diversion." *I am such a small sailboat floating next to a cruise ship. My God.* Her hand flew to her forehead, and she squeezed her temples. *He's right, his father's issues and mine seem to come to mind all the time. Why? What's worse is that I can see why good old Bob would never approve of me.*

He reached out and took her hand. "You're the only one that got me off the road, so to speak. It was my decision to stay with you. I don't tell people stuff like this. I'm not used to it."

"There's no need to hide anything from me. We'll be going our separate ways soon." *I'm crazy to think this relationship can survive the real world.*

"But we have Sacramento today and Friday, tomorrow to get your cast off. Let's enjoy what's left of this afternoon's adventure. Speaking of which, we have arrived."

24

"Preston, the railroad?"

"More like Railroad Museum. It's an affiliate of the Smithsonian in Washington D.C. Like museums?"

"I do."

"Good. Because we're going to start with the museum and then we're going on an excursion train ride that normally doesn't operate on Thursdays. We're getting lucky today!"

"I'll say. I haven't ridden a train before. Have you?"

"No. Almost. I almost took an Amtrak home once, but I changed my mind because I had a car to drive for someone."

"So, this is your first time, too. That's so exciting. Let's hurry into the exhibits so we don't miss the ride."

"Okay. I was hoping you'd like the plan."

* * *

Inside the museum, they read exhibits and marveled at the actual cars, engines, and all the artifacts, including realistic miniature model train sets of all sizes.

Admiring the information related to women's involvement in the railroad history, June shook her head. "Imagine how strong and pioneering these women were. I find this very inspirational." *Surely, I can rebuild what I've lost and get back on my feet.*

Watching the clock, he motioned her to follow. "We better head outside to board. I'm glad we've got clear blue sky above us." He reached out and put his arm around her. "Think we'll get preferential boarding due to your cast?"

June cuffed his arm with a fake power punch. "You are too funny."

He leaned over and hugged her. "Let's board and enjoy."

They sat in silence and took in the fresh air and peaceful surroundings. The traditional train whistle blew, and they looked at each other. June's eyes teared up. Preston whispered in her ear. "That sound is so melancholy, isn't it?"

June wiped her eyes. "I don't know why I'm so emotional." *Maybe my heart is breaking just a little bit right now at the sound of the train leaving—just like he'll be doing soon.*

Preston held her hand. "It's okay. You've been through a lot the past few weeks. I think you're doing fine. Look, isn't the view spectacular?"

June swallowed hard, sniffed, and reached for her earrings. *The backs are secure. I won't lose them. A constant reminder of him and how sweet and thoughtful he is ... If only life came with security.* "Just sitting in a railroad car is spectacular. I'm glad we're taking this ride. I think I would like to travel one day, and I never thought I'd say that."

"It's probably because you see that the world goes on with or without your daily schedule. I'm seeing things in a new light, too. You're not the only one."

"Really?"

"Yep. I've been so stubborn, and I couldn't stop for anything or anyone. Maybe this has changed both of us for the better?" He cleared his throat. "I mean, when we look back on these days, years from now, I will never forget them, or you."

She nodded. *Was he trying to say he would be nowhere in her life?* "I know. It's been fun. And that's where it stays. We have lives and we have plans." She put her hand on his thigh. *He's so strong and he's been such a pillar of strength for me. I'll be back on my own soon. I'm going to miss his constant company.*

He nodded. "Yes. And I'm glad we do."

"Me too."

* * *

Friday morning arrived with the sound of an alarm startling June. She sat up in bed. "Oh my God, Preston. Wake up!" It's 8:30 and my appointment's at 9:45. Hurry. We have to get moving. I can't be late. I can't wait to get this thing off!"

* * *

The doctor's reception area was tidy but almost full of waiting patients. June and Preston found a couple of chairs next to each other. *I'm so glad I'm not here alone. Before all this, I was alone for almost a year. Tanner…*

June grinned and whispered. "Glad we got here when we did." She reached for a magazine on the side table and looked at Preston. *Sports Illustrated?* "Really? I mean, look at all of us. We're maimed individuals in lobby chairs."

Preston's torso shook and he covered his mouth and spoke in a hushed tone. "Stop, June. You won't be 'maimed' for long."

The door opened and a tech with a clipboard called out, "June."

June and Preston stood and held hands.

The tech smiled. "Take your time. Excited?"

June didn't waste a second. "Yes. Oh my gosh. Let's do this. Please." She clung to Preston's arm as they walked the hallway to the procedure room. *Few more steps to freedom!*

"Sure. Right this way." He stopped suddenly. "I'm sorry. Just checked your chart. Oops. You start here. X-ray first!"

June gasped. "Oh no. What if my bone's not healed?" She gripped Preston's arm.

The tech faced her. "This is standard protocol for your doctor."

Easy for you to say. June spoke slowly. "If you say so." Following him, Preston sat in the hallway chair.

X-ray over, they returned to the hall and headed down the hallway again.

She entered the procedure room and sat on the table. "I hope you know I am so nervous that my bone is not healed." Dr. Carson poked his head in. "I heard that!"

He grinned. "Not changing our plan, June. Your cast is coming off and I'll be right back to talk things over."

June smiled. "Oh, please. I can't take this. I might have a heart attack, I'm so excited."

The tech pulled his rolling chair over to her. "I checked your chart, and it looks like you've had one cast change, right? So, you know the drill?"

Be brave one more time girl. June laughed. "More like the saw, right?"

The tech tapped the procedure table. "Love your sense of humor. I'll just put the arm rests up for safety and adjust the table for your leg."

He got the saw ready, and June wiped a bead of sweat from her face. "Is the doctor coming in?"

"He'll be in as soon as I get the cast off. Ready?"

June gulped and locked eyes with Preston. "I hope my leg isn't deformed."

The tech stopped. "Was it deformed after your first cast change?"

"No. But I'm keeping my eyes closed because it might be. It's been a longer time in this one."

"Then, my professional opinion is that it won't be. Please relax. Remember, this isn't going to hurt or cut your skin. It's just going to run up and down this cast shell and off it goes."

Couple more minutes…you can do this. "Go ahead. I'm just going to cover my ears. Sorry I'm such a wimp."

***

Was this the end of more than just her broken leg? Wasn't it more an end of the first time in her life she had been nurtured since she was a baby? Preston had doted on her. Tanner's brusque and standoffish manner had mirrored her self-reliance and now she was back in the world all on her own. Scary, but exciting and just what she was after?

Her eyes met Preston's. They looked deep into each other, and Preston squeezed her hand.

The tech carried on. "No, you're not a wimp. Not even close! No one likes this part, but they like it when the cast is off. Now, I'm just going to slide a little hard plastic skin protector down inside the cast, but no worries! This blade is not going to touch or cut your skin. Promise!" He lifted her leg, slid the protector from the top of her cast down and turned on the saw. He made the cut. He stopped and pulled the protector out and went from her foot up. He cut again. And sat back. "There! Now for the other side of your leg." Repeating it all, he finished.

June unplugged her ears. "Now you're clipping the cast?"

"You remember! First these snippers here, then the padding and voilà!" He pulled it all off and there was her leg.

June squealed. "My leg looks normal. Well, sorry, it's not perfect." she reached down and touched her calf. Her smiled faded and her shoulders dropped.

The tech reached out for her leg. "I uhm … I don't know what to say." Frown lines deepened. "I can't see anything wrong."

June giggled. "Me either. Just kidding! I do need to shave this forest, but my leg is just fine." She lifted it. "It's so light! Look, I can raise it. Oh my gosh." *Woo hoo! Take me dancin' now!*

The back of the tech's arm flew up to his forehead. "Wiping air sweat. You had me goin' there, June. You're a character."

Preston stood for a closer look. "June, your leg is perfect."

The door opened and Dr. Carson walked in with a smile stretched from ear to ear. "Hello, June. It's been a long ten weeks, right, but look. You are back to you!" He rolled his exam chair across the floor and sat close to her. He moved her leg and examined it.

"Yep. Nice and straight and I'll bet just as strong as it ever was after a little recovery time. You, young lady, are all set. I know you ride horses and there's no reason you can't get back to it, but you're going to need to make sure you have good balance and equal strength standing first. Okay?"

June nodded.

"I'd say give yourself a couple of weeks. Maybe using your leg on the horse won't be quite what it was for the first ride or two, but all should be okay without physical therapy. You're lucky you didn't need internal fixation either. You know, metal plates or screws. Big break, but excellent healing."

June beamed. "I'm just lucky altogether. Thank you so much. I'll be sure to follow your directions. No problem. A couple of weeks is reasonable. You sound like you know about horses."

He tapped her leg with his fingertips. "You're not my first rider. I'm just happy that you have such a good outcome. Take it easy at first. Then, ease back into your regular life."

No big lecture. Love it. Everyone takes risks if something's important enough. June extended her hand. "Thank you, Dr. Carson. You did a great job. Okay, I'm ready to stand up. Preston?"

Preston moved in and extended his arm. "Ready."

June pushed off the table and stood. "Oh no." She sat back down.

The doctor came closer. "Yes?" His brows raised and pulled together.

"I need to wear my other tennis shoe. We brought it. Right, Preston?"

Preston nodded and pulled her sneaker from the bag. "Here you go. I'll put it on for you. Stay on the table, June. I don't want you falling off." Preston knelt, put her shoe on, and tied it.

Dr. Carson looked at June. "I see. Has he done this the whole time?"

"He has."

"Well then, young lady. I would say this young man is golden. Wow. Okay you two. June, it's been a pleasure. Call my office if you have any questions or concerns. Moderation and common sense is the key. It was nice meeting you both." He turned and left the room.

Preston offered his arm, "Ready to get out of here?"

"Please." She stood and took his arm. "This feels so funny. My leg is so light." She took a step. "I'm walking again. Thank you, Preston. You've been all a girl in a cast could ask for."

"No problem. Now, it's back to reality."
June squeezed his arm, "Let's go."

25

Preston opened the door and June entered and walked with careful steps, holding onto the furniture over to the edge of the bed. "Dr. Carson was right. My leg is a little weak. I'm not very confident in just walking without thinking about staying strong. Anyway, I hope this feeling passes. I need to shower and shave my legs, erh … leg. Then, you know what sounds like fun?"

"What?" *I wonder if things will change between us now? I hope we have at least two more weeks together. This is harder than I thought it would be.*

"We've never been able to sit in the jacuzzi out there and it's right around the corner. I have my swimsuit. Remember you got me one on our first shopping trip for 'inspiration' that I would get back to being my old self?"

"I did and you're right. We need to celebrate and make our plans for the week. Want to go dancing again tonight? Maybe we can find some music and a dance floor at a local bar. Your cast is off!"

"That's right. We danced with it on and now I can really bust some moves."

"June! Don't say 'bust'! I'm going to be holding tight to you. No bustin' anything on my watch!" He laughed and gave her a hug. "Your parents haven't told you the day they're arriving next week. We need to know." *We are in the official countdown now.*

June stood and started pulling off her clothes. "You're right, they haven't. I'll check with my mom to confirm. I want to stall them until I am certain my leg is healed enough for me to be riding again before they get here. I'll die if it isn't."

Preston started taking off his clothes.

June looked at him. "What are you doing?"

Preston touched his face. "Am I red? I think I'm embarrassing myself."

"Sorry?"

"I'm so used to getting in with you, I uhm…just assumed."

"I got this, but you can join me if you want. Just teasin.' You're still allowed to accompany me you know."

"Oh good. This is going to take some getting used to. I need my patient."

"Sir, your 'patient' is practicing her independence."

"Details. Let's get your leg done, then off to the hot tub."

"I'm not going to race you; I can't afford a fall. But, come on. We have a plan."

* * *

They approached the jacuzzi holding hands and sank into the hot water. Steam rose and droplets of sweat beaded on June's face. Preston reached out and brushed them away.

I've become so used to his touch. How in the world is separation going to work? "Thanks. This water feels amazing. My leg is quite happy. I think my bones like it too."

"I'm sure they do. We shouldn't stay in very long. I don't want it to bother your leg."

"You are a little worrywart, you know? But okay. Sounds

good." She splashed the water on her arms. "Since you mentioned going out, what are we going to tell the server tonight we're celebrating this time?"

"How about Independence Day? Nah. Just kidding. How about our anniversary? Uhm, two and a half months."

"Sounds romantic. Okay. It will make our server smile. Let's talk about our next plans. I can't believe I can drive, ride, walk. I will never take any of that for granted. Not that I ever did, but…" Her voice trailed off. *I'm going to have to hustle to get work, call Brianna to say hi, call Mary to check in, call Mom…*

"June!"

"I'm sorry, what?"

"I lost you." He grinned. "You quit talking. I'm happy for you. How about going up to my place with me in Portland tomorrow? I'd like to check on my place, drop off this rental, and get my own car."

Tomorrow? A huge drive? That's a lot of immobility. But I can't ask him to wait. He's done enough for me. "Oh! Okay. Sure, if you want me to, I'll go with you. It's the least I can do." She sank under the water and popped up. "I love water. Can't wait to see your dad's workplace."

Preston grimaced. "Haven't changed your mind?"

"No."

"Okay. If you want to see it, it's on the list of things to do before we uhm…" His eyes looked away.

"It's okay, Preston. Say it. Before we go our separate ways. I never meant to change your life and you never meant to injure me. I'll be fine. Heartbroken, but fine." She moved her hand to her heart and batted her eyelashes. "We'll be friends, right?"

Preston cleared his throat.

"Oh, come on now. A plan is a plan. You have things to do. And I have things to do. Maybe college. Maybe back to D? I need to find out what or who's been riding him. What if he made it to Grand Prix? He's so talented, I wouldn't doubt it. Mary is so lucky to own a horse like him. I would love to have a horse like him, one day." *Good job, June. Keep talkin' with confidence.*

"You've got plans. You really don't need me anymore, do you?"

"I wouldn't say that. But 'need' is an entirely different word that we just haven't talked about. You've been there to help me get back on my feet, so to speak, and I appreciate everything." *Stay strong, girl.*

"Say no more, sweetie pie. Nothing should hold you back now. After lunch, we'll contact our parents. Geez. My dad is going to flip out."

I'm glad he mentioned his dad before I did, for once! "I think he'll be happy to see you. I don't know about seeing me again, but you? He'll be all about it."

"Think so? We'll have to see."

* * *

After lunch, Preston and June came back to their room. June flopped on the bed and patted her stomach. "I am so full and ready for a nap. How about you?"

"Me too. We better check in with the parents and see what they say." *I can't even really remember the last time I called Dad. He won't believe it.*

June picked up her phone. "I'm texting my mom."

—*Went to my last doctor's appointment today. My leg is fine. Very happy. Are you both still coming for a visit?*

"I'm making a call. Wish me luck." Preston picked up his phone and left a message.

"Hi, Dad. June got her cast off, and we'll be driving back to San Diego soon. Are you going to be in town? Thinking we could stop by sometime next week." *Can't believe I said 'we.'*

June's phone buzzed. She looked. "Oh my gosh, they said they're still coming out here. They don't know the exact date yet. Preston, what if I'm not strong enough to ride? Worse yet, what if Mary is dumping me as a rider? This is awful! What should I text back?-

Preston nodded. "If that's the case, we're barely going to have enough time to get my car and make it back to San Diego. The soonest we'll be back is in two days — Sunday. At least we're half-way to Portland, so it'll only be about an eight-hour drive from here. Just get the date from them." *There's the 'we' word again. I wonder if she'll get clingy. She can't. My world is a man's world. She'll see for herself…*

"So, we're leaving tomorrow morning?"

"Yes. We're done with this place. I'm going to check out. This is nerve wracking." *I can't tell her I've never had a broken heart; she could use that to play me like any other woman would. So what? I have to go back to work. How bad is a broken heart anyway? Stupid to worry about something that hasn't happened.*

She nodded. "I agree. Road trip it is. I'll text back to my mom for their dates. Hey! I'll be driving again soon."

"Yep. But not up to Portland. My treat."

"What a chauffeur!"

"Ha, ha. Let's get an early start tomorrow. Leave by 8 a.m.? Oh, my dad's texting back." He studied his phone. "Notice he didn't call back, June? That's him for you. But he says anytime is good. He just returned from the East Coast so we can pick a day. I'll tell him we'll pick one and get back to him. He's probably blown away by this." He shook his head.

"Well, give him a chance. I'm sure my parents are too. Yikes. What are we in for?"

"Meeting up? Fessing up about our living arrangement? I feel like I'm sixteen instead of twenty-nine."

"I know, right? I think anytime parents are involved, you go back to being some sort of kid or something. I'm not used to checking in with them anymore. That's for sure. In fact, they've never been out to California to check on me either. Not their fault, I stayed in touch enough so that they didn't feel the need to fly out—before this." She giggled.

"This was all so perfect." *Made it easier on me not having to deal with parents while taking care of her. Face it, you loved being alone with her. Control yourself, Preston.*

* * *

Relaxing with the TV on, Preston's cell phone buzzed with an incoming text message. He read it and sat up. "Uh oh, June. This text is from one of my clients in Seattle. He needs me to be there tomorrow. Some timing, huh?"

"In Seattle? On a Saturday? That's so far to travel. I …"

"This is Scott. He's an important client. Well, they all are. Anyway, he wants me to fly up. I'd like you to go with me. Want to?" *All I care about is getting two more weeks with her. That's still a possibility. Good.*

"Fly? Really? No road trip?"

"Yeah. Fly instead of driving. I'll see if I can get us some first-class seats on United. Or at least Business class. I better text him back. I'll do that right now."

"Isn't any seat, okay? I mean if you really must get there," she shrugged.

Pursing his lips, he looked at her. "I got this." He started to text, but another message came in. He read it and looked at June. "He's sending his jet here to pick me up. I'll let him know I'll be bringing you along."

June gulped. "What? His own jet? Will that be, okay?"

"It'll be fine." Preston sent his text, and a message came back. "He said for us to be at the airport at 10 a.m. tomorrow. He has a 'special project' waiting for me."

"Okay. We'll do that. And then what?"

"After I take care of his job, I'll have him fly us to Portland."

"Will he do that?"

"Yes. He will. This is working out great. I can return our rental car at the airport and then we'll drive one of my cars back to San Diego."

"Wow. Sounds like fun. I wonder what your client's special project is."

"We'll find out when we get there. At least we know what to bring with us."

"Such as?"

"Everything we have in this room." He laughed. *You're the only thing I care about bringing up there.* "We will be homeless as of tomorrow until we get to my place, get you to your place, both of us to my dad's house, and end with meeting your parents. Think that's enough?" *I'll be sweating out the part about the parents.*

26

"Preston, double check all the drawers. I'm hoping all our stuff fits in your duffel bag. I've never shared a suitcase with a man."

Hmm … makes me feel like we're a couple and we are not, sad to say. I'll be even more alone soon. Maybe riding again though! At least there's something to hope for since my show plans got squashed. "I still can't believe mine got stolen and I never needed it until now."

She opened a drawer, picked up his coveralls and held them to her face, leaning her face on them. "Aw … you haven't worn these since the day of my accident. We can't forget them. Who thought the mechanic sitting by my hospital bed would turn out to be someone so wonderful?" *My God. How am I going to let him go? I have to!* She placed them with a tender touch in the bag.

Preston came over and hugged her. "And who knew that the beautiful blonde in the hospital bed would turn out to be so sweet?" Melting into a long kiss, she let his arms wrap around her and enjoyed his warm body next to her.

"We should get moving. I think we're packed. We'll put these on top so they're easy for you to put on."

"Sounds good."

She looked around the room. "I guess we're ready to go. Say goodbye to our little place."

"It was a great little room. K. Let's move out. It's getting late!"

The door closed behind them. Checkout was done and off they went to the car to load up and go.

June looked back. "It was an experience." She got in the car.

"Seatbelt on, June? There's traffic and we don't want to be late for the airport. Our last breakfast bars and fruit came in handy."

"It's on and yes, they did."

"We'll have a nice lunch somewhere along the way. No worries."

"I'm not worried, but do my clothes look alright?"

"Yes. They still look new. You look amazing. I'll be proud to show you off! Goodbye to this place!"

* * *

They arrived at the airport car rental return and were shuttled to the executive airport where the jet was waiting. The attendant greeted Preston. "Hello, sir. It's good to see you. Scott's relieved you're on the way."

"Glad to make him happy. Oh, this is June."

June smiled, "Hello."

"Hello and follow me, please. The pilots are ready to go. Our flight plan is filed. All we needed was you, Preston."

Preston took the bag. "Let's do this."

* * *

Onboard, they relaxed for the short flight. Offered snacks and beverages, they were content, and June peered out the windows. Gosh, is this how people really travel?

The jet landed and a limousine was waiting for them. Preston grinned, "Scott thinks of everything. He must be in a hurry. I wonder what's up?"

The limo pulled up to a large, gated property. Security clearance measures allowed entry, and the limo followed the curved paved driveway to the residence. June gazed out the window, "My God, Preston. It's not a house; it's a mansion and look over there at that building. It's almost as big as the house." *This looks like something out of the movies.*

"Yeah, that's where we'll be heading in a while. That's where I'll see my 'project.'"

She gripped his hand, "I'm so nervous and excited. This is like…uhm…wow!"

The limo stopped and the driver came to open their door. "Madam. Sir. Please." He held the door.

Scott waved and walked over. "Hey, Preston. I'm so happy to see you. Thanks for being here so quickly. I'm a nervous wreck."

"You? Nervous?" Preston offered his hand to shake Scott's. "What's got you all tied up in knots?"

"It's the Rolls. Luna wants it to be their "get away" car from the wedding. She's changed her mind about ten times from a horse-drawn carriage to a Ferrari to my new Mercedes limo and finally back to something her fiancé can drive off. And so here we are. I need the Rolls checked out. They'll only be driving to the airport and then they'll be flying to a secret destination. I think it's a Hawaiian island, but that's been changed a million times, too. Now that, I'm okay with, for safety reasons. Know what I mean?"

"I do. I'll be sure to give the car a good check. Got my coveralls in my bag. Never go anywhere without them. Let's go see this Rolls beauty. Speaking of beauty. I'm so sorry. This is June.

Pardon my delayed introduction. She's going to give the ride it's final stamp of approval."

Extending her hand to reach Scott's she smiled, "Such a beautiful setting. Is the wedding here?"

"Yes, young lady. It's next Saturday. My poor wife has been in a tizzy about that too while Luna has just been enjoying her bridal moments. I do think I have a few more grey hairs to show for all of it. Speaking of hair, my goodness, your blonde hair, I must say, is quite stunning. There's not much sun out and your hair is sparkling."

Preston beamed, "It is shiny, isn't it? Frames her beautiful face." He gently touched her cheek. "Well, let's get to work, June. Come with me. See you later, Scott. I'll let you know when I'm through."

"You're the boss. Thanks, Preston. I'll have lunch waiting for you when you're ready. If not lunch, then dinner is an option. I have guest rooms prepared as well."

"Okay thanks."

* * *

They walked to the building. Preston entered the code on the keypad and opened the carriage garage doors. A collection of a dozen or more cars flanked the sides of the Rolls Royce. The Rolls' shimmering gold paint caught the glimmer of sunlight through Seattle's cloudy skies.

"June, this is my work." Preston climbed into his coveralls. He opened the hood and began checking the car. Starting the engine, the car purred. "Piece of cake. I'll finish this mechanical check, look at the tires—guaranteed not to blow." He grinned, "And then we're off for a spin."

"Preston, no wonder your hands were clean. You haven't done anything mechanical to this car. Why all this?"

"Security, June. At Scott's level, only insiders come into his circle and into his life. You're here because you're with me. He has confidence in my background and my work. He's known me for years. My dad and Scott are also good friends. Scott has a yacht, too. We're all connected somehow. Good ole Dad! There, I mentioned him before you could." He winked.

June giggled. "Your dad's going to like me. I'm making you think about him. Just teasin'. Seriously though, is Scott's yacht bigger than Andrew's and Alicia's?"

Preston scoffed, "Much bigger. Compared to Scott's yacht, Andrew and Alicia's luxury yacht is a pleasure boat. Scott has one that could keep pace with the one Tiger Woods has. And Tiger's is just an example. My dad's work world is also a closed circle of trust and exclusion."

June's face fell. "I'm so out of place with all this, Preston. I'm thinking I shouldn't meet your dad after all."

"Oh, come on. Our plan, remember?"

"I'm, I'm … a nothing."

"Don't get all hung up on that. You're a hardworking person. I've worked hard to get clients like Scott and my dad has worked hard to build a solid reputation of service and quality of his products too."

"Okay. But I'm unemployed without a horse, that's all I can say."

"So what? You're not going to stay that way."

"God, I hope not. I'm already walking better than yesterday."

"Yes, you are. Come on. Get in. Let's take a drive." *My God. He is so privileged. What's he doing with me? With all this, I can't be-*

lieve he hasn't left me, especially with my cast off now. Thank God for that. I'll be able to drive my car and find work again. Mucking stalls maybe, but I'll work! I think…haven't been on my legs long enough to test them.

* * *

"Preston, we've spent months talking about your work and how you travel. Now I can see firsthand what you mean. You pick up and go at the drop of a hat! I could never do that if I have a horse or horses in training. What about if I have a show during the weekend? Riding takes consistency." She looked out the window of the Rolls.

"I'm glad you can see this for yourself. This is it, June. This is my job. Let's enjoy the ride. Ever been in a Rolls Royce?"

"No. But gosh. What an experience. Pure luxury. First, the private jet, then the limo to the gorgeous mansion, and now all these collector cars? No barn I've ever worked in had all top-level horses. Maybe one or two, but not a whole barn full. Geez. But to get this straight…Scott just paid and went through all this for nothing? I mean, this car is perfect."

"Hey, wait a minute. It's perfect because its been maintained. That's what I do. I keep the owners' collections in pristine working order for them. Just like you would do if you had a horse in training and the owner comes to watch you ride it and all the horse does is obey the commands during that ride. It's because of all the hours you spent training it up until that moment. True? There are days that I might get my hands dirty if the car needs something. But overall, this is my business, and this happens all over the U.S."

"Wow. There sure are a lot of rich people. I'm not."

"Never say never, June. What if you hit the lottery and won millions of dollars? What would you do?"

"I guess I'd buy property, build a barn, and take in horses in training and buy a special one for me."

"You wouldn't want to travel?"

"Nope. I can't. Not with all those horses to train."

"What if you had other trainers working for you?" He grinned.

"This is way too much for me to process. My brain is stopping at getting back in the saddle, if I'm capable, and had a horse to ride."

* * *

Making it back for dinner, they stayed overnight. Sunday morning, after saying their goodbyes, the limo took them to the airport, and they boarded the jet for Portland.

"This is a super short flight, June. We'll be at my place soon. Then, we can drive for a couple of hours heading back to San Diego."

"Sounds good. I can't wait to see where you live." *Tanner was right. He is Richie Rich. And soon he'll be seeing my one-bedroom apartment? Oh my gosh. I hope I left it looking okay. I think there was a pile of dirty clothes in the laundry basket. Dirty dishes—just a few, in the sink. My parents are going to see it, too. This is starting to freak me out.*

27

Catching a limo from the airport, they arrived at a luxury condo high rise. June's neck craned backward to look up. *How many stories are there? Twenty?* She looked at the manicured and shaped boxwood hedging and seasonal annuals sprouting a burst of color. *Fully landscaped and maintained to perfection. Not one plant with a leaf or branch out of place. In dressage, I'd say it's letter perfect. Impressive but daunting.*

The doorman greeted them.

"Welcome back, sir. Madam." He tipped his hat and held the door open. "May I assist you with your luggage, sir?"

"No thanks, Buzz. I don't have any to bring in."

"June, we're taking the elevator." Pushing the elevator buttons, the doors closed. "Up we go!"

June looked out the glass wall as the elevator rose. *This is an express elevator. Whoa. It's fast and look at all the other buildings! He's a city boy for sure. No wonder he's never been around horses. We do live in two different worlds. I hate to say it, but Tanner's right about that too.* "How high up are we going?"

"To the top floor."

"The button says Private."

"Yes. It's a penthouse." The door opened to one entry door. "Welcome. This is my Portland place."

"My gosh. And you have others?"

"Yeah. Two on the east coast. Let's just take a quick look and you can pick which of my cars you want me to drive. But we better not stay too long."

"So, we'll stay like ten minutes?"

Preston laughed. "I think we should stay a little longer than that. Maybe an hour?" Wrapping his arms around her, he kissed her.

Giving him a quick kiss, she pulled back. "Preston, this is once again, way over my head. Good grief. Look at this place." *And he said he was a mechanic? E–x–c–u–s–e me!*

She ran her hands over the leather couch and admired an upholstered chair and swanky love seat surrounding a cocktail table on a Persian rug. "Gosh, this leather is so soft it feels like butter. Reminds me of my saddle when it was brand new, only it's softer."

Custom lighting could spotlight pieces of art on the shelves if it wasn't in the middle of the day. She looked across at the blackout shades that had to be remote and at this moment were tucked into housing at the top of the ceiling, allowing all the glass to be exposed. *Sexy. This is high-end stuff I could never in a million, billion years afford. Compared to my tiny apartment. Oh my gosh.* "Look! You've got art on the walls! Did a designer decorate it for you?"

"Yes. Because if I did it, it wouldn't look this good at all. I think it was done by four artists. Come here. It can't hold a candle compared to you. Let's look out this window. We can make a drink at the bar if you want."

"No thank you. What? No server to impress with an anniversary?" She laughed. "The view is so gorgeous; I love the cityscape and skyline views. What a truly magnificent city lifestyle. Wow."

"Would this be enough for you, June?" He kissed her neck and let his hands slide down her back.

She moved closer. "I love it. I can't deny that, but I'm a fish out of water."

"Not with me you're not." He scooped her up into his arms and proceeded to the bedroom. Gently placing her on the bed, he knelt at the side of the bed and stroked her hair. "I'm falling for you. I can't help it."

"I know how you feel. I've never had such a great and easy time being with someone twenty-four hours a day. We don't belong together though. We can't give up what we've worked so hard for."

She reached out and pulled his face close and kissed him. "We should savor our moments. I'll never, ever forget you. No matter what comes our way or how busy we get. You are my love, but for us, love means letting each other go. We promised not to trap each other."

"You aren't a trap, you're my destination."

"Only for the last leg of this journey. I love the way you've taken care of me. I've had no worries."

He put his fingers to her lips. "Shh…it's not over yet. Move over. I can't say no to you."

"Me neither." *We only have a short time together before he leaves. I hope a couple of weeks more, at least. I'm sure my parents will love him and see that, for once, I made a great decision, even if it was only about my caregiver. They'll want me to hang onto him and give up all my plans so I can live the life of Bri with a 'safe' job. New plan — leave out telling them about all this when they get here so they can meet him and see him for what he is and not for his money. He'll like that!*

***

Preston let his fingers trace lightly across her face. "Hey, sweetie. We better get up and get going." *With anyone else, I'd be ready to escape to freedom. Actually, there's never been another girl in this place or going to my old home. But we haven't parted yet. Don't forget Sheila used to be nice, but then again, I never spent much time with her at all. Think what she would've said or done at the casino if I had!* "We should drive halfway, or close to it, and then stop. How about staying the night in Redding?"

She groaned. "Okay. At least we'll be in California. Sounds like fun. My gosh, you know how to travel."

"I do. Come on, babe. You get to pick the car, remember?" *I know I'm wrong to worry about June. She's nothing like any other girl I've ever met. I got lucky meeting her, but it's hard to change, and then there's work. Then how do I expect Dad to? That's the problem, I gave up caring. So why is he coming to mind? It's all because of June…*

"Oh yeah. Let's go see the choices."

"They're limited. I only have two here."

"Here? Okay…No problem. That's one more than I have."

* * *

They stood at the cars. "Well, June? Which one?"

She stared. "A Porsche Cayenne or a Ferrari? Geez. I guess the Porsche has a little more room for our bag." She laughed. *Our bag? I'm going back to being single soon. Note to self—buy another travel bag!* "Other than that, I'm blown away by the choices."

"Porsche, it is." He pushed the button and opened the cargo area. It lifted. Putting the bag in, he closed the door and off they drove, talking nonstop until they stopped for lunch a couple of hours later.

* * *

With lunch over, they drove down the Interstate, commenting on the forests and mountainous terrain along the way. No big cities, but open land took up most of the landscape.

"This is so peaceful, Preston. Soon we'll be back in the hustle bustle of San Diego."

"Yeah. And on top of that, meeting up with parents. That's going to be a lot of scrutiny and questions."

"Should we really go through with meeting each other's or not?"

"You don't care if we don't?" Preston tightened his grip on the steering wheel.

"I wouldn't say I don't care, but we don't have to."

"Huh? And you don't care about that either?"

"It was always our plan. Mutual, remember?"

"Whatever. Okay, fine. Glad I was there for the time being." He tightened his lips and stared ahead. "Turn on the radio, please."

She looked at him. "I'm not trying to start something."

"I never said you were. That's the problem. You're trying to end 'something.'"

"Geez. This is not a good topic for our final days."

"I agree. No more talking about it. What happens, happens."

"Right." She tapped her fingers on the console. "Girls haven't said no to you before, have they?"

"Correct."

"Ah. Well, lots of people have said no to me before. I'm used to it."

"I never asked anyone to say yes before."

"And you're still not, right?"

"Well, that's a funny way to put it. For us, it's not a question." *We're good together, but nothing else about us lines up. Our work is pulling us apart, and we can't give it up. A man's got to work! Her, I could take care of, but she's already said, she could never live my lifestyle so it's useless to hope for a future life with her—the only woman I've fallen for.* "I won't leave until your parents do and after your first ride. I'm betting you will have your chance with Mary and D."

"Got it all figured out, don't you? Works for me."

* * *

They pulled into a hotel parking lot at Redding's Sundial bridge over the Sacramento River. June looked around. "Gosh, this bridge is amazing. My phone says the sundial works. It has a classic sundial sphere standing over 217 feet tall at one end of the bridge and is accurate between the hours of eleven in the morning until three in the afternoon."

"That's cool. Let's check in and then go see it up close."

* * *

Checking in, the clerk chatted on about the hotel's amenities, including the bridge and paved trails along the river. "Your wife will enjoy our gift shop. We have local handmade gifts that the ladies rave about. You'll have to check them out!" She smiled at June and June's face went ten shades of red. As soon as they left the front desk, she looked at him.

"At least I have a title for the night, and she didn't call me your sister." She tickled him.

"Good old Sheila!" They both laughed. *Sheila, ugh. June is such a good sport. Love her for that. Most women would be seething. But not her. She gets it. Another reason to love her for what she is.*

"Hey, Preston, they have a restaurant. What anniversary should we say we're celebrating now?"

"Uhm …. third? It's almost the end of three months."

"Works for me. I'm enjoying all our anniversaries, you know that?"

"Good. Then I'll try not to disappoint you tonight." *She's a sexy woman.*

* * *

After dinner they walked across the Sundial Bridge. June pointed. "Preston, look at the wildlife catching the last rays of the day. Fish jumping, birds, and a butterfly. I wonder what butterflies do at night. It needs to go home. It's getting late. Aw … so peaceful here." Holding hands, they walked along. Midway across, they stopped and looked over the rail.

Preston turned June's face toward his and kissed her. "This is a great way to end a long day, don't you think?"

"I agree. I love the lighting on the glass walkway. I've never seen this river before. Taking in all this beauty makes you want to ride a bike on the trail, doesn't it, Preston?" June joked.

"I'm happy just walking and holding your hand. Thank you very much."

June shivered for a second.

"Are you cold?"

"No, just happy."

28

Monday morning came and they piled back into the car. June fidgeted. "I'll call Mary and check in and check on D."

"Good move, June."

"Preston, I could be in the saddle again soon. I hope she says the end of next week would work for her. Then, I'll get my parents to delay their visit just a little. I need at least a week!

"Oh my God. That's a mighty big 'could'! All those thousand plus hours together tryin' to get me well was all for this. It's tough to be completely positive when I have no idea if I'm able or not." *My leg's pretty steady, but riding with it? I don't know. My bones had ten weeks to heal. That should be enough. I'll make it be enough. Sorry, Dr. Carson. Tryin' to go slow with the comeback.* "Geez. I hope she's receptive to my call again; especially now!"

"Fingers crossed she's got good news for you. I don't see why she'd have a problem with you. It was her horse, after all…"

***

What should I say? Am I fired from riding D? Have you given up on me? Am I out of the picture? Dialing, June's hand shook, and the call went to the car's speaker phone. Preston smiled, "Hope she's as excited as you are."

"Excited? What if she's madder than a hornet? What if she

thinks I should've been calling her and checking in routinely and more often and I'm a total flake and useless now? Does she know that my immediate riding career is teetering on the edge of impossible without D? Does she …"

A warm voice answered, "June! I saw your name and number! How nice to hear from you."

"Hi, Mary. Sorry I've been thinking of you, and D, but haven't called for a while. I've never been through so much turmoil with my health. I think it derailed my thinking! And somehow the days just flew by, and here I am today, ten weeks past all that. But trust me, I've made good healing progress mentally and physically, and I'm on my way back to San Diego!"

"I completely understand. I didn't want to bother you. I heard via the grapevine you were doing well, and I thought you'd call when you were ready. We had a few text messages back and forth, and I knew you were there. The time has passed quickly for me too. I felt so bad about the accident, it's great to hear your voice again. You sound good."

Whew. So far so good. June crossed her fingers and grimaced. "Thank you, Mary. I just got my cast off a couple of days ago and the good news is my leg looks fine. I have no idea if it will work fine, but I don't see why not!"

"That is such good news. I felt so responsible since it was my horse. You know how uptight he can be. But you always did so well with him."

"It was just an accident. I loved riding him. He was very forward and always a good boy for me. So, how is D? I haven't heard one thing about him. Of course, I haven't been talking to more than just a couple of people." June put her hands in prayer. *Please say something good.*

"Yes. I understand. Is the phone on speaker? I hear a little echo."

"Oh yes, I didn't mean to exclude Preston. Oops! He's the one that stopped to help me. After his car tire almost got me killed!" She laughed. "Don't worry, Mary. We had months to desensitize ourselves to this topic. Anyway, he's driving. So, like I said, we're on the way back to San Diego tonight."

Preston cleared his throat. "Hi, Mary. I've heard your name. Nice to hear your voice since I've heard your name, but we never got to meet up."

"Hi, Preston. I've heard yours too, via chit chat and, as I mentioned, a very active barn grapevine. I'm so happy you've been helping June. What a blessing for her."

June piped up, "It has been, Mary. Preston's in the know with just about everything. I'm dying to ask how D's been doing in training. Has he been shown at all?"

Mary cleared her throat. "You wouldn't believe this, but we discovered that D had a small crack on his right hind hoof when the vet examined him after his wild escape! Just to be safe, the vet and the farrier both agreed that he should be on rest for a couple of shoeings. He's had the same time off you've had."

"What? That's good. I mean, bad. I'm just shocked to hear that. This is not what I was expecting to hear at all. How's he now?" *I hope he's fine.*

"Well, he's ready to go back to work. Are you?"

June choked. "Do you mean riding?" Her fingers clasped together, and her knuckles went white. Taking quick breaths, her chest tightened. "I tried to accept that I might never ride again and tried to put it out of my mind, but I can't shake riding. It's what I love. I've missed it and D so much it's crazy."

"So, do you think you're ready to try riding him again? Or is it too soon?"

She grabbed Preston's thigh and released it, clasping her hands in prayer and lightly stomped both feet on the floor mat. Preston gave her a thumbs up. "Too soon? Mary, I can't believe I'm on my way back to my real life! I'm not scared, but I'm not sure of my ability until I get in the saddle." *I have a second chance?*

"I'd like to give you a chance with D. It will be nice to see how you are with him—if you're still the pair I saw before…Well, yes, he's ready for you now. I think he's missed you too. Are you still in your same apartment in San Diego?"

"Thanks to Preston, yes. I didn't lose it." *Wow. This is amazing! All my worry all these weeks and in a few minutes, I'm finding out there is true hope!*

"Well, my barn hasn't gotten up and moved either." She laughed. "The trip I made up to Elk Grove was my last. I got to see the horses I was considering buying and glad I saw them in person. I decided against them, but they sure looked tempting on the videos. I had my trailer and a vet check lined up and was ready to bring them back with me. But you know how that goes!"

"Oh, I'm sorry to hear that. I know you'd been looking for a while."

"Well, the trip wasn't in vain though because getting to see you and Sarah riding convinced me to wait it out for you. She's a beautiful rider, but I was hoping it would go your way. Granted, you're not back in the saddle yet and things could be different, but I'm willing to wait to see you and D together again. He's high strung, but I like his relaxation—if a tire doesn't blow, with you."

June chuckled. "Aw…thanks." *I'm going for it. I have to!* "Mary, how about Tuesday—next week? Would that work for you? How about 4 p.m.? She crossed her fingers. *Give me at least one week! I dare not ask for any more time.*

"I'm so sorry, June. I have a packed schedule and I'll be leaving town in a few days. Another buying trip for some horses from Germany. I'm on call to see them first once they're cleared from quarantine so I must go without delay. If you're going to coming over and try D, 4 p.m., works, but it will have to be tomorrow. That's all I can commit to. We'll have a little reunion in my barn and arena."

Tomorrow? OMG. This is it. The day of reckoning. That is way sooner than I had hoped, but I'll have to try. If I fail, I fail…Dr. Carson said to take it easy. Well, that's not happenin.' I'm not missing out on this opportunity no matter what. She squeezed her arm rest. "Thank you. I'm glad you're giving me a second chance with him."

"Of course. I saw your progress. Like I said, let's check things out and see. Stay in touch, June."

"I will. Bye and thank you from the bottom of my heart." She disconnected the call. Looking at Preston she shrieked. "Oh my God! I'm happy she said yes, but tomorrow? Yikes!"

"I know. Told ya. Do you think you can do it? I mean ride him?"

June gulped. "Well, I'm going to try. At least I'll have a job, maybe. What if I've lost my touch? I'm so scared that my ability is gone."

"Be confident. I wonder what the parents will have to say. Call yours and check on the final plans. Then I'll call my dad."

"Now?"

"Why not? We have lots of hours."

"Here goes nothing." June dialed. *Please say you can't make it until the end of next week. Please, please not this week.*

"Hi, Mom."

"Hello, dear. How are you?"

"That's what I was calling to say. I'm fine. My leg's feeling like it used to and guess what?"

"I can't guess, but I can tell you're excited."

"I think I'm getting my horse back, Mom! His owner, Mary, said she wants me back as his trainer. Well, if, and that's a big if, I'm still able to ride him. I hope so. I'll be meeting up with her and the horse soon—tomorrow, actually. So, are you guys still flying out?" She bit her lip. *Please don't say this week. I'll probably have bad news about my riding and not have anything to show you guys.*

"We are! We booked our flight after we last talked. We'll be there in three days—on Thursday! Are you sure you'll have time for us?"

"Of course. I'm looking forward to your visit. Gosh, Mom. I haven't seen you guys for two years—my big Christmas trip home." *No! Thursday is too soon! After all this recovery time, I could be at my worst, and they'll see it all with their own eyes. Maybe I can get them to hold off for at least a week longer.*

"Just thinking though, Mom, my place needs a little TLC since I've been gone and maybe I'll be working longer hours at the barn. What do you think about coming out next week instead?" *I hope she goes for it!*

"Sorry, but we have to keep our visit as is. I know it's a short visit but that's the only time we can squeeze in. Don't worry about anything, honey. We want to see your apartment and your training barn, no matter what condition they're in. We haven't watched you ride in years. You always looked so pretty up there. But oh, I worried every time you got on one."

Oh my gosh. I hope I'm capable of riding! I've hardly walked much at all with all this traveling. "I know you did, Mom. It's what I do though. I'll just give you a little demo. Nothing too long. I'd like you to meet Preston and he wants to meet you both."

"Okay. We'll meet him if you want us to. I'll send you our flight information."

"Can't wait! Bye, Mom."

She looked at Preston and scowled. "Oh my gosh. They're coming on Thursday. So, in the next two days, I'll be riding D, maybe seeing your dad, the shop, and then they'll be here? My God. Help! What if this all goes wrong? Oops. I should've let you say hi." *The day of reckoning! Yikes. Calm down. They will love him and see all his good qualities. Not that it matters since he's leaving, but they will know why I insisted on staying in California and see how well I managed my own recovery. Finally, they will approve of something I did!*

"No problem." He shook his head. "Really, it's okay. When parents are involved, things can get crazy. Anyway, at least you'll have a couple of days to get settled in."

"They're going to be the shortest days of my life. Thank you for understanding. It's your turn, Preston. Fingers crossed for you now."

"Should I tell him we'll come for a visit on Wednesday? That's the only day we'll have."

"Yes."

"Okay, use my phone and send him a text so I can get this over with." His lips curled into a soft smile.

Get it over with? Letting me see him? Or for his father to see us again? June got his phone and scrolled. "Got it. He must be "Dad" in your phone, right?"

"Yes. Say,—*Hi. Will be in San Diego and hoping to stop by with June on Wednesday. Are you in town?*—and that's it."

June sent the text and a couple of minutes later the phone buzzed. She picked it up. "He answered!"

"Okay. And?"

—*Yes. See you then.*—

"I'm nervous, Preston." *His father didn't mention me in the text.*

"Me too—about seeing him."

"Don't worry. What can go wrong with a little visit? I'll be there too." *I'll do my best to make a good impression for Preston's sake. I'm sure he'll do great with my parents. What's not to love about him?*

29

"Hey, June. Just a few more miles and we'll be in San Diego. "Still know the way to your apartment?" He laughed.

"I sure do. I'm glad I never got around to having house plants or even a fish. None would have survived. My place is going to seem like a shoebox compared to yours." *He might be glad he's leaving me when he sees my real life.*

"No worries. Let's get groceries on the way there."

"Still spoiling me, aren't you?"

"Well, you'll need a little bit of help getting back on your feet."

"I'll be okay if I still know how to ride."

* * *

Preston pulled into June's apartment complex, and she looked around. "Well, you can park here. This is for visitors. I'll tell the manager I'm back. Thanks for putting my car in the covered parking. My real spot is close to this space."

"Well at least, it's off the street parking, right?"

"Yes. And it's assigned so I never have to worry about walking in at night. Sometimes I get home past dark. How far away is your dad's home from here?" *Why does that man come to mind all the time?*

"About forty miles." He's got a view of…."

"Let me guess, the ocean." *Of course, he would live in a spectacular place. What is going through Preston's mind? 'What's a guy like me doin' with a girl like her?' What would his father say? Oh my gosh. Here I go again with his dad…*

"Yep."

They got out of his car. "Welcome to my shoebox," she laughed. "Come on in. Let's get the groceries and see if everything's okay. This complex looks so tiny and plain. Even my door is small."

Putting the key in the lock, June turned it and pushed, and the door squeaked open. "Well, this is it. The living room. And my room's to the right. At least I have a half bath for guests and my own bathroom off the bedroom and then the kitchen and a small patio in the back."

"Huh. Not bad. I like your horse photos."

"Thanks. That's my artwork. It's easy to decorate walls in an 850-square-foot place."

"It's all yours. Nothing wrong with being on your own and being realistic. I admire that. I'll help you put the groceries away. I do miss our little suite in Rancho." He opened his arms, and she went in for a long hug and buried her head in his chest.

"Me too." She kissed him. "Thank you so very much for helping me. Come on, I'll give you the grand tour now that you know the layout." *He is so sweet to me. But I refuse to be his ball and chain. I will set him free.*

* * *

Putting the groceries away and unpacking, Preston opened a beer and turned on the TV. "I'll watch TV while you finish unpacking."

"Okay. It won't take me long. I'm just taking my stuff out and then the bag's all yours." June poked her head out from her bedroom. "You'll be spending the night with me, right?" Her cheeks burned.

"If I'm invited."

June called out. "Plan on it!" *I hope I pull off goodbye without making him feel bad about leaving.*

* * *

"Preston, I can't believe it's already Tuesday afternoon." She pulled on her breeches. "I wish my favorite breeches hadn't been stolen, but these will have to do."

"They look cool, June. Don't worry."

"Thanks. My usual attire feels so odd right now, but I'll get used to them again. I'm glad we spent some time taking walks and getting in some light workouts. It's not much, but at least I feel balanced and steady. I'm doing some positive self-talk. That's what athletes do right?"

"Yes, they do."

"I can't wait to see D. And tomorrow, your dad. This is a lot." *Stay calm. You got this, June.*

"Yes, it is." Preston grabbed the keys. "Let's take my car. Don't forget about the traffic. We better leave soon. I want to see this horse up close. I'm going to take your picture with him. You're going to be very careful?"

June carried boots, helmet, and gloves. "Of course," she muttered. "It's a good thing I have lots of spares on hand. Let me grab some carrots and some sodas. I have a little thermal bag for my lunch and snacks. Oh! Here's an ice pack to keep stuff cold. K.

Ready! Let's go. How do I look?" *This is so weird. It's the beginning of the end of us and the beginning of where I belong … I hope.*

"Like a rider and like you know what you're doing. How did I look in my coveralls?" He laughed.

"Like you knew what you were doing. Although when I first met you, I secretly doubted that you did, you were so clean and handsome." *And you're leaving me soon and going back to your real life. And I'm not even sure if I'm going to have a horse to ride or, worse yet, even capable of handling him. What if D gets unruly underneath me?*

"Handsome? My, how nice of you to have noticed through all your pain."

"I was in pain, Preston. Not dead!"

He laughed. "Let's go."

* * *

They parked and pulled into the barn parking lot. "This is it. Come on, Preston. I see Mary's car. She's probably got him out of his stall."

They walked into the barn where D was tied and being groomed. "Hello, Mary!" June walked up with a sugar cube in her hand. Stretching his nose and mouth out, he whinnied softly. She fed him the sugar. "Hi, boy. Remember me? Oh, Mary. His muzzle is so soft. I could just hug him. Want me to finish brushing him?"

"Hi, June. It's great to see you. You look so good." The two women hugged. "You certainly may finish him up. He's happy to see you."

"Thank you." Picking up a brush, June motioned for Preston to come closer. "Mary, this is Preston."

"Hi, Mary. Nice to meet you." *This is June's real life. Wow. I'm kind of nervous in this barn.*

"Nice to meet you too, Preston. I'm so happy you brought June. I know she's happy to have your company."

"Thanks. I'm going to take some pictures. Can you stand next to her and the horse?" He snapped the picture. "And now you, June. Look at you. I don't have to tell you to smile." He positioned the camera. "Got it. That's nice." *June, you're a brave woman. I wouldn't even think about riding that horse!*

June proceeded to finish up with the horse. She put her gloves on and buckled her helmet. She picked up the lunge whip. "All set. I'll lunge him a little, Mary. Just in case he's got a little more under the hood than I need right now."

"I think that's wise. Let's go to the covered round pen, then we'll go to the covered arena. I have a headset for you so we can talk."

"Perfect. I'll put it on after I lunge him."

* * *

Entering the round pen, Preston looked around the covered area. The horse looks even bigger here. He stood next to Mary. His muscles tensed and his palms got sweaty.

June closed the gate behind herself and D. June grinned and hooked up the lunge line the same way she always had. "Alright D. Ready?" She spoke softly, secured the line to his snaffle bit, patted his neck, and gently dragged the lunge whip on the sand. She clucked and D walked a few steps forward then burst into a trot going fully around the circle and spontaneously galloped, throwing in a few high bucks. Firing loud popping farts, he tossed his head with exaggerated movement and whinnied. "Such energy," June chuckled. "Easy boy. I know you're excited about all this. Easy…" D carried on at the same speed.

He's acting like the same horse I saw her riding just before she fell off. I hope she's not scared. I am! Sucking in his breath, Preston watched and waited until she finished lunging and they were on their way to the arena. He lowered his voice. "It's a good thing you did that, June."

"Oh, I know him. He's a good boy but he's got plenty of power."

"I'll say. Please be careful." *I shouldn't have made her sit for hours for the past three days. She needed more light exercise to build strength. I've been out of the gym for so long I've lost my focus on strength training. What if she's too weak and falls off? It will be all my fault again!*

"I'm just going to stay very basic today. Hopefully, he'll be calm for me. He hasn't been worked much has he, Mary?"

"No, not really. We lunged him the past two days, but he's mostly been at rest."

"Okay. We'll come back slowly together. I don't have any show plans right now, do you, Mary? I think we've missed most of them." June scratched D's withers as they talked.

"It's understandable. And no, I don't have any plans for him at the end of this year. Just waiting it out to see how this goes. Oh. I might be getting another horse."

"How exciting. Buying it?"

"No another trainer wants to board and train here. I'll tell you more after your ride. Here's your headset."

"Thanks. Okay."

* * *

June led D to the mounting block. With three steps, it was tall and brought her level with D's back with ease. She put her foot in the stirrup iron and swung her right leg up over onto the saddle. She smiled, patted his neck, and waved. "So far, so good. Come on, boy." June lightly squeezed her legs and moved the horse forward. D walked on with big, forward, ground-covering steps.

Minutes later, June scratched his withers. "Together again, aren't we boy? Man, I'm going to be sore tomorrow, but this is heaven. Let's see how your trot feels. Easy there…Good boy."

Moving the horse to a posting trot, June reacted with a smile stretched across her face. No words needed; she moved in harmony with the horse. The rhythmic thudding of D's hooves in the sand and the gentle breeze propelled the twosome into a picture of horse and rider that combined strength and elegance. D's head was down and round as it should be, as he accepted his bit and shortened rein length without hesitation. He powered up and pushed from behind.

Preston took another picture. "She looks great." *She's an expert—no doubt about it. I can't expect her to leave this life and she was clear about that when I asked her. Makes sense. This is her world.*

"She does. I wanted to see that magic again. I thought she might be the best one for him. He's happy."

D'll have her, but where does that leave me? In competition with a horse? That's nuts. Going back to work is not as easy as I thought it was going to be. At least D's only a horse and not a man. "Looks like June's happy too."

* * *

The ride went smoothly and within thirty minutes the ride and cooldown were over. June patted D and got off. "I am so excited that went well. I kept it super short today for his sake and mine. But I can't wait to hear about the other horse."

Mary cleared her throat. "Let's walk and talk. Preston, there's cold drinks in the fridge in the break room in the other barn. It's the building out to the left. Would you like one? Please help yourself to whatever you want. There's sodas and water. I'll take a juice if you don't mind."

"You got it. I'll be back." Preston walked off.

"Preston sure is nice." Mary's words came quicker. "But I wanted to tell you, June, the other trainer is Tanner. He's got a new four-year old gelding from Germany. It's his, but he might be selling it to me. I'd like your opinion."

June coughed. "Of Tanner? He can't be trusted." *There! How's that? Is that man going to follow me forever? Rather unfair of me to think such things based on his past.*

Mary took June's arm. "The horse. I completely understand how you must be feeling about Tanner, but this opportunity just came up for me. Can you be around him?" Her eyes darted around looking for Preston.

Uh oh. Be professional. "Oh! Yes, I can. I've already seen him. I mean Tanner. We bumped into him not long ago. I can handle him, Mary. No worries. You've got a business to run, and he and I are over. Besides, Preston's going back to work and his life, too. We both are. After my parents' visit this week, everything is going to be back to normal."

"So, Preston won't be around?"

"No. That was our plan. He works out of town. It will be me and the horses. I can assure you that I am not only trying to make a living, but a life too, and that just has to include horses — no matter the cost to me. I can't let 'people,' her fingers formed air quotes while she was still holding the reins and walking, "get in the way."

"You haven't changed a bit, June." Mary glanced at her and grinned.

June froze, then shook her head and walked on with slower steps. Her thoughts didn't match the pace and galloped off.

Was hearing she hadn't changed equivalent to fingernails on a chalkboard? No—not gritty enough. More like biting into a large chunk of foil embedded in her favorite Lindt 78% cocoa dark chocolate bar square. This was not good. It was awful. Was telling Mary the truth going to cause her to lose out again? After all, didn't she always lose at the last minute? But why did it have to be now, after her perfect recovery?

Arriving at D's halter, still hanging as she had left it, June thrust the reins over D's neck and started unfastening the bridle and putting the halter back on. *Oh my gosh. Now I have to disclose one more thing. God help me.* "Mary, a part of me has changed."

"Oh? What's that?"

"I met up with Isabel Sheffield and she wants me to go to college with her. She's hoping to bring Zephyr here for boarding and lessons and then help each other between classes and our schedules. I have an associate's degree and I'd be working on my bachelor's in business, if all that works. What do you think?" She took the saddle off and started pulling D's Velcro schooling boots off.

"My goodness. I take it back, June. You have changed. I've never heard you talk about your parents, or school for that matter. Are you sure you could keep up with D? I want him to move up to Grand Prix."

"I'm sure I can keep up. Horses are my priority, and I'd stay up all night studying and doing homework if necessary. Isabel and I can help each other out with barn chores. That will free up some time."

"Sounds like you've done some thinking." She paused. "That's good to hear. I've seen Isabel ride and I'd love to have her. She would be welcome. And why not go back to school? One day you might have your own barn to run. The more you know, the better."

"I'm glad you feel that way." *Whew. And the truth shall prevail.*

"I certainly do—because running a training and boarding barn takes a lot of knowledge, luck, and money. Sure, you can make money, but you've got to work things right to stay afloat."

"I know you're right. Oh. Here comes Preston. Let's not bring up Tanner yet. I'll tell him later."

"I understand and I don't blame you, June." She winked. "Ex-boyfriends can be uh … something to deal with."

You took the words right out of my mouth, Mary.

30

The next day, June and Preston hurried to get ready for lunch with Preston's father.

June posed. "Preston, how's this outfit?"

"Beautiful. Come on, sweetie pie. We have a lunch reservation at one at his favorite yacht club spots. We can't be late. He hates people that aren't on time. No one makes him wait! Like seafood? Cuz there'll be plenty to pick from."

"Love it. I mean the seafood. I've heard about some of the yacht club restaurants from a couple of the super-rich boarders at Mary's barn, but never thought I'd be going to one. Aren't they for the owners only? Never mind! Preston, are you sure I look alright? Should I just let you go without me? Maybe this wasn't such a good idea after all. Oh my gosh, is Cassie going to be there?"

"No, but probably Liv will. She's his significant other. I think I already told you that."

"Whatever. I'm a little nervous. Okay. Not a little…a lot!" *What was I thinking? Seeing Bob again? I had to be crazy asking for this.*

"Don't be."

* * *

Entering the restaurant, Preston spotted his father and Liv, seated and waiting. "There they are, June." June stared at them, the other patrons, and the restaurant. *Wow. More designer touches just like Preston's apartment. What did I expect?* They left the wood flooring entryway and walked across carpet with a subdued blue pattern that corresponded with the ocean view visible from the picture windows surrounding the dining room. June noticed her footsteps feeling the cush of the rug. Feels like the float of riding on expensive springy foam footing in a fancy arena. At least I've done that a time or two. Gosh. "Hello. Hello again, June." He looked at his watch. "I was hoping you hadn't changed your mind about lunch. It's good to see you, son."

"Hi, Dad. Hi, Liv."

"Hello sir. It's nice to see you too." June's voice trembled slightly. *Uh oh. Did he mean it was good to see Preston and not me? We are a little late. Bad start. Calm down! My gosh this place is ritzy and getting to my head. Everyone here looks like they walked off the set of Lifestyles of the Rich and Famous and of course, more art on the walls.* She swallowed hard.

"You can call me Bob, June." His hand stretched outward. "This beautiful woman is Liv."

Liv extended her hand in a delicate manner. "Hello, June. I've heard all about you. How is your recovery going, dear?"

Distracted by the ambience and soft music, June forced herself to focus. She reached out with a bare touch of her fingertips. "It's so nice to meet you, Liv. Thank you for asking. My recovery's going just fine, actually. I rode yesterday. Preston went with me."

Bob cleared his throat. "I see. What can I say? I'm both surprised and not surprised that he accompanied you to a, a…barn? If he asked you to call him Preston, well…"

"Dad, please, that's enough for now, okay? Anyway, yes, I did because June is special, and I didn't want to blow her mind with your last name until she got to know me." His tone was stern, and he glanced at June. "Anyway, that's history and over. Now I have a couple of pictures to show you of June and the horse she's going to be training."

Bob muttered under his breath, "It's your name too…" He cleared his throat and spoke in a loud voice, "Pictures? Really. That's a new one." He shifted in his seat.

Preston pulled his phone out and showed them the pictures.

Bob's eyebrows shot up. "My goodness. That horse looks so big." He looked closer. "Is it an expensive one?"

June piped up. "Yes. He's imported from Germany, where he was born."

"Uh huh. I see. Just like cars and boats, right son? Top of the line is always important."

June squirmed. "Well, he's not my horse, but I hope to own one like him one day. It's just that breeding is important for performance. That's all. I'll have to save up for quite a while to get one."

"Sounds like you have your work cut out for you, then." His lip curled in a knowing smile.

This is worse than talking to my own father. Yikes. "Yes sir, I do."

The waiter came over and Preston noticed his dad and Liv had cocktails and ordered two glasses of Chardonnay. "Is that okay with you, June? We're planning on having fish. Aren't we?"

"Yes. I love seafood. I love the ocean. This restaurant is amazing. Love the ocean view."

Preston's father cleared his throat. "Come here often?"

June's cheeks pinked. "Me? Oh no, sir. I've always wanted to. It's as nice as I've heard it was." She tucked her hair behind her ear.

Liv's head turned with interest. "My goodness, your earrings complement your beautiful hair. Glistening. Love it."

June's cheeks burned. "Thank you. They're new. I don't wear much jewelry." Her fingers pinched her bracelet.

"I meant your hair, oh, and of course the earrings, but that bracelet must be very special, dear."

"Yes. It's what got Preston on the helicopter after my accident. The EMTs thought it was an allergy bracelet."

"Oh my. Such an accident and you look perfect now. It's a lucky one then. Good for you. And it's inscribed?"

"Yes. It says, 'Reach for the Stars.' I guess it must be working. My stars have been aligned lately."

"That's so positive considering your injury. But then again, your fortune is at your fingertips, isn't it?"

Preston coughed. "June's feet are on the ground, Liv. She's very realistic and has goals."

Bob's fingers tapped the tabletop. "To think that you've been in San Diego for what, the past five years, June?"

"Close to that. Yes. Since I left Florida."

"And you're a horse trainer?" He cleared his throat again.

"Yes. That's what I do."

His father and Liv exchanged looks. "And you like it, I presume?"

"No. I love it, to be honest."

He coughed. "Well, good to love your job. Preston loves his job too. How long are you in town, son?"

"Not too long. Time for me to get back to work. I, uhm … we just got back from Scott's place."

"His Seattle home?"

"Yes. Luna's wedding is this coming weekend. I had to get his Rolls checked out."

"And you took June with you?"

Preston flinched. "Yes. I wanted to show her my place and get my car so yeah, she went with me."

June fidgeted. "He's great with cars, sir."

"That's nice of you to say. He always had a knack with anything mechanical."

"You must be proud of him. He makes his work look so easy."

"I don't think I've ever heard any young lady say that before..."

"Dad, that's enough. How's everything with you, Liv?"

"Just fine. Thank you for asking. Cassie said to tell you hello."

"That was nice of her. Is her job going well?"

"Yes. Her company is growing by leaps and bounds. She's all over the U.S. it seems like."

"Oh. Good for her."

"I'm sure you'll be bumping into her in your travels."

"Sounds nice, Liv. Glad she likes her job too."

* * *

Taking their order, the server left the table. "Dad, June wants to see the business, and I wanted to show her the house."

"Fine with me. We can tour the shop this afternoon and home is well, home. Come by whenever. Will you be staying in your room? It's still there."

"Not tonight. But I will Thursday night since her parents are arriving in the afternoon for their first visit. I'm helping to get a few little things set up at her place. She's keeping me busy. And then we'll spend some time with her folks too. Right, June?" Preston nudged her foot and winked.

"That's our plan. Bob, Preston has been such a wonderful help and not just for me. Our friends, well, we met them in South Lake Tahoe, have one of your yachts and he fixed it for them. They were so excited. We watched them sail off the next morning."

Bob sputtered. "Preston! You didn't tell me. You fixed one of my yachts? Which one?"

"Waveflames II, Dad. It was the reserve gas line, that's all. They didn't have any reserve and I just made sure they had it working. But it was their honeymoon morning ride that we watched them sail off and away."

June gushed, "Bob, I just love their yacht. We had a beautiful sunset cruise. I think we told you we were going on one that evening, and we did. I love, love, love the ocean. I can't wait to see your workshop. I mean place. I mean business." She squirmed and adjusted the napkin on her lap. *Try to speak as though you have some solid brain cells. These are educated people. God. What are they going to think?*

Liv sat taller and leaned in for a closer look. "I always wanted to be a blonde. Blondes are smart, aren't they? Seems like some people hold onto silly stereotypes. I know you must be very smart to keep Preston at your side." She moistened her lips with her tongue. "Us girls have our little ways, don't we?"

"Uhm…well, yes, I suppose. Preston has a heart of gold, and he came to my rescue. He's a free man though and going back to work soon. I guess we both have lives and plans that we try to do well at. He's just a super guy." *Dodged that bullet, I hope. Get off my back, lady. Now she's almost as bad as talking to both of my parents. I can see why Preston doesn't come here more often.*

Preston's foot nudged her again and mouthed, "Thank you."

Liv dabbed the corner of her mouth with her napkin. "Well

then, I must say that you stumbled onto a 'super guy' that's turned out to have much more than just a 'heart of gold' as you put it. Unexpected surprises are always nice. Especially when they can yield so much in return. Maybe your dream horse isn't that far off after all. You, my dear, must certainly know how to erh … what is it they say? Oh, I know … work it."

June felt her cheeks burn. "I'm not expecting anything else from him."

"Smart. Men like surprises — giving and receiving."

"Right." *This conversation is over. Liv, one. June, zero.*

* * *

With lunch over, the foursome stood, and Bob led the way out. "See you two at the shop, right, Preston?"

"Right, Dad. We'll be there."

June sighed as soon as both were out of earshot. "I'm exhausted, but I'm happy we got to see your dad, Preston."

"You are?"

"Yes. It wasn't easy. But then, you haven't met my parents yet!"

"Oh come on now. What can be so hard about meeting them?" *I'll lay on the charm, and they'll see that their daughter has been in good hands. Uh … I better rephrase that.*

31

Taking June's elbow, Preston escorted her to the car and opened the door for her. He came around and got in. "I'm surprised he didn't have Cassie there."

"Preston! Your dad's nice. Maybe he would have liked to treat her to a fancy lunch as a way of including her with us and showing his affection for her. I mean, she did miss out on an elegant dining experience."

"'Nice?' June, you don't know him. He gets his way. I'm surprised he barely mentioned her. Something's up."

"Like what?"

"I don't know. He wants me to marry her, and he doesn't give up."

"All parents want things. Doesn't mean we have to do them."

"Yeah well, let's go see the business. Then I'm taking you for a tour of my house and my old room." He put his arm around her. "What on earth have you done to me, June?"

***

They pulled into Wahlberg Marine & Engineering, Inc. parking lot. "June, see that black BMW?"

"Yes."

"I think that's Cassie's car. I knew he'd be up to something." His voice raised. "I told you!"

"It's okay. She can be here. Big deal. She's Liv's daughter, Preston. That gives her every right, and it makes sense."

"We'll see what he's up to. Come on. Let's go to the office."

* * *

Preston opened the door. "Hello, Dad. Liv, Cassie. I thought I saw your car." *For Christ sakes he never knows when to quit.*

Bob's voice boomed. "Hello again. Hello, June. This is Cassie. Liv's daughter."

Smiling, June extended her hand. "Nice to meet you, Cassie."

"Nice to meet you too, June. I was surprised to hear Preston was in town, so of course I rushed right over. Hi, Preston. Fancy meeting you here!"

"I figured you'd be here." *Entrapment.*

"Hey. I thought you'd be happy to see me, Preston."

Preston shifted his stance and stood closer to June. "Sure, Cass. It's nice to see you. I just figured you'd be here, that's all. What are you up to on a Wednesday afternoon?"

"Well, I've got some exciting news to share. Your father and I both do."

"Oh, and what's that?"

"I'm taking over the financials for Wahlberg, Inc."

"Everything?"

"Yes. Everything. So, I guess you'll be seeing me around here more often. That is, if you stick around."

Yeah sure. Am I a glutton for punishment? "I might be in and out. You never know. Well, good for you. Another feather in your cap."

"Your father was ready for this move. He can't run all this by himself."

"I see, Cassie. And I'm never around?" *Sure. Play the pity card. Is that all you can come up with?*

Cassie's arms flew open and flopped to her sides. "Preston, no problem. I'm just doing the books and all the corporate tax and financial projections. That's all."

"Whatever works. You were always good with numbers. Beats me why you liked them so much."

"That's okay. To each their own. How's your business?"

"Oh. It's fine. Keeps me traveling. Erh … just the way I like it."

"And you, June. I hear you're a horse trainer?"

"Dressage. Yes. I am. I just got my client's horse back in training as of yesterday."

"Well, it's an elegant sport. It must keep you busy. I mean, in the saddle?"

"That's correct. Being in the saddle is a rider's number one priority, for obvious reasons. My leg is a classic example. But yes, that's what I do, along with five thousand other slaving things at the barn. Horses don't have owners, they have staff!"

While everyone was laughing, Preston spoke up. "June's an amazing rider."

Cassie added. "I didn't know you knew anything about horses or riding, Preston."

His eyes bored into hers. "I didn't. Until I met June. She can educate anyone about the sport. You should hear her talk the talk."

Blushing, June chimed in, "It's just that riding is so much a part of my life, it's like never leaving your job or your passion, all at the same time."

Cassie cleared her throat. "Beautifully spoken, June. We should all have work that reflects our passion. Preston followed his interests too and that's worked out for him."

Smiling, Preston added. "Thanks. Nice of you to notice."

Bob stood. "Well, now that we're all introduced, shall we take the tour?"

* * *

June looked around. "Your facility is so big." She looked up at the immense height of the building. *I swear my voice echoes in here.* "I never knew what went into building a boat, let alone a yacht. Love the waterfront location too." She took a deep breath. "There's nothing like the bracing smell of the ocean. We're so close to the water." She took another deeper and exaggerated breath. "This is fascinating, Bob. The engine fabrication is so involved. Glistening metal just about everywhere. I never knew so much went into engine design and the operations. I can see where Preston learned to be a mechanic. You probably miss him." *I hope I didn't say too much.*

"I do, but that's a sore subject at times. Isn't it, Preston?"

"Not all the time. Come on, Dad." Preston reached out and stroked an engine under construction. "Cold metal that leads to warm experiences." His hand lingered on the machine. "Huh…June made some good observations about shipbuilding, wouldn't you say?"

"She did." He locked eyes with Preston. "Never knew you appreciated the process so much. And what could you add?"

"I would have to say that shipbuilding includes many tasks and calls for intensive scheduling, material planning, and integrative engineering."

"Son, you're a natural."

"Thanks, Dad. Glad you like what I had to say. I guess this

stuff has been in my blood for a long time. But, how about a little fun and taking a short cruise?"

Bob stood back. His mouth dropped. "Son, 'this stuff' is most definitely your blood! Glad you can see that. You want me to take you guys out on the ocean? Go for a 'warm experience'?"

"Yes. Let's give June a ride."

Bob shook his head. "June, I'm liking what I'm hearing. Sure. Come on everyone. Let's board and go. Preston, you're full of surprises."

"I surprise myself at times lately, Dad. Come on, June. Now you'll be boarding a real yacht. Much bigger than Andrew and Alicia's. Isn't it?"

June stood still and eyed the vessel. *Compliments are usually a safe topic. I hope so. Nothing but the truth. All of this is way above my expectations.* "It's gorgeous. How big is this, Bob?"

He turned and grinned. "Eighty-five feet of pure luxury and I think it will be sold soon. Glad you approve, June. Preston, take the wheel. Show June your boating skills."

"Dad. You take the wheel. We're going to watch the ocean."

"Come with me, Liv. You heard my son. Let's go."

* * *

Sailing along the water made June gasp with pleasure as the wind and ocean waves worked their magic. Tipping her chin up and closing her eyes, she took a deep breath. "The briny smell of the sea..."

Preston's arm wrapped around her and closed the distance between them. He braced as the boat crossed the white tipped waves, building momentum and motion. "I can't help myself, June.

I want you to be close to me. You're beautiful and happy. I love watching you more than watching the ocean. You know that?"

"Preston, how could you not be in love with being out on the ocean? It's almost like riding. Such a thrill and feeling the wind brush against your face and body, yet the power beneath you isn't hampered."

"I never saw it like that. I thought it was just a boat ride."

She laughed. "Oh you. Good grief."

Preston whispered in her ear and they both laughed and snuggled in tight.

* * *

Bob gave the wheel to Liv and hurried over to them. "Son, I'm impressed you've been on two yachts lately. That's more than I've seen you do in the past three years."

Preston beamed. June pulled away a little. *I can't interfere with Preston's moment of approval. It must be rare, and I hope he has more of them. Maybe my parents will approve of me too. Would be nice.*

* * *

Arriving back at the dock, the sea breeze picked up and the setting sun provided a refreshing atmosphere. Bob beckoned to all of them. "Joining us for dinner at the house, Preston?"

Making up for lost time with the old man. He looks strong and healthy. Three years didn't touch him. "Yes. Thanks. I can't believe I'm getting hungry again. Must've been the sailing."

"We can have steak and lobster. Gotta have a little fresh catch. I'll call and tell 'em there's five of us on the way."

"We love steak. Don't we, June?" Preston's fingers slid through her hair. *I could go for a little alone time.*

June's cheeks flamed and she stammered, "We do."

They fell behind the others and remained on the dock. "You got a little sunburned. Just a little tiny bit." He gave her a quick kiss. His fingers traced the side of her face. "I like it when you say 'we.' You look good next to the ocean too. Let me take another picture. Stand and smile."

Obliging, June posed.

Bob turned and called out, "Let's get moving, Preston."

"Okay, Dad. I'm sure the kitchen staff has plenty to do until we get there."

"Cassie's already in her car!"

"Got it. We're coming."

Preston squeezed June's hand. "Come on. We better catch up. He's worried about Cassie."

"No problem, Preston. We're the last ones on the dock."

"Yeah, so what? Cassie's a member of the family. They're always all about her. That will never change." *Cassie this. Cassie that. Ugh. She's okay, but it gets old.*

32

"Well, June, the day goes on and we're on the road again. You'll see where I grew up."

"I'm excited to see your house. Does it have a nice big backyard?" She looked out the car windows and saw that the real estate was changing. *Upscale. Secluded properties behind iron fencing. Close proximity to the ocean. The money is in the air just as much as the sea breeze was. Wow. Tanner was right. Preston is Richie Rich. How did he turn out so nice? Well, Sheila didn't think so.* She bit her lip.

"Yeah. It's got some pretty sweet views too. You can see the terrain, and the ocean too. Kind of an inspiring place. For my dad's life that is."

"Why do you say that? Because if this gate is the entry to your house, I say it looks like there's another mansion ahead." *No wonder he always ran from expectations.*

Preston stopped at the keypad and entered the code. The eighteen-foot-high black wrought iron gates with a large gold W emblem on each, moved open. An Ocean waves design was entwined in the ornate custom ironwork. Flower beds, Sega palms, and other flowering shrubs, including fuchsia and red bougainvillea, and a variety of tropical and indigenous trees flanked both sides of the gate on the inside and outside as the asphalt drive led cars up the hill and wound its way to the house. "It is a mansion, June. But it's not mine and I don't live here anymore. Before this trip, I hadn't been here for at least two years. Longer than that, I must say."

If I lived here, I would have never moved out! "What about Christmas? Oh my God, another long-paved driveway and oh my gosh. Look at the lush landscape. I love Tudors. God, the windows are super tall. You must have an ocean view from the back that's to die for. How beautiful is that! Wow. Does your dad have cars too?"

"Not like Scott does. But he's got more than one, I can't lie. He's more into boats."

"I can see why he sent you to Yale. I can see why he wants you with Cassie, Preston. He wants you to have the best." *This place is a showstopper. No wonder Bob asked if D was expensive. That's all that man knows.*

Turning off the engine, Preston turned to talk. "Hey. Give yourself some credit, June. Those are his choices. Does my apartment look like this?"

June sputtered. "Apartment? Your 'apartment' is a penthouse luxury condo. What about my little place? What do you think my parents are going to think about my choices?"

"The one thing we had in common, even before we met, or your accident, and that we still have, is our common interests."

"Meaning?"

"We both pursued life choices of our own and I think we've done alright. So what if your family isn't based on millions, billions, whatever. You're happy."

"Weren't you happy before you met me?" *A bit of a playboy I can only imagine. Okay. More than a bit.*

"I was. In a way. I don't know. I was too busy being free and living the life of a bachelor to give 'happy' much more than a thought. You heard what Sheila thought about me?" He shook his head. "I admit. I wasn't very caring about anyone. You're the first one I've ever stopped for. I was always going on spur of the moment trips, jobs, events with people like that David guy at the restaurant. I know lots of people like that. I could call them and do whatever and that's all I was about. That's my life and that's what it'll be when I go back to work."

"Oh. Well. You're not thirty yet. Maybe you'll change when you're older. That's what people say about turning thirty. I'm two years behind you!"

"Yeah. I'll always be the older man. Did you know Cassie's two years older than me? That girl was bossy from day one. No wonder my dad loves her."

"She seems nice to talk to."

"Nice, yeah. But she's been around my whole life."

"It sounds like you two are a match. Similar backgrounds." *I don't fit in here.*

"Yeah. I told you. Like a corporate merger." Preston cleared his throat. "One last thing."

"What is it? You look worried." *It's me. That's why he's worried.*

"I've never brought anyone home before. Dad might be a little unnerved by it. Try not to take offense at anything he or Liv says. You did great with them at lunch."

I did? Yikes. "Thank you. Fair warning. Besides, my parents might be just as bad. All you've had to put up with so far is Tanner. He was pretty awful at the show. Braggadocios character. So full of himself. God. My parents…well, add them in." She giggled. "I think we should go in now. They're probably looking out the windows somewhere wondering what's taking us so long."

"Okay. Come on. I can't wait to hear what my father's going to say at dinner. Kick me if I lose my cool."

* * *

"Hey, Dad! We're here. I'm going to take June on a quick tour." They entered the study.

Bob closed his laptop. "Sounds good. I'm not in the mood to look at the books anyway. I'm glad Cassie's here to make me." He laughed.

"She loves books and numbers. Yuck. But someone's got to do it. Not me. No siree."

"Me either. Enjoy the tour, June. I'll see you guys in the dining room."

"Okay."

* * *

Preston entered his bedroom. "Welcome, my lady. This is it."

"Geez. Your room's ginormous. French doors overlooking the ocean with your own private balcony and chairs? Come on! Second story living with such a view. Huge bed." She patted it and looked around. Motioning him to come close, she kissed him. Her lips parted and she felt his lips caress hers ever so tenderly. She whispered in his ear and let her lips brush his ear, "Do you ever miss home?" *He's a hot guy.*

"No."

She left him standing, watching her. "I see your diploma on the wall. Is this a picture of you and your mom?" *I'm the first girl he's ever brought here? To a place like this? Unbelievable.*

"Yeah. I was about eight. It was taken at her house."

"She's pretty. That's where you got your blonde hair. How old were you when they divorced?"

"I was about two. Dad was a good parent and of course, I had good nannies. At least he never had a revolving door of women in his life. He was a good role model in that respect."

She held his hand and took a deep breath. "It's nice to hear you say something positive about him. I get your pressure feelings though. Mine were so pushy too."

"I call it like I see it. His work consumed his life though. It's weird being here. My current life is much better."

"I see you played sports."

"Yep. I had to. Looks good on a college application. Sports weren't so bad. Soccer and baseball. Some golf. Not much. Too slow for me, but one day I'd like to play. How about you?"

"It's outdoors. I think I'd like to try it."

He moved close and took her hand. "Here, sit on the bed with me. How's this going to work, June? Are we going to be seeing each other?"

"I don't know. You can't quit your job, can you?"

"No. I own the business. My boss wouldn't like that." He laughed.

What if we didn't have such impossibly different work worlds? He's the kind of guy I could spend the rest of my life with—minus the travel. But without travel, he would be living a trapped life that he couldn't tolerate. It would break us. "Of course, you can't ditch your job, Preston. Just teasin.'" She giggled. Her eyes looked down. "I never expected any of this."

"Me either. Let's just meet your parents and go day to day."

"Perfect."

* * *

Tapping on his crystal champagne glass, Bob raised his glass. "I'd like to toast Preston's visit. I haven't seen my son at this table for a long time and it's a great sight to my eyes. Cheers!"

Raising her glass to toast, the glasses clinked. June sipped and smiled. "It's lovely to see Preston's childhood home. My parents are coming to California for the first time tomorrow, so I understand your excitement, Bob."

Preston added, "June's been getting her place ready for them." *It would never meet his standards but who cares. It's none of his concern.*

"It's only a one-bedroom apartment, but we picked up a few things and Preston was a big help getting it ready. I haven't seen my parents since last Christmas."

Preston sank in his chair and took a big swallow of champagne. *Don't give him any ammunition, June.*

Bob's sly grin lifted the corners of his lips. "I see. Another child living across the country from parents?"

"Yes, sir. I came for a visit, a few rides, and stayed. I love California. My parents have properties in Florida, but no horse properties. They never will. But I hope we have a great visit just like this. Only this is, is … is, uhm … quite the place!"

Bob laughed. "That it is. Glad you approve, June."

She fiddled with her fork. "Well, I sure do."

Clearing his throat, Bob turned his head and looked at the staffer coming into the room. "And here comes our first course. Let's eat."

* * *

Driving home, June was quiet.

"Penny for your thoughts, June." *I love it when we talk things over. He's been my best friend the whole time we've been together, and so supportive because he knows this visit has been a lot to take in.*

"Oh. Just thinking about tomorrow. I'm excited to ride D again. I bet my legs will be sore."

"Like a cowboy's?"

Laughing, June patted his thigh. "Sore, but not bowlegged if that's what you mean. I'm sure I'll feel it, even though I tried to go easy. Hey. We're back. Yes! There's still a place for you to park. Good thing we have visitor parking off the street. I don't want your nice car on the street."

"Thanks. Let's go to bed. I'm tired and I bet you are too."

"I'm exhausted."

June got her key out and opened the front door. "Good. I was hoping you'd be ready to jump into bed."

"Preston!" She reached out and tickled him. "Race?"

"Bring it on, woman."

"No problem. I've got legs now."

"Boy, I'll say." He slammed the door behind him.

Running to the bed, they jumped on it and piled on top of each other laughing and wrestling. Preston tickled her. "I thought you were tired."

"Not anymore!" They wrestled and messed up the bedspread, blanket, and sheet. The pillows fell off the bed. Clothing—yanked off and thrown, landed on the bedding strewn on the floor while only the sheet remained. She held his arms down and climbed on top of him. Her long hair flowed freely, scantly covering her and her bare waist. "I got you!" Leaning down she kissed his face and his neck until he quit moving. "What have you got to say now, mister? Give?"

Laughing, he grabbed her and rolled on top. Skin to skin, he held her to him, and his hands pulled her tight and close. His breath was warm on her neck. "You want to know what I have to say? Huh?" He covered her neck with kisses. "You have a great apartment, know that?"

"Oh, so, you like it? I liked your room, too." Her voice softened and slowed as her fingers traced his face and chest, letting them slide even lower and explore the muscles she had become familiar with. His body heat radiated and shifted her intentions into a new depth of awareness of all he was to her. "Thank God you paid the rent, and I still have it." She kissed him until they became quiet in the darkness and words were no longer needed.

* * *

The next morning, June made coffee and brought a cup to Preston. "Here you go. Coffee in bed. Did you sleep well?"

"I did. Crawl back in here before the day steals you away." *She's got me spoiled and used to all this routine.*

"Okay." She scooted in. "Whatcha got planned?"

He kissed her. "For now? Or for the day?"

"For the day, silly. Drink your coffee. Let's talk."

"About what?"

"Thursday has arrived, and your parents will be here this afternoon." *Countdown. I've never really had to meet a girl's parents. No need. Never stuck around long enough. Wish we could have had at least one week alone…*

"I think we've done everything we can. I'll just pick up more breakfast items and hopefully all the dinners will be out! I never was a good cook, even though I must admit our leftovers have reheated nicely."

"Yeah. Good food hasn't been the problem. You know, June. Good anything hasn't been the problem. Makes me wish they were staying at Dad's while they're here so I could stay with you." *What a sorry way to end our time together—separated. We made a promise that I had no idea would be so hard to keep. I still can't believe she hasn't gone clingy on me. Are horses more important to her than I am?*

June burst out laughing. "Like your dad would tolerate that. He hardly put up with me, and don't think I couldn't tell. I deal with horses. I'm used to reading body language. But wow, I'm going to miss you. We've only spent a couple of nights alone. Our first two nights at the suites, remember?"

"I know. It's going to be weird going to my old room. I tell you; I feel like a kid all over again doing that."

"But you still want to stay for their visit and meet uhm…my parents—Randy and Ann, in person?"

"What do you want me to do?"

"Be honest and tell me what would make you happy, Preston. You've done so much for me, and I don't want to hold you up any longer. You're right, reality is here."

"It is. I still want to meet them. I'll be staying in town for a few more days and looking forward to getting to know your parents a little. I hope I can manage not to argue with my Dad. I expected much worse than it's been, to tell you the truth. I mean about his scrutiny and constant opinions." *So far, June is still the same sweetheart she's always been. Unreal.*

"I'm glad you've had some time with him. I want you to meet mine after all you've heard about them. Dinner tonight, right?

"Absolutely! My treat."

"I'm looking forward to it and I'm sure they'll enjoy the outing. Hey! Maybe we can talk to my sister on the phone and that'll take care of my whole family. Good old Bri. She kept her word and never told them my leg was broken. Come to think of it, I never really admitted it to them. I just couldn't. Oh well. Too late now. Isn't it weird? My broken leg was my whole world, and now everything is almost like it never happened—except for us and our little world and your dad, Liv, Cassie and my parents, Mary, and D. Yikes! And then what are you going to do?"

"Then, after your parents leave, I have to go back to work. I'm sure everyone's cars will all need little things taken care of. Yep. Back to work after Sunday."

"Gosh. Remember when I didn't even think I'd ride again?"

"Yeah. Are you scared at all now?"

"No. Not scared, just taking it slow for D's sake and mine. Glad my first ride on him is over and was a success."

"You're considerate."

She snuggled next to him and put her head on his shoulder. "Aw. What are you going to do for these next few days?"

"I don't have a clue. Probably hang around the boat shop and hear the latest buzz on the biz! Those mechanics can talk the talk just like you. All mechanical stuff. I wonder how my car knowledge will fit in?"

"Knowing you, you'll blow 'em out of the water—ha ha, with your fancy mechanic talk. But at least we'll be having dinners together."

"All of them! June, you, and I have always eaten together. I like that. I've never had it before. Even at home, Dad was always buried in work and put in mega long hours. I'd sit there in the kitchen and eat with the staff just for company. I don't want to give that part of us up."

"That's so sweet of you to say, Preston. I'm always eating on the run alone too and I agree it's been so nice. Also, for a person with a broken leg, what other entertainment could have been more fun?" Heat flooded her face, and she fluttered her eyelashes with a coy smile. "Uh…other than…"

Preston reached out and hugged her. "You're so cute. But anyway, your folks will probably want some alone time with you during the day."

"I bet your dad will, too."

"It should be interesting, to say the least." He leaned over and gave her a kiss.

She sighed. "Our last morning alone together."

33

The afternoon brought the classic sunshine of San Diego and June headed for the international airport at one in the afternoon and parked in the short-term lot. *It's only Thursday and it's crazy busy here. I better hurry or I'll miss their entrance.* Rushing to the lobby, her fists were clenched, and her stomach was in knots. *I hope this visit is drama free.* She scanned the incoming arrivals. Waving and smiling, her parents spotted her and rushed through the crowd to greet her.

"Hi, Mom and Dad! Big hugs."

June's mom, reaching out hugged June. Her dad, following suit squeezed and grinned. "June, you look so good. California life must suit you, no matter what."

"Thanks, Dad. You guys look good, too. Love your tan, Mom. It sets off your blond hair. I love your haircut, too."

"Thank you. I got it just for this trip to surprise you. I've never had a bob cut before. I thought it was classy."

"Totally, Mom." June's fingers touched the ends. "Looks good on you. How are you keeping in shape? The gym still?"

"Yep. Yoga, lately. I'm always in new kicks, not like you, just constant with your horses."

Randy cut in. "Well, what about my haircut?" He burst out laughing. "It's nice but not as nice as my daughter's beautiful hair."

"Aw, Dad. That's nice. You look slim and trim. Been working on those renos?"

"Oh yeah. The properties keep up busy. But at least we're getting good turn around on them. So, you're doing okay, honey? You had us worried."

"I've been through a lot lately, but I really feel fortunate that I'm getting things back in order. And I have some big news to tell you both."

Her mom stood back. Her brows raised and pulled together. "Are you engaged?"

Let the inquisition begin. June laughed. "No, Mom. Preston's a great guy and you'll be meeting him tonight, but that's not it."

Her dad held her arm, "Still just about horses, honey?"

Oh no. They're here for two minutes and this is how it starts … "Kind of. But that's not it either. There's more. Come on. Let's go to my place and I'll catch you both up on all my potentially exciting changes in my life."

Her mom hugged her. "Can't wait to hear and I'd like to thank Preston for helping you during your recovery. June, I do get the feeling you were hurt far worse than you let on."

"Eh, I'm healed. No sense in worrying anymore. See?" She held her arms out and twirled. "All better. Preston's a wonderful guy, Mom, but I can't say more. I think you should meet him first."

Her dad cleared his throat. "Sounds like a nice young man to me. But he doesn't live in this state. Does he?"

Knew it. Here it comes. "He's great, but no, he owns several businesses and travels all the time."

"Really? Pretty good for uhm … how old did you say he was?"

"Twenty-nine. He's got his act together."

"Huh. Does he own real estate? That's what we value, right Ann?"

Her mom nodded.

Her dad continued. "June, you need to find a man that wants to put some roots down. I don't trust traveling people that can't commit. You don't need anyone like that interfering in your life."

Little does he know he's taking off right after they leave. I'll probably be in tears. I better enjoy the happy times with Preston and them for the next three days. "Okay, Dad. We have days to talk about it. Let's go get your bags from baggage claim."

"We only have one. Surely, it's going to be a quick pick up and go."

"I hope so. On my way over here, years ago, they lost my bag in transfer! It took two days to get to me. Gosh. I hope yours made it."

"If not," Ann laughed, "we'll have to do some quick shopping."

June's cheeks burned. "Been there, done that. Uh…long story."

* * *

The baggage claim carousel spun until no bags remained on it. Standing, the threesome stood in amazement. The carousel went around three more times, empty then stopped.

June spoke up. "Told ya. I knew it! They did the same thing to me. It's okay, guys. You both look great."

Her mom looked at her leisure sport attire. "I only have tennis shoes on. I need every single thing in that bag. This is awful." She scowled.

Her dad's frown lines appeared and deepened. "So do I. All I've got is this polo shirt and jeans."

June looked at the carousel one last time. *Show up, you dumb bag! This is not a good sign or start for their visit.* She tried to sound positive. "No problem. Come on. Let's go fill out the lost claim report and give them my address. We'll just stay casual for dinner. Pizza maybe?"

Her dad laughed. "All the way from Florida for pizza? That's travel for you."

* * *

June' cell phone was buzzing, and she checked the text message. "Oh, hey. It's Preston. He wants to take us out for dinner. How does that sound?"

Her mom smiled. "How nice of him. Oh gosh, I don't have anything nice to wear. Tell him that maybe tomorrow night would be better. First impressions last forever you know."

"Mom, you look fine."

"June, you know how your mother is, we better just take it easy and meet the young man tomorrow night."

"Okay, Dad. I'm sure he would have understood and could care less what you guys are wearing, but if that's what you both want." Her words dragged.

"Please. I don't want your mother fretting over this."

"Okay. There's a cute pizza place not far from here. I'll tell Preston we'll plan on tomorrow night." *I miss him already. He wanted to have dinner together every night. We haven't had one meal apart since we met. Not even at the hospital, come to think of it. This stinks. I'm disappointing him and he doesn't deserve it.* She pulled out her phone. Her fingers moved in slow motion as she typed the text message and added a sad emoji to the text. Answering right away, he texted back that he'd let his dad know he'd be at home for dinner after all. She stared at the message, and bit her lip. *Separated already. Let him go, June. You have a life that won't include him after these three days pass.*

34

Preston's phone rang. Dad's calling? That's unusual. Where's the usual text response? "Sorry your plans changed, son. But that's okay. Liv had invited Cassie tonight for dinner anyway. Guess we'll be a foursome!"

Preston grimaced as he listened to his chipper voice. "Hi, Dad. Okay. I guess we will. See you later. I've got some things to check on." *Lie number one. No sorrow on your part huh, Dad? I didn't expect this to happen and now it's even worse. Think I'll go for a drive and kill time until dinner.*

***

Seated at the table for dinner, Bob stood when Cassie walked in. "Hello, my dear. How nice to see you." Glancing at Preston, his expression beckoned him to stand as well.

Acknowledging the order, Preston stood. *Commands. Ugh.* "Hello, Cassie. You're staying here?"

"Yes. Surprised? Your father said you'd be here for a few days. You don't mind my staying, do you?"

Preston gulped. "At the house?"

"Well, yes. Why not? Just like old times. I still have my room here, too."

Preston's chair scraped on the floor as he sat and moved forward to the table. "I don't have a problem with it."

"Oh. Good to hear, Preston. I hear June's parents are here but…"

"I'll meet them tomorrow night and I won't be here for dinner. Can we just eat, Dad?"

His dad's eyes maintained contact with Preston's. "Don't you mean 'May we— …'?"

"Whatever." Preston grumbled. "Let's eat. I'm hungry." *Figures he'd try to pull something. These are going to be the longest three days of my life. Face it, you're going to have to let June go soon anyway.*

Cassie added, "Me too." Giving Preston a smile, she picked up her fork.

Preston looked at the empty chair next to him. *I wish June was here. She would've helped me out as well. But at least Cassie showed some inkling of support. Alone, she's not so bad.*

* * *

Dinner over, Cassie came over to Preston and talked softly. "Will you take a walk with me?"

Sighing, he stood. "Okay." As soon as they were out of earshot, he jump started the conversation.

"Why are you here?"

"The truth?"

"It better not be because of a set up for us. I'm going back to work."

"No. It's not a set up. Calm down, Preston. I'm on your side. Let's drive to the shop. I want to show you something."

"Sorry, Cass." *I'm going a little crazy without June. Maybe things already went to hell in a handbasket with her parents and she just couldn't text the truth. Or, maybe she's seeing me as a* guy on his way out the door and it's ridiculous for me to meet her parents after all. Well, there's dinner tomorrow. I'll find out which way it is.

* * *

They parked at the shop and started walking. "Follow me. You have to see this. It's in the planning and design room." Cassie turned on the lights and waved him over to a worktable. "Look at this drawing."

Preston leaned down and studied the print. "It's Dad's newest engine. The one with the superturbo performance intake valves. I heard about it. Ah…for the flow." Preston's fingers traced the prints flow arrows. "This is great, but it will never work as is."

"I knew something was wrong. That's why I'm here, Preston. Your dad thinks his new engineer has it figured out, but if we do an engine prototype and an install that fails, our production will be behind a year. That's also going to kill the profit margin on the line and the word will leak out. I just studied the ops books, and this line is running thin as it is."

"Meaning we'll take a hit not only in production but in reputation too? Isn't Gregory's shop kind of pursuing a similar thing?" *I can see the problem right off the bat. Still got it!*

"How would you know that? You're right!"

"I overheard one of Dad's phone calls and he said enough that I got the picture."

"Preston. I knew you'd be able to see all this. Can you help?"

"Technically, I could, Cass, but I need to get back to my own businesses. Speaking of which, I've ignored them. I've got a lot on my mind lately, and it's not all about my work." *If you only knew.*

"Oh." She reached out and touched his arm. "About June?"

"It's getting complicated, especially now that her parents are here. I feel like our 'life' is under a microscope. And with Dad hovering all over us, good God."

"Your father doesn't have any one team member that I truly trust. Not as much as you would oversee things." Her hand stayed on his arm. "Please." Her eyes searched his.

His stare was blank. "His millions and billions are fine, Cass."

"I know, but don't you want to help keep it that way for him? For you? For your legacy?"

"For him, yes. I've got a full plate. Right now, my answer must be no. I need to leave town and I'm planning on Monday."

"Sorry to interfere then."

"You're just doing your job. You know what? I want you to keep this issue quiet for now."

"Wait. What do you mean? About you looking at the design? Leaving on Monday? Or June?"

"All of it for now. Dad is such a schemer, and I can't get my hopes up that he'll behave himself, aka not butt into my involvement with June, or without trying to throw a monkey wrench in my relationship with her that is rocky as it is right now. Long story." He ran his fingers through his hair. "But anyway, I like to keep my travel plans to myself, just because."

"I will try to keep quiet, Preston, but what if they pressure me about something? I've got my own stuff going on to worry about and I can't talk about it either—yet."

Preston laughed. "Okay. Fair enough. No sharing nothing with no one. Ha!"

"Okay. Let's head home. There's some peach pie in the fridge. Want dessert?"

"Sure. We can eat on the patio and star gaze."

"It's just pie, Cass."

"I know. And they're just stars. I have dreams too you know. What if there's a shooting star, and I see it, and my wish comes true?"

"You're still the same as you always were, aren't you? What is this thing with girls and stars? June has this bracelet…" He grinned.

"You know me very well. I've always had big dreams."

"True and I've always admired you for having dreams. We have history, that's for sure."

"You're not mad at me for dragging you here, are you?"

"No."

* * *

Back at the house, they got their pie.

"Cass, want to join me with a glass of wine?" *Hope she doesn't take this wrong.*

"Sounds sophisticated doesn't it, but no thank you. You have one and I'll just stick with iced water. Actually, a glass of warm water sounds better."

"Warm water? Are you ninety years old?" Preston shook with laughter.

"I am not! I'm thirty-one and you know it."

"You'll always be the older woman." He chuckled.

"Little brat, aren't you?" She pretended to glare at him and moved to the veranda next to the pool and looked up at the stars.

"Okay. I'm sorry."

"It's nice having you here, Preston. I missed you and I know your father does. Well, in his own way." She laughed.

"I miss him too, at times. I don't know, Cassie. I've never hesitated about leaving before, but between your little update on that engine design and uhm — ..."

"June? Is that it? Are you in love with her?"

"I'm not talking. Besides working here, why did you rush to be here today?"

"The truth? To see you." She put her fork down and set her plate down. "All the cities you go to, are the same cities I go to. Most all your clients have boats and yachts too, right? So, our offices are located on both sides of the U.S., just like you've organized your businesses. I travel all the time too. I really like traveling."

"Good to know. I mean for you and for what you like to do." Preston looked up and noticed the light on in his Dad's room. "We're being spied on, Cass. Don't look up at the house. Dad just moved back from their bedroom window."

"Oh gosh. My mom's probably standing right there next to them and they're talking about us. Those two. You've got to admit they're a good couple."

"Yeah. If only they could leave us out of it. What is it with couples? Why do they have to fix up other people? No one can be happily single?"

Cassie laughed. "Preston, you have changed. You never talked like that. It was always about cars and going out and everything else under the sun. Geez. I think June has influenced your life more than you're willing to admit. She's a lucky woman."

"Think so? Huh. Well, whatever. I'm leaving soon." *This is bad. I need June tonight.*

35

The next morning, June made scrambled eggs and toast. "Mom, can you get the plates? They're in the cabinet next to the sink." Motioning her dad to the table, June pulled the chair out for him. "Come on, Dad. Have a seat. Food's done."

"Such service. I'll eat quick. I'm looking forward to going to the barn to see this horse I've been hearing about."

This is a first! "Good to hear you say that. I would hate to make you do something against your will. Ha, ha. Anyway, Isabel, the girl I want you both to meet, just texted me that she's going to be there too. She's trailering her horse to the barn so I can give her a lesson. Cha ching! I'll be making a little money from two rides today." She giggled. "Big news! I'm thinking we might be teaming up and going to college together. Thoughts, Dad?"

"Did I hear you say college or are my ears playing tricks on me? You're serious?"

"Yes. We saw Isabel at a horse show, and she mentioned college and that we might both be pals and go together. But then Isabel's the one that got me seriously thinking about school too. Seeing her made me realize if she could do it, then so could I. Oh! Preston went to college."

"Was it a good school?"

"Is Yale a good school?"

"He went to Yale? I'll say. What was his major, or did you ask?"

Gosh. No confidence in my ability to think about other things besides horses. "Give me some credit, Dad. Yes, I asked. He's a Mechanical Engineering major with a Business minor."

"Sounds like a solid education. Okay, honey. No attitude from me. Sorry. We're just happy you're healed. This horseback riding thing is so dangerous."

Here we go again. "Dad. I could get killed driving to college. I refuse to think like that." She stood and gathered the plates. "Sorry, guys. Did you want more to eat? Mom, you haven't said anything."

"No sweetheart. Just listening to your good news. Let me help you clear the table and tidy up." She went to the sink and started washing dishes.

Randy took a sip of coffee. "Good point, June. Life is unpredictable. You can improve your chances for success with college though. But then, we could have died in a plane crash. Glad that the only thing that happened was they lost our bag. And our bag's still not here."

"No bueno for sure. We'll check on it before we leave, but hurry. At least you have new clothes for dinner tonight. I want you to meet Preston. We need to go soon." *I wonder how his conversations are going. I can't wait to see him tonight! I miss him. Good thing my couch was so small I could pretend he was next to me last night.*

* * *

Pulling into the barn parking lot, June chatted on and led her parents on a tour. "Okay, let's start with the arena where I'll be riding. Then, we'll look at all the horses and end with seeing the horse I've been riding—D."

They went to the arena. Her dad exclaimed. "It's bigger than I thought it would be. When you said a covered arena, I didn't expect it to be this nice and open. Impressive."

Her mom spoke up. "It's very nice. And it looks like you would have fun riding in there."

June smiled. "Yes. I enjoy riding and I'm glad it's my job. Okay, let's go to the barns."

Peeking in the occupied stalls they discussed the horse's names, gender, and breeding. Her dad sucked in his breath before he commented. "All these people probably pay lots of money to keep them here. Talk about income property!" He laughed. Just then, Mary walked up.

June beamed. "Mary. These are my parents—Randy and Ann." They shook hands.

Smiling, Ann looked at Mary. "Thank you for welcoming June back, Mary. She is so excited to be back."

"My pleasure. Your daughter is a fine rider and I'm not just saying that because she's standing here. It's true. June, why don't you tack up D and I'll take your parents to the newest barn. I've got a new horse coming in and it's going to join some others that are there. Then we'll meet you at the arena. Isabel's coming in about an hour, right?"

"Yes. I'll go get D." Her steps were quick and lively. *Well, so far, they seem impressed with my choices. Wait until they meet Preston! They're going to be even prouder of me. They'll know it was best to do my own planning and realize how capable I was of handling a crisis.*

* * *

Returning with D in hand, June led him by the reins and brought him to the edge of the arena. "Here he is!" She patted him.

Her father gasped. "Good grief. That horse is a giant!"

"I know he is, Dad, but he's such a sweetie and a good mover. I'm hardly back in the game, but I'll show you my riding. Nothing upper level, though."

"We don't know the difference, honey. Show us what you want."

Mounting up, June settled into the saddle and smiled. *Let's hear his praise now that he sees me in control.*

Her dad shook his head. "June, you still have no fear. I wonder about your judgment right now. I don't think it's very sound—just thinking about your accident. I'll be happy to see you sitting in a classroom instead of on that monstrous animal."

June's expression changed from happy to mad. "Dad, the horse is sweet."

"Was he sweet when he took off with you and seriously injured your leg? What if you would've broken your neck or your back?"

"He was scared. That's understandable."

"'Understandable?' Yeah, well. I'm sorry. I'm not convinced. I need a drink!"

Her mom gasped. "Randy!"

"Hold on, Ann. I mean water. Mary, is there any water close by?"

"Yes. Just go back to where we were, and you'll see a little kitchen. There are cold drinks in the fridge."

* * *

Her dad left and June's ride started and ended just as he returned. Mary left to take care of some issue in the office. June dismounted with a huge smile. "D is wonderful. I'm nuts about him. He loves me too. I can tell."

June's father chuckled. "Young lady. You are still horse crazy. I can't wait to meet Isabel and see how on earth the two of you horse-crazy girls are going to pull off going to college. Not only that, June, but there's someone else here that knows you and that I just met."

June's mouth dropped open. "Who?"

"I met Tanner."

"Oh no. He's here?" *That's Tanner. He didn't hesitate for a minute to make his presence known.*

"Yes, indeed. He seems like quite a nice young man."

"Dad! He's my former boyfriend! We 'broke apart' because he dumped me and ran off with a rich woman. Geez."

"Well, he's young. He probably just made a big mistake. Young people make mistakes sometimes."

"Dad, it took me a year to get over him. I don't know."

"Well, he seems nice to me. It couldn't hurt to have a man's help, now and then with your horse, would it? I watched him take a horse out of the trailer and it was all he could do to handle it. It was kicking the walls and snorting. He went right in and got it out. It came out all high headed and pawing the ground. He held onto it no matter what. Scared me, and I wasn't any closer than ten or twelve yards away and I wasn't about to take one step closer. If I was you, and this is your thing, I would at least consider working with him—as a business option. Sounds like a wise move. And a safe one too."

'A man's help?' 'Business option?' What! Come on. You'll never ap-

preciate what I, or a woman trainer, can do! I could train a horse just as well as any man. Good grief. I wonder if the horse is as unruly and untrained as Dad makes it sound? June traced her boot toe in the sand. "Maybe, Dad. I know you're worried. It wouldn't hurt to talk to Tanner about possibilities. I'll meet up with him some time."

"That's what I think. Ann?"

"I agree. I would like to meet him."

Randy looked up. "Say no more, here he comes."

June looked. *Oh my God. It's him—a stately frame and an authoritative walk. Add handsome face with an arrogant attitude and there he is.* She held the lead rope so tight that her hand went numb. "Tanner. What are you doing here?" *I don't believe you have such nerve. Actually, I do and that's the problem with you!*

"Hey, June. I wanted to surprise you. The word spread that you'd be training soon and sure enough here you are. I just met your father." Tanner extended his hand to Ann. "Hello, ma'am. I'm Tanner. I can tell you're June's mother by the beautiful resemblance. You two could pass as sisters. Has anyone told you that?"

Ann's cheeks reddened. "Thank you, Tanner. It's nice to meet you. We've heard about you."

"Uh oh. Am I in trouble? I hope all can forgive a few moments of stupidity on my part. June was the best thing in my life, and it was all my fault for messing that up."

June coughed. "That's enough history, Tanner. So, what's this I hear about you being here?"

"I have a new horse for you. For us, I mean. I thought he would make a great joint project. He's four and his name's Devlin Deshyer. He's pretty sweet."

Randy interrupted. "Sweet? I don't know about that, but what a stunning looker he is. Seems pretty wild to me though. It worries me June would be riding him."

Tanner adjusted his cap with a first-place emblem on the logo and looked Randy in the eye. "Oh, not right away, sir. No worries. Devlin needs a few days and a few rides to acclimate. June knows the drill with young and new horses. Don't you, June? You could handle him. Couldn't you? You're capable."

"Yes. But I haven't said yes to working with you. There's something familiar with the name Deshyer. I can't place it right now."

Tanner's smile faded. "Well, I hope you will consider my offer. Just like old times. We really were good with the horses, weren't we? Good rides and all that. Lots of ribbons to show for our work."

D pawed. June adjusted the lead rope in her hand. "He's ready to be untacked. He's been patient long enough. Isabel's on her way. I'll talk to you later. Bye, Tanner." *I can't believe I used to think we had a future. The only issue is the reality of horses—I need them to make a living and love them, but I can see that love doesn't include Tanner anymore. I might have promised Preston I would let him go, but I didn't promise I would never fall in love with him.*

"Oh. Sure. I'll be looking forward to showing Devlin to you. See you around, June." He walked off snapping his fingers and whistling.

June shook her head. "Well, come on guys. Isabel's bringing her parents too. They're looking forward to meeting you." *Deshyer? Where have I heard that name?*

36

Isabel and her parents piled out of her truck and came over to June and her parents. Her horse stood quiet in the trailer.

June's smile stretched across her face. "Hi, Isabel. You're right on time! Awesome."

"Thanks! I tried. Oh, Mom, Dad. This is June and her parents."

June's arm raised and her hand pointed outward. "Mom, Dad. This is Isabel and her parents. Oops! I should add Mom and Dad are Ann and Randy."

Isabel chimed in, "My Mom and Dad are Nova and Josh."

Both sets laughed and shook hands.

Ann smiled. "I love your name, Nova. It's so beautiful."

"Thank you, Ann."

June didn't hesitate to speak up. "You can unload Zephyr, Isabel. I'm ready to get started if you are."

"Definitely." Isabel unloaded Zephyr from the trailer. June smiled as she watched Isabel let the horse look around, relax, and put his head down and nibble on the grass. "Way to get him comfortable, Isabel. Good for you. He's young and you're showing him the right way to act. Ground manners count!" *I hope Dad sees the difference!*

"Dad, this is how horses should come out of the trailer. Quiet and well behaved!" June motioned Isabel to bring Zephyr a little closer.

"Okay, June. I see your point. Horses have your attention. Now, what about school?"

June's grin was lopsided, but her excitement was obvious in her sparkling eyes. She faced both sets of parents. "We've been talking about San Diego State. Since we don't have much time, we're hoping to meet at the campus tomorrow and take a look."

Randy added. "I'm up for that." And all the parents agreed.

June smiled. "Super! Then our Saturday is now booked with a tour of the campus. This is exciting. I'm beginning to think my leg was a lucky, uh…happening." *God, I don't dare say break!* "But Isabel's here for a lesson, so we should get started."

June watched the moms walking and talking about how happy they were for their possible enrollment and the whole group walked together, heading to the barn. *So, I'm finally getting some approval. Of course, it's never just about horses. Oh well. I wonder what they'll say when I give Isabel her lesson.*

Putting his arm around June, Randy gave her a loving squeeze. "I'm happy you're finally considering going back to school. We want you safe."

"I'll do my best, Dad. I'll be on my own, you know."

"That's right. We haven't met Preston, but it seems like he'll be history soon anyway, at least from the little you've told us about him. Traveling and all that, huh? You need a solid man in your life, like Brianna has."

The perpetual comparison. I love Bri but I hate that. June bit her lip. "That was our plan all along, Dad. Preston's always been there for me, but we have a plan not to interfere with each other's future. I have a riding career and I've been successful all these years. I'm trying to grow my business."

"Fine, but don't forget, Tanner has a great horse for you."

Isabel overheard and stopped dead in her tracks. She frowned. "Tanner? Tanner Harmon? What? June, you didn't tell me about him. What horse?"

June shook her head. "Tanner showed up here with a horse. Top of the line, of course. He says he wants to co-train it with me. I don't know about that, Isabel. Whatever. I haven't even seen it yet. Too much detail for now. Get tacked up and I'll see you in the covered arena."

"Yes, madam trainer. Me and Zeph will be right there."

* * *

Walking to the covered arena, Randy and June fell behind the others and talked. "June, was Isabel raised with horses?"

"She was. They have about seventy acres and quite a few horses."

Randy lowered his voice. "I didn't know her parents were horse people too."

June rolled her eyes. "'Horse people'? Dad, it's not a bad thing. You sound like it is. They buy, sell, raise them, and train them. One-stop shopping. They have ranch hands and trainers break them and get them ready to go. It's an amazing lifestyle." *For someone like me.*

"Oh. Is their place far from the college?"

"No, they don't live too far from here. Maybe an hour or so. Isabel will be living at home and driving everywhere. She's planning on boarding Zephyr here though."

"Oh. Sounds reasonable, I guess."

June shook her head. *Glad it meets with your approval.* "Okay, everybody. Let's take a seat. I'll be right back with a headset so I can coach Isabel."

* * *

June watched and coached Isabel through some new moves. "Isabel, show me Travers and half pass at the walk." She watched. "Good job!" Hearing her mother talking, she tuned in.

Ann kept her voice down. "Maybe June should be a regular teacher the way she's issuing commands."

Nova nodded. "And her instructions are working. Looking at Isabel's expression, she's pleased with Zephyr and the lesson. This is going well, Ann. I've watched Isabel take many, many lessons and this one is noteworthy."

"Oh, so kind of you to say that."

"I mean it. June's obviously very skilled and knowledgeable."

* * *

After the lesson, heading to their cars, Randy spoke up. "How about going to dinner? Our treat, Josh, and Nova. I'm sure the girls will have plenty to talk about."

June frowned. "Dad, we were supposed to go to dinner with Preston tonight."

"I know honey, but this is very important. We'll be looking at your college campus tomorrow. Your mom and I are looking forward to seeing it and it's our only chance. I'd love to meet Preston before we go, but he's leaving soon, isn't he? I know he was a nice guy for you, but your future is here and now. Wouldn't you agree? We've got your college expenses, June. You don't have to worry, but I think this is an excellent opportunity for all of us to sit down and talk, undisturbed."

'Undisturbed?' Oh my God. Dad's set on it and if Preston joined

us, he'd be made to feel like a third wheel. I don't want to disappoint him again, but I'm stuck. They're going to pay for my college? That's big. I hope Preston understands this is the only reason I'm agreeing to eating without him.

"Okay, Dad. I'll text him. But let's plan on tomorrow night with him for sure, okay? Promise, Mom?"

"Okay, honey. Saturday night will be dinner with Preston, promise."

* * *

June walked a little away and texted Preston. I feel like he's drifting away from me already. More like being pushed away by the circumstances. And Tanner's in because he's here and has a horse for me? I'll have to see the horse. Gosh. I don't know about all this. And how about Bob, Liv, and Cassie? None of them are crazy about me! This is not going well on both sides. "Sorry, Preston. Dinner will be with Isabel's parents tonight. I made my parents promise that tomorrow night is our dinner. K?"

* * *

Preston's phone buzzed. He read the text and scowled. Cassie caught the look on his face and came over to his side. "Something's wrong, Preston?"

"Yeah. I guess I won't be having dinner with June and her parents after all. I'm bummed. I was looking forward to seeing her and meeting them."

"That's too bad. Seems like you're almost out of her life, doesn't it?"

Preston swallowed hard. "That's a lot for you to say, Cassie. I wasn't even in her real life. I was just helping her out." Preston stared in the distance and his mind drifted to their race to the bed in her apartment. Their kisses, the loving night, and then talking together in the morning over coffee. *She couldn't change in twenty-four hours, could she? I could sign up for that for a lifetime. Someone that understands me and doesn't judge me. I've got to brainstorm this problem out. Just like school. I can do it, somehow.*

"I know. Sorry if it's a sore spot. Do you want to go to the shop and take a look around again? It's Friday and everyone's probably gone. We could have the whole place to ourselves and..."

"Perfect!" He grinned. *A light bulb just went off. I see a glimmer of what could turn out to be the best thing after all!*

"Whoa. You perked up, Preston. What are you thinking? You're freaking me out! I just said we'd be alone there."

"So? We're not kids anymore. Calm down, Cass. We won't do anything you don't want to."

"Preston, are you okay?"

"Yes, I'm okay. You'll see. A private tour and the perfect opportunity…I'm going to change my clothes and then let's go! I need to see things in a different way."

"If you say so."

* * *

Returning to the apartment, June fixed a cup of tea and sat on the couch. "Mom, I'm worn out."

"You are, dear? Why don't you rest?"

"I think I just need a little bit of time to process everything that's going on with me. I mean, since I got my uh…leg healed, my world has gone, and is continuing to go, upside down."

"It's that boy, Tanner, isn't it?"

June frowned. "Maybe. But then again, Preston's on my mind too. Even though there's no way he fits in my real life. He never said he could, and I don't expect that, but then again, I don't trust Tanner."

"Like your dad said, maybe he just made a mistake with you the first time around. Men can be idiots."

"Mom! I can't believe you said that." June was cracking up. "Okay, that puts this situation in perspective. A potential man on the run and an idiot! I could never bring myself to call Preston an idiot. But he is leaving me and going back to work and out of state, I'm sure. But Tanner, no problem. Idiot material. That guy has a bad track record with me! Only problem is, he's dangling a horse in front of me."

Shaking with laughter, they hugged. "June, you'll make the right decision. You've done a great job on your own out here all these years and even after a serious injury—and don't tell me it wasn't, June Tarlin. I know you haven't told me the extent of your injury. Have you?"

June's head hung low. "Not entirely, I guess. Well, I broke it. I was in a cast for ten weeks."

"Oh my goodness. And Preston stood by your side through all of it?"

"Yes. It was his idea because it was his car tire that blew."

"I see. I can imagine the words your father and I would have said to you."

"I know. You would have been worried."

"But still, we don't need to be protected from bad news, June. Don't ever make that mistake again. I'm glad your leg healed with no complications. I think now that it's behind you, you need to look at your new possibilities."

"Thanks, Mom. This talk helps me more than you can imagine. Would you and Dad mind if I took a drive over to Preston's father's shop? It's a business, and a business should be open on a Friday. He mentioned the other day that he would be spending some time there to make his dad happy. Maybe he's there and I could surprise him. I do miss seeing him. Thank goodness we're all having dinner tomorrow night. Your visit has come and gone so fast and tomorrow is your last night before you fly home. I'm so glad you made the trip. I hope the airline calls soon about your lost bag."

"My goodness, I hope they found it. I'll call them in a little while. Oh! Go ahead and take your little drive. We'll be just fine waiting at the apartment for you. Anyway, I can't wait to see the college campus tomorrow."

"Me either. Just think, one day soon it will become half of my new life!"

"Alright. You should go now. Your dad and I will rest up and be ready for dinner."

"Bye! I won't be too long." Heading to her car, her steps quickened. *"Woo hoo! Oh, how I've missed him. I'm going to give him the biggest kiss ever."*

* * *

Following each other to the facility, Preston and Cassie parked their cars side by side.

Cassie jumped out of her car and slammed the door. "Ha, ha, Preston. I beat you getting out of the car."

"Only by a second or two! I'm not a slow old man. No bragging rights about that, Cass."

She giggled. "This is exciting. Where shall we start?"

"Let's head to fabrication. Then to the warehouse, and we'll end at engineering so I can see the plans again."

"Let's go." She held out her arm and they walked arm in arm to the first building.

* * *

Preston let out a low whistle. "My, my. This place is hopping with projects in motion, isn't it? Look at the desks and workstations. I haven't seen it in a couple of years. Dad added on to the building, didn't he?"

"Yes. He's going after more models and more upgrades to the lines. All of them."

"Huge changes." Preston walked and ran his hands over the machinery. "Cool stuff here. I've got to hand it to him. This is impressive. Challenging to keep his eye on all this, I'll bet."

"I agree. Want to see the warehouse?"

"Sure." He held his arm up so she could take hold of it as they walked. "Cass, I have an idea that's getting better by the minute. Not sure what your reaction's going to be."

"Tell me."

"Well, it's going to be a test for us."

"Us?"

"Yes. For the two of us."

Cassie froze and looked at him. "Preston, I…uhm…never expected you to say something like this."

"I told you; I just came up with this idea. You inspired me.

I'm thinking out of the box now. Come on, let's go in the warehouse."

They walked in and he whistled. Dropping her arm, he moved to look at the shelves and stations. "Good grief. Stockpiled and ready for assembly."

"Is that bad?"

"I don't think so. Do your numbers say anything 'bad'?"

"No. This business is solid and in the black from head to toe. However, if the new engine design fails— …"

"Okay. That's not a worry."

"Why not?"

"Because, I said so." He laughed. "I just need to look at the drawings one more time. Let's go to stop number three."

* * *

Arriving in the parking lot, June's chest tightened, and her jaw stiffened. Only two cars here? Preston's Porsche and a black BMW? It's got to be Cassie's car. What? Cassie and Preston are the only two here? This place is deserted except for them. My God. Are they in hiding together? She opened her car door and walked to the only building she could think of—Engineering and Design.

* * *

Preston walked over to several stations and turned on the computers. Logging in, he accessed up-to-date status reports and reviewed the latest edits. "Cass, everything looks good, except I am worried about that newbie."

"Oh, 'that' one. I know. Just as we said. But you could fix it, right?"

"Probably. But more importantly, because my idea for us would have to come first. That is, if you say yes."

Cassie's mouth dropped. "'Us?' Oh, Preston. I didn't mean to lead you on. I didn't mean to cause you to believe—…I feel so bad."

Preston came close to her and placed his finger on her lips. Their bodies were so close they almost touched. Cassie trembled and Preston held his gaze. "Don't be worried. I'm here. I got this. Don't know what took me so long to see it, but that was the past."

* * *

Meanwhile, June entered the building. Tennis shoes silenced her steps. She heard talking and moved in the direction of the sound. Spotting Preston and Cassie, she hid behind a corner, straining to hear every word. I feel sick. He is after her. Figures, two Richie Riches would belong together. I'm the only idiot, not him. She turned and stopped…Preston's words came through loud and clear.

"Shh…no need to feel bad, Cass. What I'm after is something only the two of us can understand and pull off, together. You and me and no one else. Dad was right. We do belong together. I'm ready to settle down and give up traveling. This is going to be perfect. With you, I can actually see myself working for Dad again."

Cassie remained close. "But how? I can't believe it. Tell me, quick, Preston and then I'll tell you something I've been holding back revealing; until now that is." Her hands wrung in agony. She lowered her face to her hands and covered her eyes.

* * *

June's eyes filled with tears. *I can't listen to this anymore. My heart is broken into pieces. Best friend, lover, whatever we were, I've—…I've lost him.* Slinking away, she left as quietly as she arrived. *I can only tell Mom and Dad what I learned. Never, ever Preston. I can't give him the satisfaction of ending it with me. I'm going to end it first, but it's going to be in my own way.* She bolted as quick and quiet as a cat after a mouse.

* * *

"So, here's my idea, Cassie. I think I'm convinced that my presence is needed here at the shop. At the same time, I have a thriving business in multiple states and locations. I can't give that up. That hasn't changed. Since we're both business graduates, I figure if anyone can be a partner to my newly created masterminded idea, it's you."

"So, you're not in love with me?"

"Cass, you're like a sister to me. Don't you feel the same way?"

She laughed. "Of course. And I'm relieved to hear you say that, Preston. I haven't told Mom and your dad, but I'm in love with a wonderful man. We met about a year ago, and we're quite serious about each other. We've been living together. He's my Mr. Right. I didn't want to get Mom's hopes up for me that I finally found a man or crush your dad's hopes for you and me to become closer.

"Don't pass out, but I just bought a pregnancy test and I'm waiting for him to get here before I use it. I'm going to introduce him to them. He wants to marry me and ask your dad's permission. And then if I'm pregnant, well, we'll be together and tell them that about that, too. I hope Mom doesn't faint!"

Cracking up, Preston high fived her. "Congratulations! A man and maybe a baby? Wow. No wonder you haven't been drinking anything besides water."

She nodded. "Anything else makes me nauseous. If it was up to me I would eat pie—any kind, and saltine crackers all day long."

Preston grinned. "I hope I can work things out for me too."

"With June?"

His cheeks got hot, and his palms got sweaty. "Yes. But I don't want her to think I'm undermining her independence or sidelining her. She belongs on the centerline."

"I don't understand. Centerline?"

"Oh, sorry. It's a dressage term. It's in the court. I mean, the show ring. The arena." *God, I'm even talking the talk like her. Basket case!* "Anyway, what I mean is that I don't want to interfere, but I must be with her … somehow. She brings something out of me that I never thought I had. I care more about her than I do myself. But first, I have to get my businesses rearranged in order to make it all work out. Ready to hear where you come in? You have to say yes, Cassie. This is my future we're talking about."

She grabbed his arm. "God, Preston. This is the real deal for you. You're in love and you can't bring yourself to say it, but I know you are. I'm a woman and I'm all ears. Start with business and then work your way into the part about the woman, bro." She giggled. "I've never seen you like this. What's your 'mastermind' of an idea?"

"I want to convert my businesses to franchises. Yes, there are many steps and regulations that must be followed, but I have an exclusive clientele that would most likely work with my franchisees, knowing that I am backing them with a new and solid corporation and my own name and reputation. You and I have many friends that went to Yale and other Ivy League colleges that would most likely love to have an established business. All they need is to have a mechanical and engineering background and, of course, their buy-in fees. With their backgrounds, they'll fit right into my business model. They'll have a sweet ride of a job so to speak. Thoughts?"

"Brilliant! I can handle all the accounting and financial requirements and we can get your father's corporate attorneys to help with the legalities. We're going to have multiple states' regulations to deal with. It's going to be a little complex, but that's okay. I can handle a business challenge and I'm up to it!"

"Yes! I was hoping you'd be on board. Now, all I have to do is find June and convince her that I'm going to be getting off the road as soon as the businesses can spare my presence. Got time to speed this process up?"

"Sure. Let's call it a capstone graduate project and move!"

"Love it, Cass. Hey. What's your man's name?"

"His real name is Steven, but he goes by Beau. I can't wait until you meet him. I've told him all about you and how we grew up together as 'only children'—biologically speaking. Ha, right? He's an only child too—only a real one. I love him. He gets me."

"This is too much. Wait until Dad hears my news, too."

Cassie reached out and held his arm. "Preston, this is a drastic change for you. Are you sure you're ready to give up traveling?"

"Being with June isn't 'giving up' anything. I would be gaining. I've had time, erh…months to think about this. It's nothing overnight. I'm just glad your news plus mine will smooth over that you and I aren't a couple and will never be."

"I should hope so. We're adults, Preston. Talking with you is such a relief. Let's go home and have dinner with the parents."

"Let's!"

"Don't tell my dad, Cass. I want to surprise him myself. One day, I hope I can tell him I appreciate all he's done for me." *It's true, but things change when we're in the same room talking. Nah, it's more like fighting.*

"You got it."

37

June threw open the front door and let it slam closed. Running to the couch, she dove onto it and cried. *I've never been sadder in my whole life.* Ann and Randy came over and sat next to her. Wrapping her arm around June's shaking shoulders, Ann shot a worried look at Randy.

"Sweetheart. Tell us. What's wrong. Are you sick? Do you have a migraine? Sometimes I…"

"No!" June wailed. "It's nothing like that. I'm sick alright though. Sick to my stomach. Preston's in love with Cassie. That's ridiculous! She's practically his stepsister. Okay well, his dad and Liv aren't married—yet. But they will be one day! Oh my God. I'm always falling for the wrong man. How can I be so naïve?" Tears rolled down her cheeks.

Ann cooed and smoothed her hair away from her face. "Aw…I'm so sorry. Did you hear him say he loved her?"

June sniffed and wiped her nose on the back of her hand. "Yes. He…he…He said they belonged together. What about us?" She wailed. "You don't understand, Mom. He filled my heart with so much happiness, like the wind filling a ship's sails on a blustery day in the ocean. My heart aches like the pain in my leg right after the accident. *I lied to them about the fact I broke it. I deserve to be punished, but it's too late anyway. I'm healed.* What have I done to lose him in that way? He has no problem committing to her, but not to me! I wasn't supposed to feel this way, but I do, and I can't help it. And now, I'm the loser, again." She sobbed.

Randy touched her arm. "You've got Tanner, sweetie. And how about the horses, and Isabel, and everything else? That guy, Preston can't take all that from you."

"Dad, I don't know. I'm just so mixed up. I hope I can make it through dinner tonight. If you guys weren't leaving so soon, I'd cancel all our plans." *I am going to look like the fool I was the first time Tanner dumped me. Déjà vu. Disgusting!*

* * *

Arriving home, Preston and Cassie laughed and talked nonstop as they entered the house. They both laughed harder at the shock on Bob and Liv's faces.

Liv spoke up. "What's going on you two?"

Preston smiled. *Only the best news ever.* "Oh, just some good news. Right, Cass?"

"That's right."

Bob bit his lip. "I can't wait to hear what's up. Dinner should be almost ready. Preston, go tell them, we're ready to eat now. If it's going to be long, they can just bring us grilled cheese sandwiches and soup for all I care."

"Right away, Dad." Preston walked quickly to the kitchen.

* * *

Seated at the Italian restaurant's window booth, the Italian music set the mood along with the traditional décor of Italian paintings, pottery, and plants. The parents admired the San Diego weather while Isabel looked at her phone and intermittently at June. June moped and stared out the window. She broke her gaze and spoke. "Glad we were all able to have dinner." *Preston would've been here. But, no, not now. I've lost him and he's with someone else tonight. I could be sick.*

"June, June, honey," Ann caught her attention. "Our server just asked what you would like to drink."

"Oh. I'm sorry. A glass of water."

"With ice?"

"No ice, please." Her fingers toyed with the edges of her menu, but she didn't read it.

Randy shook his head and pursed his lips into a thin line. He ordered a variety of appetizers and soon the table was buzzing with talk about school enrollment, majors, classes, and the fact that it would be so easy for the girls to commute.

June shifted in her seat and toyed with the food on her plate. "This decision has happened so fast. I'm not sure I'm ready for homework, but signing up for classes sounds exciting." Her voice was dull, and her eyes looked down.

Isabel perked up. "June, we need to meet with our advisors on campus. Let's go on Monday and check it out. We don't want to miss any deadlines."

"Good point, Isabel. You're on it. Okay, I'll find out about having my transcripts from the community college transferred. I'm sure the advisor will ask me to do that. I looked online. I can start in the Spring next year with my GPA, and I know I have all my transfer units completed. You should be able to start in the Fall. I'll go on my own though, so I can work in a ride." June tapped her fingers on her water glass.

Isabel grinned. "Lucky dog. Wish I was starting as a junior."

"Well, you're lucky you're starting as a freshman. I need you, Isabel. You're so on the ball about God, everything."

Randy spoke up. "I don't see a problem with you starting in the Spring next year, June. That will give you time to get your work hours finalized and be ready to start."

"I'm glad you're okay with that, Dad." *He's never disappointed in me when it's about school, no matter what I say.*

After ordering their entrees, everyone resumed talking through the meal and on through dessert.

June crinkled and smoothed the cloth napkin on her lap. *Endless meal…*

Randy and Ann admitted that June's California move had been for the best. Her education with this arrangement was no problem and they could pay for the tuition and expenses.

June added, "Gosh, Mom and Dad, I appreciate your help. Thank you." *I feel like this is a runaway train. I'm lucky they still want to pay for college. That's one promise they've never backed out of. Anything to get me off horses. Well, they can't buy me Bri's lifestyle. But that would include a boyfriend and that's not happenin' for me.* She blinked back a tear.

Looking at June, Isabel reached for her purse. "Let's freshen our lipstick, June. There's some hot guys in here."

"I hadn't noticed," June grabbed her purse and scooted out of the booth.

The parents laughed and June and Isabel left the table.

"What's up, June? You're anything but happy. I can tell. Did your parents do something?"

"No. Preston did. He's fallen for his stepsister."

Isabel stopped and grabbed June's arm. "What? Isn't that against the law?"

"Okay, so she's not legally, but she might as well be."

Releasing her arm, they continued walking. "Girl, you are not making sense. I can't believe that sweet guy, Preston, could do any such thing. You can see that he's nuts about you."

"Ha! No, he's not. I heard him say that him and Cassie, the stepsister, are meant to be."

"That's crazy. I mean, I didn't hear him, but no matter what, I'd believe in him any day. That guy's no liar. He gives off good vibes. Now, Tanner…"

"I know. He is just a manipulator. But the manipulator is proving to be someone that is interested in the things I love—horses. Ugh. How does he get me to even listen to him after what he pulled on me in the past? Answer to my own question—horses, horses, and more horses. Even though I feel like a fool talking to him, if I pass some great horse opportunity, that's foolish too. Hey, we better get back to the table."

"Okay. Tomorrow, see the advisor. You're doing the right thing. You're going to have options and no men are going to stop you."

"Thank goodness I bumped into you. Without Preston, I never would have all this because I wouldn't have bumped into you up north and then that led to all this. I would've probably had to recover in Florida, or worse yet, I don't even know how or where. Oh my God. I better forget about him. He's out of my life."

"Not buyin' it, but I'll be supportive, June."

"K. Thanks."

* * *

The Wahlberg dinner table was alive with conversation. Bob and Liv were animated and joyful. Cassie bit her lip and Preston fiddled with the cutlery. Cassie cleared her throat and Preston let her see that he crossed his fingers for her. I should've been with June tonight, but that loss will pay off in the end.

Smiling and sitting taller in her chair, Cassie cleared her throat again. "Mom and Bob, I have something to tell you. I think Preston does too."

Preston shifted in his seat. *Go, Cass.*

Liv's smile was so wide that her tiny laugh lines edging the corners of her eyes deepened. "We thought something was up, dear. Go ahead."

Bob sat as still as a statue.

Continuing, Cassie twirled her napkin holder. "Well, let me be point blank. I've never been one to hold back my words, until lately. And that's the reason I'm here. But I must say, it was so hard to come to this house alone. I'm glad Preston was here."

Preston sat taller. *And here it comes.*

Bob grinned and reached for Liv's hand. "Go on, honey."

"It was so hard to be here alone because for the first time in my life, I am in love."

Liv gasped. "Oh sweetie. You and Preston…"

Preston swallowed hard. *The pressure and expectations are surrounding us. God. Can't they see it? It's too much.*

"No! I'm not in love with Preston. I have a wonderful man in my life. He's coming here tomorrow. I asked him to give me a few days. He's a great guy and we have a lot in common."

Liv stammered. "What? Well, why were you hesitant to tell me, or us, about him? Is it his background?" Frown lines crossed her forehead.

"No. He's a businessman. And a good one. He's working in his family business. He's going to be running it one day."

"What made you hesitate?"

"Expectations. You all would expect more out of our relationship than I have. I'm happy with how it's been. But you've always wanted me to find someone and have children. Mom, I'm thirty-one, don't you think I'm aware of my own body clock?

"I've never meant to push you."

Preston laughed to himself. *My whole life has been a push. That's what 'pushed' me away!*

"No, you've just been uhm … disappointed."

"Not in you. But in the fact that your life choices have led you to …"

"Business decisions. But not this time."

"I'm so sorry, Cassie. Where have you been with this man? I mean, where is the business?" She bit her lip.

"In Garden City, Georgia."

"Ah," Bob cleared his throat. "A good city is always close to waterways. Not that I'm a little biased or anything like that."

"Of course you're not, Dad," Preston chuckled.

"I've been looking for a new place to expand."

"Dad! Cassie's trying to say something. Can we just hear her out?" *Think of a future with June. Make him listen and see the possibilities.*

"Sorry, Cassie. Preston's right. I didn't mean to interrupt. Please continue."

Cassie pressed on. "Anyway, Mom, Beau's dad started a plastics factory there many years ago."

"Isn't that where Pennington Plastics is located?"

Cassie perked up. "Yes, and that's his business! Beau, well, his real name is Steven, but Beau's dad owns that. Beau's been shadowing his father and learning the operations. They're getting ready to expand into another state and there's a lot going on."

"That sounds big."

"But that's not why I love him. I love him because he's genuine and smart and gets what I'm about."

Liv stammered, "Okay, I see what you're about, but what about Preston?"

Sitting right here, with a plan of my own, Liv. Seconds are ticking by, and the glorious details will be out on the table, so to speak.

"Mom, Preston and I are going to be…"

Preston jumped in. "We're going to be business partners. Dad, I want to help you in the business. And I have a new plan. And I'm thinking about settling down in the area."

Bob stared and his eyes bore into Preston's. "Son, this is your home and I want you involved in the business. It's your place to be there. I'm confident your business plans have potential and I'll hear you out."

Preston tapped his foot and waited. *There's got to be a 'but' coming…*

Bob eyes bore into him, and he frowned. "But when you say, 'settling down,' I take it you're including June in your plans?"

"That's a big question mark right now. There's no guarantee for any of this. June loves horses and they are her life. I don't know if she can see that I would be the right man for her. It's all kind of early. We're in unchartered waters here."

Bob exploded. "'Unchartered' is a massive understatement. This woman came out of nowhere and you barely know her. I'm stunned that you're even considering this step. I'm not sure what else to say. I've missed you and have wanted you here, but I don't want you to make a mistake."

"So, what you're saying is that you're afraid June's a 'mistake'?" Preston's lips pursed tight. "She's clueless about all this."

"And that's what I'm worried about. There's a lot to this family."

His voice escalated. "Oh, it's okay for Cassie to bring someone in, but not me because my someone doesn't have a business or big degree attached to her background? Oh sure! Just say it, Dad." He scoffed. "We live in a mansion and June lives in tiny apartment 2A in the Oceanside Villas. Not good enough? Don't even answer!"

His chair scraped against the floor and flipped over. He jerked it upright and tossed his napkin on the table. Turning and muttering under his breath, he stormed off.

Cassie's chair scraped as she got up and fled after him.

38

The next morning, June picked up her phone and turned it on. *It's Saturday, already…* She almost dropped it from shock. *Preston sent five messages yesterday? Oh my God. What does he possibly have to say for himself? Sorry, I've been such a liar? Sorry, I'm no different than Tanner? Sorry, you thought Tanner was bad and I'm much worse? Sorry, I wrecked your life? Sorry, I'll be on the run again soon? June! Read the messages before you flip out and make up even more bad stuff! Okay, okay, Preston, let's see what you have to say.*

> Hi, I'm miserable without you. Please call me. (6:30 p.m.)
>
> Hi, me again. I need to talk to you. (7:00 p.m.)
>
> Hi, still me. I have BIG news. (8:20 p.m.)
>
> Hi, come on, June. Call me! (9:25 p.m.)
>
> Hi, PLEASE CALL ME! I'll settle for a text, but I need to hear your voice. (10:30 p.m.)

How could he send me those texts after practically declaring his total love and devotion to Cassie? This is just not like him, but I know what I saw and heard. Only one thing can cure these blues. June hustled around the kitchen, hastily making coffee, pancakes, and bacon. Randy and Ann came and joined her. "What's up? You're energized."

"I am, sort of. I don't know. Nervous energy? I'm happy about school but bummed about Preston. If it's okay with you guys, I thought I'd run over to the barn for a little while before we meet up with Isabel and her parents. I need some barn time. I'm hoping D can help me. Is that okay? I made you breakfast."

Ann gave her a hug. "Very thoughtful of you, sweetheart."

Randy took a cup of coffee and sat at the table. "Well, I've never had your cooking, especially for me, well, for us, until this visit. Makes my trip worthwhile. By the way, the fact that you're wearing breeches was a giveaway to your destination. Yes, it's okay." He winked.

"Alright, thanks. Here's a plate. Hope you enjoy. I better run. I shouldn't be too long. Just a short visit. I want to sneak in a peek at Tanner's horse without him knowing I'm looking."

Randy grinned. "I see. Get going little lady. Just be careful around those monstrous horses."

"I will."

"Okay. This horse thing…I want to see my little girl happy. Well, have fun and ride safe. Is that what people say?"

"No, they just say 'Have a good ride!'"

"Okay, then 'Have a good ride!'"

"Oh, okay. That works. I'm glad you didn't say a quick ride because that's a sure-fire way to get your plans, erh…your ride to blow up in your face. I'm a little suspicious, that's all. So, forget what I said about quick or short or hurrying, I'll see you when I see you." Grabbing her keys and purse, she headed for the door.

* * *

Arriving at the barn, June headed straight for D's stall. "Come on boy. Glad you had your morning hay. How about a little ride?

Let's get you groomed and gorgeous." Putting the halter on, she led him to the cross ties.

* * *

Tanner pulled into the parking lot and parked next to June's car. He headed for the barn and then to the arena. At the arena gate, he paused and watched for a moment. He called out, "Gate please!"

June looked over. *Surprise, surprise. Huh.* "Tanner. Ha, ha. What are you doing here so early?" *He's up to something. He never used to ride early unless he had to.*

"I could say the same thing. But when I pulled into the parking lot and parked next to your car, I wasn't surprised to see that you were here early, just like the old days. So, I hurried and got Devlin groomed, tacked up and here we are! He's a real show-stopper, right?" His grin was wide and mischievous. "How's your ride going? Looks pretty good to me."

June scoffed. *Knew it. He knows my riding preferences.* June patted D. "Thank you. We're coming along. Well, aren't you coming in?"

"Do you want me to?"

"It's an open arena."

"Of course, I'm coming in. I came here hoping to see you. What do you think of Devlin?"

He mounted up and rode close.

"He looks like a handful. What's his story?" *Dangling the pretty boy out in front of me. Tanner, you are such a player.*

"He's from Virginia. That's where he was started. Imported from Germany. His owner bought him without riding him. She just went off the trainer's and the owner's word and a video if you can believe it. She fell in love with him and just had to have him. Needless to say, he's just a bit much for a novice right now. But for you and me," he whistled, "the sky's the limit with this one."

Is he thinking about rekindling our relationship? Preston might be in the doghouse, but Tanner, you're not even in the yard! "Yeah, but I never said there was ever going to be a 'you and me.'"

"I'll get you to change your mind, June. Come on. Let's get them warmed up."

I'm not that naïve! "Okay. Keep your distance with Devlin. He's just a little too much for me right now."

"Alright, but you're already looking great in the saddle, and it's only been what, days? Lucky for you that stupid Preston didn't get you killed with his fast car. Dummy."

I might be mad at him, but he is not dumb. "Hey. He's not a dummy. And don't call him stupid. Just ride and keep your comments to yourself."

"Sorry. Didn't know you cared so much about him."

And you will never know how I really feel because I can't trust you. What's that saying – 'Fool me once, shame on you; fool me twice, shame on me.' "That's enough, Tanner." She turned and started her warm-up trot.

* * *

Preston pulled into his usual parking space at June's apartment and glanced at his watch. *It's 9 a.m. and she never called me back. I hope she's home. Is she okay? I can't believe I haven't heard from her. What gives?* He bolted from the car, slammed his car door, and walked as fast as he could to the front door. He knocked loud and hard. I think I hear the TV. He knocked even louder. "June! It's me, Preston. Are you in there?" He rattled the doorknob, and the door flew open. Preston's hands immediately fisted at the sight of a man answering the door and another person peeking out behind him. "Who are you people?" Where's June?"

"Hold on there, mister. June's our daughter and she's not home. Who are you?" He held the door firmly.

Preston relaxed. "Oh, my goodness. I'm so sorry, sir. Where are my manners?" He stretched his hand out. "I'm Preston. I was hoping we would have met before now."

"Hello, Preston. I'm Randy, and this is Ann, her mother. Come in." He wiped sweat from his forehead. "You scared us."

"I don't mean to barge in. I was worried about June. She could have been hurt or something. I haven't heard from her."

"Son, she's fine. We've been busy every minute that we've been here."

"I'm sure. I had been looking forward to meeting you both though. I thought we'd meet over dinner. But anyway, I was hoping to talk to June. Is she at the barn, maybe?"

"You guessed it."

Ann motioned him to the sit on the couch. "Not to delay you or interfere, but I want to share something with you." Her eyes bored into his. "June was very upset yesterday."

Preston blinked but didn't look away. "Sorry to hear that. Like I said, I haven't talked to her. About what?"

"Well, I shouldn't intrude on your personal business, but she came home in tears."

"Came home? From where? I thought she spent the day with you both, and Isabel and her parents."

"She did but then she went to your father's workplace to see you. She wanted to surprise you." Ann bit her lip.

"I never saw her."

"I'm sure you didn't." Ann scooted a little further away from him on the couch. "Preston, she heard you talking to Cassie. I think that's all I should say."

"I don't know what she heard. But I don't understand why it would make her cry."

"No clue?"

"None. Cassie's like a sister to me."

"Matches what June said."

"Then why she would cry is beyond me. I really don't know."

"Preston, whatever she heard made her upset."

"But what I said to Cassie was only meant for Cassie to hear."

"No doubt about that either." She huffed. "June was devastated."

Preston's hand brushed through his hair. "She must have left before we finished talking."

"She didn't say that in particular."

"I think she misinterpreted whatever she heard. But please don't tell her I came here. Let me go find her. I'll explain what she needs to know. I'm sorry. I've got to go."

Randy stood and walked him to the door. "June has a lot on her mind, son. I think she's in turmoil over college, her riding and well, now this between you two."

"Again, I'm so sorry about that. This has been such an experience together and now things are out of hand. I'll see what I can do." He stood. "Thank you for listening."

* * *

Walking him to the door, Randy opened it for Preston. Preston stopped and turned. "Has June told you about she and Tanner? I don't mean to break her confidence, but he hurt her by leaving her for another opportunity, erh … woman, horse, money — whatever. Bottom line is, I would never do that. She knows I'm leaving to take care of my business, but I'm not running out on her. Surely, she must have told you about our plan. I'm not lying, but if she runs into Tanner, in my opinion — and hers, I believe, he can't be trusted, and she might be making a mistake. I know we're out of time and you're visit is almost over, and since we never met, I just want you to know I only want the best for her."

Ann looked him in the eye. "We appreciate your concern, Preston."

The door closed behind Preston, and he hurried to his car. *Things are getting messy, but I need to know what's going on. They don't know what Tanner is up to. I hope I'm not too late. On my way, June! I'm glad I told them not to tell her I was there. I want to find her and make things right.*

39

Preston pulled into the parking lot at the barn and flinched. *Oh no. June's car and a big truck — license plate — TOP T, are parked right next to each other, at the end of the parking lot, and no other cars are here. I don't like the looks of it.*

* * *

Walking to the covered arena, he could see two riders' helmets bobbing in the distance. *Ah, maybe she's here with Isabel. That's it!* Coming closer he clenched his fist. *She's riding with a man that looks like Tanner.* He stopped and studied the man's face. *It is Tanner!* He immediately turned and headed back to his car. *I'm out of sight for two days and she's already running back to him? I'll just wait for the ride to end, and I'll meet her in the barn.* He looked at his watch. Ten minutes later, heading back, the arena was empty. *Yep. Time to go find her. Tanner will be history when I'm done with him.*

Taking deliberate steps, he walked softly down the barn aisle to D's stall and tack room area. Just outside the tack room, he heard Tanner's voice. He peeked around the corner and saw Tanner's standing behind June with his arms wrapped around her shoulders. He froze as Tanner spoke.

"Come on, June. I've said it all along." His head was inches away from hers and his mouth was close to her ear. "I've missed you."

June pulled away from him and faced him. "You're the one that left me."

"And I told you, that was my biggest mistake. I'm here. I love you and I have no plans to leave. I have more horses lined up for training. You and I would be great together. Think about it. You'll be a Grand Prix trainer soon."

"I haven't shown at Grand Prix, Tanner. Isn't that the first step?"

"But I have, and I can coach you and together with top horse flesh, we'll have it in the bag."

June sighed. "Are you being honest, Tanner? Do you really love me? True love wouldn't have walked out and left for money."

"I'm here to make money with you. I'm not Wahlberg. That guy's had it handed to him. Besides, he's always leaving, and no way is that lifestyle a match with what we're about. I figure we can buy some land and build our own house and barn. We love this life. I know I do, and you do too."

"Yes. I love this life. But I'll be in school too."

"Eh, for what? You're going to be too busy with all our horses. You don't need a stupid degree. What's a piece of paper got to do with what makes you happy? It could never, ever take the place of a horse."

"Of course, it can't. I never said it could or would."

"Well then, June. What do you say? Pick one or the other. You've had a while to think over your next move and I'm offering you a world of top horses. Unlimited. All for the two of us. Please, June. Please give me one last chance." Tanner came closer and reached for her. He spun her around slowly and held her while he talked with his mouth inches away from her. "I want you back, June Tarlin. I want you now more than anything I've ever wanted. I can make you happy."

"I can't deny that horses are my love, Tanner. But my heart…"

"Your heart would be empty without horses. I know you can't be without them, and you don't have to be anymore."

"Okay, Tanner. I'm in. But I'm in for the horses."

Preston held his breath. *'Horses'? Yeah, right. She's back with him without even asking me about what she heard yesterday. Just assumed I had dumped her, choosing what—Cassie over her or God knows what? That's it. No communication whatsoever? Well, you can't lose what you never had, and I never had her. That's obvious.* He turned and walked away as quickly and quietly as he could.

* * *

Arriving home, Preston pulled into the driveway and headed for his room. He heard his dad's quick footsteps coming down the hall. God. Not now. I'm in no mood for any lecture. Bob spotted him and rushed to talk to him. "Hello, son. You're up and moving fast early on a Saturday morning. Preston? Son, what's wrong?"

Preston turned. "I'm leaving." He moved to the dresser and pulled open the drawer so hard it almost fell out. He reached in and tossed the clothes on the bed in a pile. Moving to the closet, he grabbed his weekender bag and started throwing the clothes in. Closing the zipper with force, he yelped, "Ouch! Caught my finger." He bit his lip and continued filling and closing the remaining pockets.

* * *

June returned home. Rushing to her, her mom was anxious to talk. "Hi, honey. How was your ride? Feel better?"

"Hi, Mom. Yes, and I had a good ride. Then, I bumped into Tanner."

"Oh, is that all?"

"What do you mean? That's a lot. He sure had a lot to say."

"And he's the only one you talked to?" Ann's fingers clenched.

"Yes. But anyway, he wants to bring more horses in, and he wants us to get together and train them. He says he has big plans for the two of us."

"Oh. Did you tell him you're going to be busy with school, too?"

"Yes. I told him."

"Is he supportive?" She bit her lip. Randy lowered the volume on the TV.

"Not about college, he's not. He has big plans for horses for us though." June sat on the couch and fiddled with the armrest.

"That could mean anything! Buying horses together? Property? Marriage? Your future is at stake." Her mom's fingers rubbed the side of her neck as she looked at Randy's darkening expression.

"Well, that's it for now. I told him I was with him just for the horses. It can't be more than that. Not with him."

Randy scowled. "I don't like what I'm hearing. Are you changing your mind about college?" He turned the TV off and faced her.

Give me a chance to sort through this. I'm doing the best I can. "No, Dad. I'm going to go back to college. My life is my life and if he doesn't like that, well, I'm capable of supporting myself. He talks big and I do want in on the horses, but him ... that's another story. I'll have my own horses to train with or without any that he's got anyway. I'm not going to depend on him 100 percent like I used to. I learned my lesson."

"Oh. But you're still in love with Tanner or erh…at least have feelings for him?" Ann grabbed a horse figurine and toyed with it.

"Love takes two people, doesn't it? I don't have the deep feelings I had for Tanner anymore. As for Preston, he was just being nice and responsible, that's all. Preston's someone that I'll always fondly love," reaching to her ear, she stroked her empty ear. *Proof of my loss. Took it off and now I don't even have an earring to show for all we had together. Thank God I still have my bracelet. She twirled it.* "Even though I was madder than a hornet yesterday and his deceitful behavior. I can't ignore the fact that he took care of me when I needed him the most. Mom, I can't be on the road and traveling. I need stability. Our two lives and work could never be what I need. Preston and Cassie are two peas in a pod. I don't belong in their circle or their world. I'm a dressage rider, trainer, and soon, college student. Right now, I'm pretty broke. But that's okay. I'm going to make it."

Her dad came and hugged her. "I'm starting to have big doubts about Tanner too. I don't like someone not supporting your future or seeing the importance of your education. Your mom and I struggled without college because we couldn't afford to go and got lucky with how our lives worked out. I know we frustrated you, and probably insulted you, but I'm sorry, June, we vowed our daughters would have more security than we ever did. So, we've got you covered for school. All you need to do is get yourself there."

Tears welled in her eyes. "I'm going to. Next Spring—if all

goes as planned with Admissions. I'm grateful for the help. I'm so glad you and Mom came here."

"Well, sweetheart, we have a college campus to see today. Let's get ready. We can go out for a nice lunch and then see it."

"Sounds good, Dad. Thank you. I'm going to take a shower." *Lunch? What happened to going out to dinner and meeting Preston? That's so over. They'll never know how handsome and warm and wonderful he is. I mean was. It's so stupid thinking about him. He loves Cassie, not me. Thank God Mom and Dad live across the country. It's not like they'll ever see him again even if they had met him. For that matter, I'll never see him again either.*

"I guess you guys will never get to meet Preston. It probably was for the best, right?"

Ann swallowed hard, looked at Randy, then looked at June. "Sometimes, honey, things just go the way they're supposed to and not the way we plan."

"You're right." June left the room and headed for the bathroom. Just after the door closed, she turned on the shower, moved back to the door, leaned her head and back on it, slid down in slow motion and slumped to the floor crying.

* * *

Preston carried his bag and walked to his room to check for anything left behind. Bob followed him. Preston went to the dresser to close the open drawer. He pushed it hard and smashed his finger as it closed. He swore. "Okay, Dad. That's it! I've had enough. I'm going. Say goodbye to Liv and Cassie for me, please."

"Son, I know you're still upset about June."

"That's not it. It's not just 'June.' It's that you'll never fully accept my choices or ideas. I give up." *My efforts are always squashed when it comes to him. His expectations are my downfall around here. I was strong with June at my side, but now that she's gone, nothing's going the way it should be.*

"I accepted everything you said."

"It didn't seem that way. June will never be an Ivy League kind of girl. She could be if she wanted to. Forget it. I have things to take care of and I need some time."

"Her college background isn't an issue. Come on. What about your business plans?"

"Plans are plans, Dad. Some come to fruition and some don't, I guess."

"And yours?"

"That's where I'm at right now—plans and planning. I'll be in touch. I'm heading home to sort things out." *I've got to act whether it's step up or step out. A man's got to do what a man's got to do. Philip, your life was cut short. I can't help but think I should do more, not less, with mine.*

"Listen, I'm sorry if there's hurt feelings. I'm not much of a conversational father." He put his hand on the edge of the chest of drawers and took a deep breath. "Drive safe, son."

Picking up his bag, Preston turned. "Bye, Dad." *One day, you might be proud of me as Axel thinks you would be, but today sure isn't the day. I can't say I blame you right now either.*

40

Sunday morning arrived and June made an omelet for breakfast. "Dad," she called from the kitchen, "breakfast is ready. Thought I'd surprise you both one last time."

Randy walked in and hugged her. "Whoa. What a sendoff. This omelet looks delicious. Thank you, honey. Better than any airport food, that's for sure."

Ann came and sat at the table. "Wow. What a beautiful presentation. I'm impressed."

"Aw, thanks guys. I've enjoyed your visit. I'm glad we all got to walk around and see everything that we could. I'll go back to the campus tomorrow. Every office should be open on a Monday. No worries. I know you're both concerned, but I got this. School is my new plan. At least I've got a few months before it starts. I looked at the transfer requirements online. I'm glad I think I'm all set to transfer in. I'm also glad I squeezed in some extra credits at the community college so I shouldn't have any classes holding me back from starting. I need to get organized at the barn too. I'll talk to Mary. It's good to have her in my corner."

Ann sipped her orange juice. "What about Tanner?"

"Speaking of him, I think I'll pop over to the barn after I drop you off at the airport. I'm sure he'll be around there. I need to clear the air, so he understands the way it is." *Tanner, you're not the one in charge. I'm equally as strong as you are with or without your horses. I got this.*

There was a knock at the door. Leaving Randy and Ann sipping the last of their coffee, June hurried to the door. Looking through the peephole, she giggled and opened the door wide.

"Hello. Just in time."

The delivery man smiled. "I'm happy to hear that. Many of my deliveries aren't met with such a warm greeting. If you sign here, I'll be out of your way. Here you go!"

June reached out and signed. "Thanks."

Closing the door, she called out. "Mom, Dad, your suitcase just arrived!"

Ann rushed in and burst out laughing. "Oh, thank goodness I get my clothes back. I missed my favorite jeans. And, I didn't want to tell you, but we brought you a little gift. That's why I was so sad about them losing our bag."

"How sweet."

Ann unzipped the bag and inner pocket. She brought out a small box. "Safe and sound. Open it!"

June's hands fumbled as she unwrapped the box and opened it. She shrieked, "Wow! A necklace. I love it. My initial J. Are these real diamonds?"

"Yes, a little diamond J for our precious youngest daughter."

"Mom, Dad, I always loved Bri's B necklace and now I have one too. Put it on me."

Ann fastened it and June reached up for it. "Let me run and see it in the mirror. I'll be right back." She came running back. "It's so me. I l–o–v–e diamonds! Thanks." She kissed them both.

Randy laughed. "Better late than never. At least we don't have much to pack. Want our new suitcase, June?"

"Sure. I'll take it. It might come in handy. I lost my old one." *And Preston has the one we used to share. I miss him so much I ache. My world is upside down right now. I wonder how he is?*

***

Hours later, they pulled into the airport's short-term parking. Walking to Departures, they reviewed the plans for college tuition and other details. Randy continued talking with one arm around June and the other pulling his bag. "I'm proud of you, June. Surprised?" He grinned.

"I am."

"You've done very well on your own and we know you can manage without us now. However, we are planning on a return visit!"

June grinned. "I hope so. I'll have more horses to show you and uh…a stack of books probably from my first semester or two."

"Sounds good."

"I've thought about a lot of things, and I've made some decisions. I'm going to follow through with everything that is important in my life. You guys, Isabel, college, Mary, D and most of all, Preston.

Ann gulped. "Preston?"

"Yes, Mom. I can't bring myself to just walk away from him without at least hearing him out and sharing how I feel. If he officially walks away from me for the rest of his life, that's going to hurt, but at least I'll know I told him the truth about how I feel about him. He's the man I love.

"Tanner, forget it. I just can't trust him. My gut says no. I don't want to be involved with him. Besides, he's not supportive about my college plans and I don't need an anchor. I need someone that, well," she twirled her bracelet, "believes in destiny, and will help me reach for the stars. These new earrings came from Preston, and I hope they bring me luck. I'm going to meet up with him, wherever he is."

Ann's face was beet red. "Honey, we must tell you something—even though we promised Preston we wouldn't."

June's mouth dropped. "Preston?"

"He came to see you yesterday morning and made us promise not to tell you he was there. He was going to the barn to find you."

"He did? I never saw him. Maybe he changed his mind about me and never went there."

"Honey, we must go. Our flight! But, sweetheart, what if he went there and saw you and Tanner talking or thought he heard something?"

"I don't know. That's lame and so dumb of him. If he did, he could've at least asked me about it!"

"Now, June. Isn't that what you did when you heard Preston talking to Cassie?"

"Mom! Oh my gosh. Talk about dumb. I was unfair to him. He deserved a chance to at least explain himself, even if it was something horrible or he dreaded telling me. Isn't that what you taught me?" She winked and her smile reached her eyes. "Have a great flight. I've got to find my guy. He may be with Cassie, but he's going to tell me to my face. If so, I can end it on my terms. I've had it with being dumped. I want the last word! Today, tomorrow, as soon as I can! Love you both! Bye!"

Exchanging hugs, they parted.

* * *

Rushing to her car, June sat and texted Preston. Hi, I know things didn't go the way we planned. I want to talk to you. I miss you. REALLY, REALLY miss you.

* * *

Arriving home, she changed into breeches. She picked up the phone. No response from Preston. Disappointed, she picked up her phone and dialed. Two rings later, her call was answered.

"Hi, Mary."

"Hello, June. Is everything okay? You sound tense."

"I'm okay, sort of, but not really. I wanted to talk to you about me and Tanner and of course, the horses, his plans, and all that."

"I'm glad you called. Tanner gave me some highlights of everything. Sounds like big plans alright."

"I know. But Mary, his plans won't be including me. I'm going to be on my own. With you, D, Isabel, and college—whenever I start. I'm hoping to pick up more business, but I just can't be associated with Tanner."

"No?"

"No. I can't say bad things about him, that's not fair of me, but I just wanted to let you know."

"Okay. Keep me posted. June?"

"Yes?"

"You're going to be fine on your own, and I can't say bad things about Tanner either! Our plans are solid and stay as we discussed." Laughing, they hung up.

* * *

Driving to the barn, June's mind was on D. Pulling into the barn parking lot, she spotted Tanner's truck and a silver BMW Z4 convertible parked next to it. There it is – BIG T. Huh…Steps crunching on the gravel, she headed for the barn. Hearing laughter and talk getting louder, she continued, getting closer to the conversation. Seeing a halter missing from the mounted wall hook and a horse stall door partially open, she paused. Oh no, now what? Tanner's in there? Peeking into the stall, Devlin's halter was on. His lead rope, held by a woman with long dark hair wearing skinny jeans, an exquisite couture equestrian blouse tucked tight into her super tiny waistband and held by a black leather belt encrusted with bling, dangled in her hand.

Noticing the woman with the whitest teeth on the planet, hair and nails done, makeup on and accessories made for any place but a horse's stall, June gulped as the woman cooed at Tanner and laughed at whatever he whispered in her ear. In return, he took the rope with his right hand, pulled the woman in close with his left arm, and planted a long, wet kiss on her waiting lips. Beaming, she reached up and wiped traces of her red lipstick from the corners of his mouth while her finger traced his lower lip.

June's hand flew over her mouth for a nanosecond. *You dog. Sorry excuse of a man. Ugh!* "Hi, Tanner."

Tanner jumped and the horse jerked back.

"I saw your truck, so I thought I'd come looking for you. Imagine that. Little old me, finding you. Surprise! Hello." She grinned at the woman. "Tanner's such a flirt, right?"

"A lovely flirt, I would agree."

June laughed. "He's just so fun. Aren't you, Tanner?"

"June. That's enough. What are you doing here?"

"I could say the same, but it's obvious why you're here. I'm here to ride. So, I'll leave you two. Sorry, to startle you, Devlin." She reached out and patted him. "May I give him a horse treat?"

The woman smiled. "Of course. He loves treats."

June pulled an oat and apple treat from her pocket. "Here boy. This is from D, your barn mate. Bye, Tanner. Oh, by the way, I just told Mary, I'm going to be exclusively working for her and Isabel. So don't worry about my riding. It's none of your concern. See ya! Oh," she reached her hand out. "My bad. I'm, June."

The woman stretched out her hand. "I'm, Blythe Deshyer. Nice to meet you. I'm so happy to have Tanner…uhm…I mean handling my naughty horse."

"Nice to meet you too. If anybody can handle naughty, Tanner can. Have a lovely rest of the day." She turned and walked off. *I knew it. Liar. You're not foolin' me twice!*

* * *

Making her way into D's stall, she haltered him and led him to the cross ties. "Let's do this, boy. I missed you, since yesterday." Laughing quietly, she patted his neck then buried her face into it and inhaled. Nothin'—no aftershave or men's cologne especially, smells as good as a horse. You're sweet, you're soft, and you're all mine for now. She finished tacking him up and used the mounting block outside the barn. "Oh, you are my boy, aren't you. Come on. Let's go out on the trail today. Just a fun ride. No arena and no work."

The rhythm of his walk rocked her body and her mind drifted into a peaceful place as they thudded along. D could have passed for a twenty-five-year-old Quarter Horse trained for a lone cowboy riding the open range and he delivered a quiet ride. *Thanks, boy. Love ya. We're gonna be at shows together one day. Jus' me and you...*

* * *

Back in her car, she reached for her phone. No messages. *I'm all alone with no one left here. I miss Preston so much my stomach's in a knot and my heart aches. I hope I can handle seeing him with Cassie. Hey, I just dealt with Tanner. I can handle myself just fine.*

* * *

"Another crazy, busy parking lot. Front row, primo spot? I'll take it, thank you very much. Now to find the Admissions office. *Huh, there's a lot more people here on a Monday than there were on Saturday, that's for sure. Note to self, always leave home early when classes start!* She located an advisor. *I wonder if anyone will notice I'm wearing riding breeches. Hee hee. Just a little confidence booster. Besides, I'm being true to who I am.*

Within an hour, registration paperwork was started, and she was on her way to being a junior with Business as a declared major. *Whoa. This is quite amazing. It's weird that all I have left to do is wait to register for Spring classes once my transcripts arrive and registration opens. I should have done this a few years ago! I'll text Mom and Dad. They'll be stoked!*

Driving home, she looked at the freeway signs and her car turned toward Wahlberg Marine & Engineering, Inc. *What am I going to say to Bob? I misjudged your son, completely messed up, and I'm looking for him? Think fast. Here it is.*

Entering the parking lot, she parked, and headed to the office. Opening the front door, she looked down at her paddock boots and breeches. *Talk about a fish out of water!*

A receptionist looked up. "Hello. May I help you?"

Tongue tied, she stammered. "I uh, hello there, I uhm…I'm looking for Mr. Wahlberg. I'm June. He knows me." A weak smile quivered.

"I'm sorry. He's not in. Did you have an appointment?"

"No. I just thought I'd stop by. No problem." She turned and headed to the door.

"I can take a message."

"No. That's okay. Sorry to trouble you. I'll uhm…give him a call a little later." *That's a lie and this was a stupid, hopeless idea. Preston has not responded to my text messages. He probably already left town as he planned to. Okay, time for Plan B. No giving up, June Tarlin!*

She stopped halfway to the door. "Could you confirm Bob's cell number? I thought I had it, but I've only got his son's." She pulled out her phone and scrolled. "Yeah, silly me. His son's number is here, but not Bob's." She pleaded with her eyes.

"I can give you Bob's cell number. He always gives it to his clients anyway. Ready?"

June got her new Contacts on the screen, "Ready!" She entered the number and smiled. "Thank you! I appreciate your help." She turned to leave.

The receptionist cleared her throat. "May I tell Bob, your full name?"

June stammered. "Uh…of course. I'm June Tarlin. Bye!" She hurried out. Got into her car and pounded the steering wheel. "Yes!"

* * *

"Uhm … hello, Bob. This is June." She waited.

"Yes, June?"

"Uhm … I've been trying to reach Preston and he hasn't answered any of my calls or texts. I was wondering if he happened to still be …"

He cut off her sentence. "He's not here. He left on Saturday."

"Oh. Earlier than planned. I'm sorry I missed saying goodbye to him."

"Uh huh."

"Did he happen to say where he was going?" She stood and started pacing.

"No."

"Oh, okay."

"June, he did mention he was going home to take care of things. He's never missed work before, and he took a lot of time off to help you, so I imagine he's very busy."

June broke into a sweat. "I'm sure he is. I, I uhm … really appreciate all he did, and I just wanted to thank him and wish him well." She cleared her throat. "Okay, thank you for answering my call. If you do happen to hear from him, please tell him that I … uhm … hope to hear from him whenever he gets a chance."

"Okay. Bye, June."

"Bye, Bob." She hung up and tears rolled down her face. "Preston went home. End of story. Well, that's it. At least I know where he went." She changed and grabbed the new bag from her parents and started packing. Dialing Mary's number, her hand shook. "Mary, hi. I'm going to look for Preston."

"Okay, June. Where is he?"

"I have no idea. It's sounds crazy, but I need to find him."

"Is he out of town?" Her voice was concerned.

"I'm almost positive. Listen, Isabel can ride D, if you approve. This will be a little test for those two because I just registered at the college today. She's a good rider; light hacking for him until I get back."

"No problem. She called and she's bringing Zephyr here to board. Glad my trip got delayed. I'm anxious to see her."

"Really?"

"Yes, so that she won't have to trailer him, and she wants him to settle in."

"That girl is on the ball! I'll call her, but in the meantime, I'm going to keep packing. I have to get on the road soon. I'll stay in touch. Okay?" Grabbing at clothes, the pile of possibilities stacked on her bed grew taller.

"Okay. Be careful."

"I will. Thanks, Mary."

"You're welcome. Bye."

"Bye."

41

June barely slept through the night and stumbled through most of Tuesday. *I'm at my wits end. This is my first road trip alone, and I don't even know where I'm going except*

I won't stop until I find Preston. Gosh, he must be mad. It's all my fault.

Her phone buzzed with an incoming message. "Preston!" She grabbed for the phone and grimaced at the text. *Oh no. It's not him. I recognize the number, it's Bob. I'm scared to read it.*

Hello, June. It's Bob and Liv. We would like to talk to you. Are you available?

June swallowed and almost choked. She texted back. *I am. When do you want to talk?*

Is now a good time? We don't mean to overstep or scare you, but we're outside your apartment.

What? Running to the door, June opened the door and saw a white four-door Maserati with tinted windows. The driver door opened, and Bob waved as he stood. The passenger door opened, and Liv stood and waved. June waved and motioned for them to come in.

"Hello, Bob. Hello, Liv. Please come in."

Walking with energetic steps, the twosome approached and came in.

June pointed to the couch. "Please have a seat. Would you like something to drink? Iced tea?"

Liv answered. "Oh no, dear. We're not here to trouble you. Please have a seat so we can talk."

Bob cleared his throat. "June, I'm afraid Preston left because of me."

"No, Bob. I'm sure he left because of me."

They both stared.

Bob said. "Listen, Preston had some business plans, but got upset when he thought that I wouldn't approve."

Liv said. "I think it wasn't, well…we know it wasn't the business plan. He thought we, erh…your dad, mostly, didn't approve of you. But we're here to say that we do."

"Yes, June. My son had disappeared for years basically, and it wasn't until you came along that he wanted anything to do with me, quite frankly, or the business. And just when he mentioned it, I opened my big mouth said the wrong thing and he, well…"

June plunked into a chair and gripped her knees, "He ran?"

Bob looked down. "So, you know how he is?"

She bit her lip. "I do. And he knows how I am too. I'm far from perfect. But we got to know each other."

He sat taller. "I want you to know that he has never brought anyone home before. I guess my question is, how did you get him to come home? I'm trying to say, how did you get him to change, June? I've tried everything with him…"

June smiled. "He knows that. He's very smart. He told me about all the wonderful opportunities you gave him. And also, he always treasured his time alone with you. Waffles on Sundays…"

Bob's eyes got glassy, and he cocked his head. His eyes bored into her. "And we never found that kind of time again." He shook his head.

"Anyway, I don't have anything to offer except that when I train horses to come to me, I might have to chase them for a while, but then, I stop the pressure and they realize it's better to just come to me instead. Not to say he's anything like a horse, and I've never been a parent, but my parents put a lot of pressure on me too and until this visit, when they eased up, I made a decision that they wanted me to."

"And what was that?"

"To finish my college. Once it was my idea, the rest worked out."

"Ah. I have pushed him really hard."

"But he knows you love him." She gasped. "Oh no. I hope I haven't said too much."

"No. it's clear you two have talked, a lot."

"Anyway, sadly, I think he overheard me saying something stupid to my ex-boyfriend at the barn, but that's completely over. I'm packing, see? I'm going to find Preston. So, I'm on the run too. I want to tell him the truth." She looked at Liv. "I just want to apologize and clear the air with him, Liv."

Liv smiled. "What a relief. June, you may think that he and Cassie are an item, but Cassie just brought her boyfriend home for us to meet him. They're officially engaged!"

June beamed. "Engaged? Wow. You must be very happy about that."

Bob added. "He's a fine young man. And you're a fine young lady. I've never seen Preston be so proud of someone, and that someone is you."

"Thank you for telling me that. My parents met Preston, on their own. He came here when I wasn't home. Yes, they were concerned that his lifestyle and mine didn't mix, but I think they got the right idea just before they left. I'm going to ride and go to college. I have plans, but first and foremost is to explain things to Preston and apologize for any misunderstandings. I care for him very much."

"We know he feels the same. He left on Saturday. He's had a while to 'take care of things' as he said he was going to. Can you think of a place to meet him besides his condo in Portland?"

"Yes. There's a hotel in Sacramento. It's a very nice hotel with an elegant restaurant. We went there and he wanted to go back there with me one day. He gave me a gift coupon and he said he wanted me to have it for a 'fancy dinner' one day, and I think that day has arrived. It would be a great meeting place."

"Alright. Were you planning on driving there?" His mouth gaped.

"I'm driving until I find him, wherever that might be. I'll start there. It was a special place for us. The beginning…"

"I can send you in my jet, June. That way, if you need transportation, the jet will take you and you can leave your bags on it. Please text Preston and hopefully, he'll come back to meet you. He's very resourceful in getting around."

"I'm sure he is. I don't want to trouble you, but that would be helpful. What if he doesn't want to see me? He hasn't talked to me for a couple of days. This may not work. We have never been through anything like this. Never."

"You two need to meet and talk, just like we are. Please. I won't be worried about you being in the jet. Besides, driving for hours on end with your leg newly out of the cast doesn't sound ideal."

"Okay, if you're sure. I'm almost packed. Is this evening too soon?"

"I don't think so. Text Preston right away and give him as much time as possible to meet you at the restaurant. He could be out of state, or not. I honestly don't know. He hasn't talked to me either. I'll call for my pilots. A car will come for you in about an hour or so. The driver will text you the time. Thank you, June. I'm so sorry Preston ever thought we didn't approve."

"No worries. I know how parents are. And I am just a horse trainer and riding instructor. But whatever, I have dreams and I'm always reaching for the stars."

Liv hugged June. "And your dreams are all going to come true. Stay in touch. I hope Preston responds."

"Me too, Liv. More than you can imagine. But what about Cassie?" Worry crept across her face and her brows knitted together. "I thought you wanted her to marry Preston."

"Oh my. Us mothers can make mistakes too. But now, to be honest, I want her to marry the father of my grandchild!"

"What?"

"She took a home pregnancy test once Beau arrived and yes, she's expecting according to the kit. I'm so excited that I could just explode with happiness. I hope that kit is reliable."

"Oh, my goodness. Congratulations. A baby! How exciting for you, Liv."

Bob cleared his throat. "We'll keep our fingers crossed for all you kids. I hope I can take all this excitement. You better get moving, June. We don't want Preston getting any farther away."

"Yes, sir!" She stood. "You got it!"

Closing the door behind them, June sank on the couch and then jumped as though a taser had just touched her. *Oh my God. What am I going to wear? Not jeans, not tennis shoes. Not barn boots or breeches.* She went to her closet. *Got it!*

42

Her cell phone buzzed, and she grabbed it and tapped on the message.

> Hello. This is your driver. I'll be picking you up in thirty minutes. Does that work for you?

Texting back approval, she gathered her bags and got a glass of water. *Why is waiting the hardest thing to do when you're nervous?* She texted Preston. *I'll try one more time! No giving up, June.*

> Hi. I am asking you to join me for dinner at 7 p.m. tonight. I have no idea where you are, but I want to take you to our first fancy place. I know you'll remember it. My gift coupon is for us, and this is my treat, of course. We have lots to talk about. I miss you.

Enduring more radio silence, she sighed. *This is awful. We have never stopped talking since the minute we met. He must be furious, and this is probably a water haul. Poor Bob. Counting on me to make Preston see the light? Failure with a capital F.* Her cell buzzed. *Preston? Oh, it's the driver again.*

> Hello. Five minutes, and I will be there.

* * *

Opening her apartment front door, she pulled her suitcase outside and was just about to close the door. No! She stood in the doorway and checked her purse. Whew. Keys are there. Not doing that again. She grabbed them and locked the door behind her. A white limo pulled up and the driver came to the doorway to take her bag.

"Hello, Miss. The pilots are ready and waiting. Excited?"

"I am. This is not my usual mode of transportation as you may have guessed."

"No problem." The driver opened the car door. "Please," he motioned her inside. Closing the door, he got in and drove off.

* * *

Escorting her to the waiting jet, she climbed the stairs, and her bag was carried inside. Buckling up and looking around, she shivered. Calm down. This must be how Cinderella felt in the carriage going to the Ball. All the magic goes away—not at midnight—without Preston. I don't care. It's not the magic that I want; it's the man.

The jet taxied and took off for the short flight. Arriving at the familiar executive airstrip and runway, she knew the drill and exited the plane once it stopped, and the door opened. Another limo awaited her entry and soon departed for the downtown hotel. As she checked in at the restaurant's reception desk, she took a quick look around just in case he was already there. *He's not.* Her heart was heavy but hopeful, giving her name and adding that a guest would be joining her. *If he shows up.*

She sat alone and waited. The server brought two glasses of sparkling water, two menus and a wine list. June didn't touch any of them. *I don't like being alone in our special place without him.* She waited and then realized she hadn't texted Preston the exact time the jet took off. *I couldn't. I was in flight!* And on top of that her phone was zipped in her carry-on bag on the jet. *I'm not thinking logically. I could've texted him again when we landed. What if he doesn't care? Oh my God. I would give anything to look into his blue eyes again and see his handsome face.* The server headed her way. With eyes conveying sympathy for the obvious that June was being stood up, she stopped at her table.

"Would you care to order some appetizers? We have a wonderful charcuterie board. It's one of my favorites for snacking. In fact, I often order it as a meal and it's easy to pack up as a 'to go' for a midnight snack."

Recognizing the gesture as a face-saving move, June nodded. "That sounds perfect. Thank you."

The server moved off and June adjusted the menus. Looking up at the entrance, she gulped. *He's here.*

Her gaze riveted on him as he walked toward her. Wearing dress slacks, a button-down shirt, and a sports jacket, he was as sophisticated as an executive of any major corporation. June smoothed her little black dress, gathered her legs and high heels under the table so that she would sit taller. Her long blonde hair flowed freely in the glow of the candlelight and subdued lighting overhead.

***

"Hi, June."

"Hi."

Clearing his throat, he sat next to her at the table. "This has been the longest five days of my life."

"Me, too." She trembled.

"I'm so glad to be with you. I was going out of my mind with crazy thoughts."

"I wasn't exactly thinking clearly either."

"Between your text messages, the pilots, and the drivers, well, I knew the timing could work, so all I had to do was get here. And I forgot to mention my father." He laughed.

"Oh, my goodness. I guess we caused quite a stir."

"It was worth it." Looking around, he reached for her hand. "I like your restaurant choice. Since this wasn't an 'anniversary,' I knew this would be the place. The gift coupon, was the final clue and I drove like mad to be on time."

"Aw … You're so smart."

"And you are too. Never forget that fact, okay? I guess I have connections that work. Look at you—so gorgeous. I have a lot to explain."

"Thank you and so do I. Or did your father tell you my side of the story?"

"No, he just wanted to make sure I made it here so that we could talk things over. He called me, June, and we talked, not texted. Amazing. He told me not to be late and not to blow my chances with you."

"Whoa. That is amazing!"

Preston grinned. "Tell me about it. Good old Dad. Bossy as ever. But in this case, I wasn't going to argue with him." The charcuterie board arrived. "Would either of you care for a beverage other than your waters?"

Preston cleared his throat. "Champagne, June?"

"Yes, please."

He smiled at the server. "A bottle of your finest, please."

"Yes, sir." She hurried off.

Preston picked up his water glass and took a sip. "Let's get started. There's lots to say. I was traveling south on Interstate 5. Heading back to San Diego. Coming after you."

"You were?"

"Yes, and this is where it gets interesting."

"I want to hear it all." The champagne arrived and their glasses filled. After toasting, he continued. "I was so mad when I heard you talking to Tanner in the barn. I wanted to yell and punch him out. But I didn't. Instead, I left because I decided to fight back in my own way. I have new business plans. I can tell you all about them, but what's more important is that I'm moving to San Diego."

June coughed. "Wow. Such big news. That's great."

"I was hoping you'd say that. Because, for once in my life, I didn't run away. Okay, maybe for the first two hours on the road when I left my house, but after that, no. I left intentionally to change things up and I'm doing this so that I can be with you. I love you, June." He reached out and took her hand again. "I'm leasing my penthouse, long term, and I'll be doing the same with my other places. I'm not going to be just a traveling mechanic anymore."

"Gosh, that is a lot of news and changes. I love you too, Preston. You were fine as a mechanic. I'm just sorry for excluding you from joining me and my parents at dinner. That was so insensitive on my part. We planned on having all our dinners together. You could have easily joined us. My Mom would have gotten over her wardrobe issues — long story, their bag got lost in flight. Anyway, not inviting you wasn't meant to hurt you. But when I heard you say you and Cassie were 'meant to be,' I guess I just flipped out when I should have talked to you. I'm guilty of doing my own running and avoiding."

"What? But are you running from Tanner now?" He shifted and a worried look crossed his face.

"I'm not running from someone who's already been left behind—permanently. He lied to me again and, with or without his lie, I knew he wasn't the one for me anymore."

"Okay, I'll accept that." He reached out and took her hand. "I should have faced him and the situation and talked to you in private so we could work it out. My running had to come to an end—with or without this trip."

"Preston, I'm sorry about that too. I promise I will never hold back talking to you."

"I believe you, and for sure you're the only person in my life that hasn't wanted anything from me and have appreciated everything I did for you. But how do you know you're really over Tanner? You said you were before and then there you were alone with him and saying you were 'in' on the horses."

"That's it, Preston. It was all about the horses. Not my heart. I didn't see him as a boyfriend, it was just going to be business. But even that was ruled out."

"I don't want you to have regrets."

"Regrets? I won't have any. I can handle my horse career on my own. Besides, I never trusted him, and I shouldn't have even listened to his insincere words. He's only true to himself. I knew it and once again, I heard it and saw it with my own eyes. I'll tell you more later. You can ask my parents; I told them at the airport I was going to find you and tell you about my true feelings for you. You've been the only one to get me to take my blinders off and see that I'm capable of handling more than one obligation at a time. You inspire me and believe in me and have never hurt me. I shouldn't have doubted you. And I won't ever again."

"I'm glad to hear it. I was deep in conversation with Cassie because I came up with a fantastic business idea, but I needed her help with the details. She's beyond good with books and I'm good with engines and design. I came up with a plan that would enable me to get off the road and be living in one place, keep my businesses, and work in the family business. I can do both too. Ever hear of franchises? Cassie, the newly engaged and hopefully pregnant big 'sister' of mine, I must add, is going to help with all the legal and accounting requirements. I'm so excited. I'm going to have a new life and hopefully..."

"Hopefully, what? It all sounds wonderful." They held both of their hands even tighter. He pulled one hand away and reached for his pocket.

"Hopefully, settle down. And I don't mean 'settle' as in accepting the status quo. This is for you." He brought a small box out of his pocket and set it on the table. "Should I kneel?"

June's eyes sparkled. "Not necessary. You did plenty of that when I had my cast on." Her cheeks burned and her heart pounded.

"You got it." He opened the box. "I want to build a new life with you. Will you accept this ring and marry me?"

She gasped. "This is the most gorgeous, beautiful ring I've ever seen."

"I was hoping you'd love it. It's a four-carat emerald cut diamond. I thought a rectangular shape looked like a dressage court, so that every time you ride down centerline, you would think of me, and of us."

Leaning over, they kissed.

"Preston, I think of you all the time. And I can't imagine a life without you. Yes, I'll marry you. I love you." She extended her hand.

"I love you too. You've changed my life and I can't be without you either." He slid the ring on her finger. "You are my everything. Is this just as good as getting your dream horse?" He grinned.

"Better! Uhm…for now." She giggled.

"Well, we'll have to tell Liv that," he chuckled, "and now, Dad's got two weddings coming up."

"You sure don't miss anything, do you? I love your dad for all he did to help us find each other."

"Oh, I would have fought for you on my own, June Tarlin. No worries. Yes, it's always nice to have the parents' approval, but I was in love with you and wild horses couldn't have stopped me."

June reached for his hand. "Sometimes a girl gets a lucky break after reaching for the stars for a long time."

About the Author

Centerline Love is J.C. Malik's debut romance novel. Growing up, her dreams of owning and riding horses came true when she moved from an Alexandria, Virginia suburb to Northern California. Finding a passion for dressage, scenic mountain and lakeside trail rides added to the excitement of horses, dressage, and competition. J.C. is a USDF Bronze medalist. A memorable Third Level Freestyle and beginning Fourth Level were achieved with her first and beloved Hanoverian gelding—Lanciano.

Love and horses seem to go hand in hand for her and now J.C. has her own website, www.jcmalik.org. Other titles in the works, as well as her second dressage romance—*Love in Deux Time,* continue her dreams and hopefully, those of her readers.

9 781966 641438